BLACKLEG RANGE

BENNETT FOSTER

SAGEBRUSH
Large Print Westerns

First published in Great Britain by Chivers
First published in the United States by William Morrow

First Isis Edition
published 2020
by arrangement with
Golden West Literary Agency

The moral right of the author has been asserted

A catalogue record for this book is available
from the British Library.

ISBN 978–1–78541–862–4

Published by
Ulverscroft Limited
Anstey, Leicestershire

Set by Words & Graphics Ltd.
Anstey, Leicestershire
Printed and bound in Great Britain by
TJ Books Limited, Padstow, Cornwall

This book is printed on acid-free paper

CONTENTS

Cast of Characters

Price Thorn . . . came back to the Teepee spread, sore as hell.

Will Thorn . . . his father, scared stiff of —

Ed Pothero . . . X Bar owner, fat, Texas, and tough

Jule Pothero . . . his younger, double-crossing brother.

Hank Kuhler . . . X Bar big shot, not too brainy.

Jim Harvie . . . Teepee 'puncher, gruff and eager for a scrap.

Tony Troncoso . . . just a fair cowhand but loyal to the death.

Claude Pearsall . . . a banker, cautious but not afraid.

Duke Wayant . . . young Thorn rider, snappy as a bronc.

Neil Redwine . . . just a kid with lousy luck.

Enrique Lucero . . . hard-bitten sheriff.

Donancio Lucero . . . under-sheriff, with a face mild as a monk's.

Ben Utt . . . he was wanted in Texas, but nobody gave a rap.

CHAPTER
ONE

Homecoming

Price Thorn rested his low-cut shoes on the dashboard and cocked his derby hat lower on his head to shade his eyes. The sun was in the west and the wagon was pulling directly into the sun. Old Lunt Taliferro, sitting on the right-hand side of the wagon seat, spat over one creeping wheel and idly flicked at a horse fly on the broad rump of the off-wheel horse. The wheels creaked in the hard ruts of the road the wagon followed, the road which was the winding stage trail connecting the railroad town of Coyuntura with the little inland settlement of Pichon.

Price Thorn knew Lunt Taliferro but it was evident that Lunt did not recognize Price. Four years at college in the East, four more years — one spent in a laboratory doing research work on animal diseases, the other three in the Argentine on the llanos — had changed Price, put new lines in his face, added a close-cropped mustache, padded his body with muscle and toughened mental and moral fiber. He had left the Rana country a gangling kid, all arms and legs and eagerness; he was coming back a man, composed and sure.

1

"There ain't but one store at Pichon," Lunt Taliferro complained. "I don't reckon you can sell no goods in that town."

"No?" Price asked, and grinned inwardly. Lunt had him sized up as a drummer, a traveling salesman, and all along the fifteen miles they had traversed since leaving Coyuntura, Lunt had been trying to pump his passenger.

"No!" Lunt grunted and spat again. "We'll hit the Dobie line-camp in about half an hour. I'm goin' to lay up there tonight. Mebbe you can get 'em to hitch up a buckboard an' take you on in to Pichon."

"Maybe," Price agreed. "How are things in this country now, Mr. Taliferro?"

"Betwixt an' between," Lunt answered. "Bunch of new people in here in the last six, seven years. New men come in, crowdin' out some of the old ones. It's open range, you know, an' a man has got to be on his toes to save his grass."

Instantly Price's mind was alert. He had sensed something wrong in the last letters he had received. For a year or more the letters from Will Thorn had seemed a little strange. Price looked at the grizzled veteran sitting beside him and for an instant was tempted to disclose his identity and to ask questions. He restrained the impulse. New people caused new alliances. Perhaps Lunt Taliferro was lined up with the newcomers.

Price watched the flat country as they moved along. There was grass in plenty, rippling grama stretching away on either side of the road. Close beside the road Price saw the skeleton of a cow, the bones scattered by

2

coyotes and buzzards. Further on another skeleton, the bony framework of a calf's body, lay in a little muddled pile of bones. There were many such bone piles — little, pitiful heaps — tombstones of a cowman's hopes.

"It looks like there ought to be enough room for everybody," Price commented.

Taliferro shrugged. "Shows what you know about it," the old man answered. "Got to have twenty acres to carry a cow through the year in this country. The country is all right now — it ain't overstocked — but if the old-timers had made a fight an' kept up their herds, an' if the blackleg hadn't cleaned out the calves last Fall, you wouldn't see any grass a-tall."

"Blackleg?" Price questioned.

"Blackleg," Lunt grunted. "It cleaned out most of the calves. They died like flies that was caught on fly paper. Just *eggs-actly.*"

There was silence while the wheels crunched the shale of the road. Price Thorn sat musing. Blackleg! He knew something about blackleg, knew what that dread scourge could do to a range and to the men who lived upon the range. In his last years in school he had become interested in the work that was being done to control animal diseases. He had seen men dressed in laboratory aprons, poring over microscopes, inoculating animals, working from early morning until late at night, trying to solve a problem. And out there on the flat, in those little bone piles, was evidence of the thing those calm, impersonal men fought. For a year after his graduation Price had helped in that fight. Then had come the Argentine offer and Price had taken it. But

3

during that year he had learned and helped. The calm laboratory men had been hopeful. They had been on the trail of the disease, had been running it to earth. Perhaps by now they were successful. Perhaps . . .

Lunt Taliferro spat over a turning wheel. "The blackleg an' the Texas men," he answered. "I never seen blackleg so bad as last Fall. But the Texas men was worse."

"How do you mean?" Price asked.

"I mean that the old-timers had to give up or fight," Lunt said succinctly. "It wasn't so long ago that all this was Teepee an' Double Loop country. Now you don't see no Double Loop a-tall an' the Teepee is just'a whisper of what it used to be."

"The Teepee?" Price Thorn questioned.

"Will Thorn's brand," Lunt explained. "Now you'll find Ed Pothero's X Bar an' Tate Merriman's Key cattle all over, clear from the Rana hills on down across the flats. There's more brands in here, too."

"And the blackleg didn't hit them?" Price asked curiously.

"Hit everybody." Again Lunt spat over a wheel. "But the Texans had more money an' more riders an' . . . well, hell, they're just tougher! There's the Dobie camp." He pointed ahead with his whipstock to where a tiny square block stood beneath a cottonwood clump. "Merriman's camp," he said. "I aim to stop there."

The Dobie camp was a single adobe shack, two corrals and a shed, the shed and corrals hidden in a draw. The cottonwoods to the west made a windbreak for the building and as Lunt Taliferro's freight outfit

4

creaked into the yard and came to a stop, a gangling man, mustache trailing from his lip like a weeping willow branch, dirty and with a battered felt hat pulled down on his head came stooping through the door of the shack, then stood leaning against the door jamb.

"Hello, Joe," Lunt Taliferro greeted.

"Hello," Joe answered. His eyes, bright and small, belied his languor as he watched Price Thorn.

"Goin' to stop with you tonight," Lunt announced. "This here feller wants to get to Pichon. You got a rig you can take him in?"

Joe Nixon shook his head. "Got nothin' but a saddle horse," he answered, his little eyes taking in Price Thorn's derby hat, his low cut shoes, his salt and pepper suit with the heavy watch chain across the vest. There was a twinkle of malicious amusement in the little eyes.

Price Thorn got down stiffly from the wagon seat, stretched, took a tentative step and stopped. "I'd like to get to Pichon," he said mildly. "Could you lend me a horse and a saddle?"

Between Lunt Taliferro and Joe Nixon a look flashed. It seemed to Price, watching from the corner of his eyes, that Lunt nodded his head. Nixon straightened from the door jamb and shambled out toward the wagon. "I reckon," he said.

"You could take my grips on in to Pichon tomorrow," Price elaborated, looking at Lunt. "I'd see that the horse got back here."

"I'll bring him back," Lunt offered suddenly. "I'll be comin' back from Pichon the end of the week."

5

"And I'll pay you . . ." Price began.

"Don't want no pay." Joe Nixon's voice was suspiciously brisk. "I'll loan you a horse. Got a extra saddle too. Ben Jorgenson's saddle here. Ben's in town. He got piled an' had his shoulder bone broken."

"I'll be obliged," Price said. Again he noted the exchange of glances between Lunt and the man at the camp.

"I'll just unhook an' take my horses down to the corral," Taliferro announced briskly. "Give me a hand, Joe. We'll bring you a horse, mister." Joe shambled forward, stooping to unhook the tugs of the wheel horse. Lunt busied himself with the tug hooks and possessing himself of the lines, drove the four-up toward the corral, Joe Nixon following along behind the man and horses. Price Thorn, a twinkle in his blue eyes, watched them go. Something was up between Lunt Taliferro and Joe Nixon; Price knew it and suspected what it was.

When the men were gone, Price, climbing up on the load, opened a grip. From it he removed certain appurtenances, socks, a handkerchief or two, hesitated over the blue steel and black rubber of a long-barreled thirty-eight Smith & Wesson in a leather scabbard, shrugged and pulled out the gun and belt and strapped it to his waist beneath his coat. The holster settled familiarly against his hip. In the Argentine a man goes armed, particularly when he is boss of five hundred thousand acres and of fifty gauchos. Spirits can flame wild on the llanos and a gun sometimes can compensate for a knife or a lead-tipped cattle whip.

6

Price closed the grip, grinned slowly and climbed down from the wagon box. He could, he believed, reach the Teepee before dark.

From the corral Lunt Taliferro and Joe Nixon were returning, Nixon leading a horse. The horse was a tall roan, hammer-headed, with muscles that were stringy and gaunt under the reddish hide. The horse carried his hammer-head low, and his ears flopped. Price Thorn was not fooled.

"Here's the horse," Nixon drawled. "Stirrups ought to be right for you. You and Ben are about of a size." Nixon tendered the reins.

Taking the reins, Price Thorn placed one over the roan's neck. The roan perked up his hammer-head, let it hang again. The roan would waste no effort trying to keep a man from mounting. It was after the rider was astride that the roan exploded his fireworks.

"I'm obliged to you," Price said. "You'll bring the horse back, Mr. Taliferro?"

"I'll bring him back," Lunt assured. "You just follow the road an' you'll reach Pichon. It's about fifteen miles."

Price nodded. Now his movements were certain, sure, deft. He gathered the reins against the horn, twisted out a stirrup and possessed himself of one of the roan's drooping ears. As he went up he twisted the ear and the horse, surprised at the movement and the pain in his ear, stood still. Price settled himself in the saddle, released the ear, and straightened.

The roan took two steps, sank his hammer head between his knees and humped his back. Then he came unbuttoned, pitching viciously away from the wagon, circling, sunning his sides; he stopped short, sucked back under the saddle and broke in two again. Price Thorn rode the roan. Joe Nixon and Lunt Taliferro, fleeing to the shack for safety, stopped at the door and, their eyes wide with wonder, watched the horse and rider.

Handicapped because of his lack of spurs, Price rode the roan straight up. The horse bawling his rage, swung his head, snake-like, from side to side, unleashed a new fury, and Price, pulling off the derby, slapped at the horse with the hard hat, fanning him. Recognition came to Lunt Taliferro's eyes. "That's . . ." he began, and stopped. A canny customer, Lunt Taliferro. He had at length recognized his passenger but he kept that recognition to himself.

The roan horse straightened out, jerked up his head and giving in to the futility of bucking, lined out toward the north. Joe Nixon running forward, yelled a warning.

"Hey . . . that ain't the way to Pichon!"

The answer was a waving hand as the roan horse took his rider down into the draw.

Very slowly Nixon came back to the adobe. Lunt Taliferro was stuffing his pipe, paying particular attention to his blunt forefinger as he packed in the tobacco. Nixon watched Lunt, then drawled, "He ain't no pilgrim anyhow, Lunt."

Lunt shook his head. "No," he answered, "he ain't a pilgrim."

"Hell," Nixon's voice was disgusted. "He rode ol' Dynamite straight up. Never seen a crack of daylight between him an' the saddle. He could of set up there an' rolled a smoke. Who is he, Lunt?"

"He never told me his name," Taliferro answered cannily. "Joe, I got a pint in the wagon that ain't never been drunk yet. What say we sample it before supper?"

"Git it," ordered Nixon succinctly. "Lunt, he ain't goin' to fetch Pichon, the way he's headed. He'll wind up at the Teepee."

"I reckon he'll make out," Lunt grunted. "I'll fetch the pint." He walked off toward the wagon. Joe Nixon, shading his eyes, watched the dot that was the roan horse and his rider disappear into the northwest.

Price Thorn, riding toward the Teepee, picking out familiar landmarks, thrilled as he crossed the old familiar country, country a little strange now because of his long absence from it. Price felt the roan horse stretch out and bunch under him, and he grinned. Tomorrow he would be sore and stiff — he had not ridden for a year — but now it was good, mighty good, to get the feel of those bunching muscles through the saddle, to feel the surge and swing of the roan.

It was growing dark as Price crossed Arroyo Seco, the roan scrambling up the further bank. Five miles from Arroyo Seco he would be at the Teepee. Price sent the horse along.

Then the roan slackened pace, hesitated, stopped, and peering through the gathering dusk Price saw the thing that had halted the horse. Here, before him, where never a fence had been, now stretched a line of wire and poles. A little bleak glint came into Price

Thorn's eyes. He swung down from the roan and walking forward examined the fence.

It was a new structure and surely had not been erected by the Teepee. Price sensed that, even as he looked at the poles and wire. Anger formed hotly in his mind, anger that grew and grew until it was a flame. The fence coupled with what Lunt Taliferro had told him as he rode the creaking wagon, spoke eloquently to Price Thorn. This fence was not a barrier raised by the Teepee against encroachment. Rather it was a defiance flung at the Teepee, a boundary mark barring the passage of Teepee cattle toward the south. Deliberately Price began to kick down the wire and then, thinking of a better idea, went to his saddle. There was a rope on the saddle. Nodding his satisfaction Price took down the rope. He broke the topmost strand of fence wire, fastened it to the rope and, mounting and fastening the other end of the rope to the horn, started the roan.

For a full half mile Price Thorn pulled down the fence, taking a strand at a time, letting the wire tangle and ensnarl, careless of how he worked. He would have been glad for a pair of fence pliers. Equipped with them he would have cut the fence in a multitude of places. Lacking the pliers he did the best he could, which was very good indeed. Finished with the fence he coiled the rope and rode on through the darkness. Tomorrow or the next day, within a short time at least, he would return and destroy that fence, tear it all down, burn the posts and throw the rolled wire into Arroyo Seco. Now he must be content with what he had done.

10

Riding on into the night, the ground gradually sloping up before him, Price could not make his anger die. This had always been his country. Old Will Thorn had settled it, fought for it, starved with it, and blossomed with it. By right of heritage, by right of battle, by usage, by every custom that governed the range, this country was Will Thorn's, and so too belonged to Will Thorn's son. And Price, riding home across his own country, had struck a drift fence, a barrier raised against the man who had tamed the land.

A pinpoint of light showed ahead, grew, became a lighted window. The black bulk of familiar buildings was outlined against a blue-black sky. Price Thorn reined in the roan horse and lifted his voice in a shout. "Hello the house!"

There followed a moment of quiet after that, while the call echoed faintly from the sheer wall of Muralla Butte behind and to the west of the house. Then light streamed from a door and a harsh voice answered, a voice which was cracked from yelling at many a recalcitrant cow.

"Who's out there?"

Price Thorn got down from the roan. "It's me, Jim," he called. "Price."

Again silence from the house while the butte wall echoed, "Price . . . Price . . . Pri . . ."

"It's about time you was gettin' home," Jim Harvie called from the doorway. "Put up yore horse an' come on in."

Deep in Price Thorn's chest a laugh formed and came bubbling to his lips. This was as it should be. This was right, just right. How many times, in the years that were gone, had old Jim Harvie scolded him from that door? How many times had Jim Harvie called, "It's about time you was gettin' home. Put up yore horse an' come on in!" The man in the door was pushed aside and another man, a man who moved slowly, as though crippled, took Harvie's place.

"Price?" a booming voice called into the night.

"Coming, Dad," Price answered, and led the roan toward the house.

When Price reached the light that streamed, fanlike, through the doorway, Will Thorn had descended from the stoop to meet him. Harvie too, small and gnarled and sharp-faced as a hawk, was waiting. Price let the roan go and shook hands with his father and with Harvie, the grip of Will Thorn's hand strangely weak, Harvie's grasp like that of a wolf trap. Will Thorn put an arm about his son's shoulders and drew him into the light and there, speechless, examined the man who had come back in place of the boy who had gone away. Jim Harvie hovered around the pair, and from the bunkhouse below the house, light came and presently there emerged the bulky figure of Granny Davis, who from time immemorial had cooked for the Teepee. Granny too joined the group and shook hands with the prodigal, then hastened away to make coffee. Will Thorn took his son into the house and Jim Harvie, muttering something about "a man lookin' after his own horse," led the roan away toward the corral.

12

In the house Price had his first real look at his father. Will Thorn, moving back from his son, surveyed the new arrival from head to foot, and as the father made survey and estimate, so too did the son.

Will Thorn saw a man, square-faced, decisive, blue eyed, the dark mustache close clipped above his mouth. He saw a man with a smoothly compact body neatly covered with a modish suit, a man who would be bigger out of his clothes than he was in them.

Price Thorn was shocked at what he saw. Will Thorn had been a big man. Once he had towered in a crowd, standing out like a pine among dwarf cedars. Now but a ruin of magnificence remained. The great muscles that had been so strong were shunken, the full cheeks were hollowed, but worse than this the brightness was gone from Will Thorn's eyes. They were the eyes of an old man, of an old man who has been beaten and who no longer has the will to fight.

Jim Harvie came hurrying in. From the kitchen Granny padded, carrying a coffee pot. He planked it down upon the table and poured the steaming beverage into cups which he brought.

"Now," commanded Jim Harvie, "let's hear about it. What brung you home? When'd you get to Coyuntura? Whyn't you let us know you was comin'?"

Price Thorn picked up a coffee cup, grinned over it at Harvie and made answer. "I came because I figured it was time," he said. "I got in today. I didn't say I was coming because I wasn't sure till the last minute. And I'm damned glad to get here."

Harvie grunted. Will Thorn was smiling at his son and old Granny Davis beamed with pride. "There yuh are, Jim," Granny said. "In a nut shell. How you been, Price? How was the Argentine? How'd yuh like it back East?"

Price Thorn sat down, took a sip of the scalding hot coffee and grinned at the three. "I'll tell you," he said.

He did tell them. Prompted by questions from his father, from Jim, from Granny, he spun the tale of the last eight years. Now and then one of the three nodded, familiar already with the tale through letters that Price had written. Now and then one of them asked a question, demanding elaboration. It was midnight and past when the first rough sketch of the story was done. Jim Harvie got up.

"An' so you come home," he said. "Well, yo're welcome, Price. I reckon we'd better turn in now, Granny. Mornin' comes early around these parts." It was just as though Jim Harvie, foreman for the Teepee, was speaking to a full crew instead of to his owner, his owner's son, and an old fat cook.

"Guess so," agreed Granny. "The rest of it'll keep. Yo're goin' to be here awhile, ain't you, Price?"

"From now on," Price answered quietly.

"That's good," said Harvie, and turned toward the door.

Price got up. "I'll be back in a minute, Dad," he said to Will Thorn, and followed Harvie out of the door. Granny was already moving off toward the bunkhouse. Price caught Harvie's arm when they were off the stoop. The old foreman stopped.

14

"Why didn't you write me, Jim?" Price demanded. "Why didn't you tell me how he was?"

"Figured you wasn't interested," Harvie answered with asperity. "You stayed away plenty long."

"But I didn't know!" Price expostulated.

Harvie relented a little. "No," he agreed, "you didn't know. Mebbe I should of wrote you. Will's slipped bad, Price. Mighty bad. He just don't give a damn."

"But the ranch," Price said. "He was always so proud of it. He . . ."

"You wasn't here an' I reckon he thought you didn't care no more." The grimness was back in Harvie's voice. "An' last Fall the blackleg hit us. We lost a lot of calves an' a lot of cows. It's kind of hard to ride out an' find yore cattle dead, no matter how well you take care of 'em or how much you try. It kicked the props out from under Will. That — an' you bein' gone."

Silence hovered between the men. "The blackleg," Price said softly. "I know something about blackleg, Jim. I . . . Never mind now, I'm here and maybe I've got a hole card against the blackleg. And I'll make it up to Dad. I just didn't think, Jim."

"Kids don't think," Jim Harvie agreed. "Well, yore bein' here will be enough for Will. I reckon there ain't much you can do about the outfit. It's slipped. Me an' Granny an' Tony Troncoso up at the Mule Pen camp are all the crew we got left. There's mebbe four hundred head of cattle." The old man spat. "Hell," his disgust was in his voice, "we used to keep six riders steady an' run three thousand head. We been crowded, Price."

15

"We'll do some crowding," Price Thorn promised grimly. "Good night, Jim. I'm going back in with Dad awhile. I'll see you tomorrow."

"Good night, Price," Jim Harvie answered, and walked on through the darkness toward the bunkhouse.

CHAPTER
TWO

Good Neighbor

The following morning, when Jim Harvie had rattled away in the buckboard to bring Price Thorn's grips from Pichon, Price stood on the stoop and looked over his domain. Will Thorn stood beside him, bent-shouldered, some of his listlessness gone because his boy was back at home. Price still wore the derby hat and the salt-and-pepper suit, but he had discarded the low-cut shoes for boots. His feet had not grown during his absence, albeit the rest of him had filled out. His old boots still fit and they felt good on his feet.

"What horses have you got, Dad?" Price asked.

Will Thorn cleared his throat. "Just Muddy is left of the bunch that was here when you were," he answered. "I keep him up for what ridin' I do. There's some young horses in the pasture an' Tony's got some horses that he's ridin' at the camp."

"I'll go out an' run in the remuda," Price said. "I want to look the place over, Dad. You go along?"

Will Thorn shook his head. "I guess not," he answered. "I don't do a lot of ridin', Price. I guess I don't do much of anything."

"I'll do what there is to be done," Price promised, stepping down from the stoop.

"You'll find things changed," Will Thorn said listlessly. "It ain't the same in the Rana anymore. Schuster is gone. There ain't any Double Loop outfit. Man named Pothero came in and bought what was left of Schuster's brand. I been dickerin' with him a little too."

"Are you going to sell out, Dad?" Price said quietly.

Will Thorn shrugged. "I've thought of it," he admitted. "I'm gettin' old an' it seemed to me that a younger man was needed here."

"I'm a younger man," Price announced. "Seems to me that they're crowding you, Dad, I struck a fence when I came in last night."

"That's a drift fence that Pothero put up," Will Thorn explained. "It saves a lot of work when we round up; kind of keeps the cattle from mixin'."

"And our cows would drift into it in a snow and bunch up and get killed," Price said succinctly. "I pulled down a half mile of that fence last night. When I go out with a pair of clippers I'll cut it all down."

The older man shook his head. "Pothero . . ." he began.

"He can like it or not!" Price's eyes glinted like flint shards in the sun. "That fence splits right across the country we've always used, and unless I'm mistaken the spring in Arroyo Seco belongs to you. Didn't you buy a homestead around the spring?"

Will Thorn nodded. "I own the Seco spring," he admitted. "But Pothero . . ."

". . . is using our country," Price snapped. "I'll have a little talk with him. I'm going out to get the remuda, Dad. Then I'll ride up and see Tony. I'll eat dinner with him."

The older man said nothing and Price, with a nod and a grin to his father, went on to the corrals.

Old Muddy was in the big pen and Price, bringing his old saddle and gear from the saddle room, saddled the horse and rode off into the horse pasture. He picked up a little bunch of horses, brought them back to the pens and selecting a bay, a full bodied, heavy horse that stood fifteen two, changed his saddle and let the others go. Will Thorn did not come from the house and Price, mounting the bay, rode off toward the north and the Rana hills. The Mule Pen camp was just at the foot of the Ranas.

As he crossed the rolling country toward the Mule Pen camp, Price began to encounter cattle. These should all have been Teepees but there were others mixed in, some branded X Bar, some with a Key and some carrying an O Slash or a Flying U. The O Slash and Flying U were familiar to Price. They did not properly belong in this country, for the headquarters of both brands were below Coyuntura. Dave Appleby owned the O Slash and Enrique and Donancio Lucero ran the Flying U as a sort of community affair for the Lucero clan. There were not enough of O Slash and Flying U cattle to worry about, but there were plenty of Keys and X Bars. The cattle under the strange brands were for the most part young animals, hustlers, but the Teepees that Price saw were old cows. Most of them were milking and there were good calves scattered here and there across the range. Price scowled at the strange cattle but grinned when he saw the Teepees.

When he reached the Mule Pen camp he found Tony Troncoso in the corral. Tony was a squat, heavy-shouldered native with a seamed and wrinkled countenance that resembled nothing so much as a monkey's face, but no one in the Rana country made the mistake of calling him "Mono." The last man that had tried that had been confronted with six inches of shining knife blade and a grinning Tony behind it. Following that occurrence the nickname craze had died down so far as Tony was concerned. Troncoso was a fair cowhand. He was not a good rider but a man could put Tony on a job and be sure that when he came back all the fences would be up and all the cattle there. Tony had worked for the Teepee since he was a kid of eighteen. He was about thirty-five now but to look at his wrinkled face a man would have judged him fifty. Tony came from the corral, stared at Price, and then, recognition blooming on his face, came at a bowlegged run.

"Meester Price!" Tony exclaimed, pump-handling the arm that Price had extended. "W'en deed you get back?"

"Last night, Tony." Price grinned and dismounted. "How are things with you?"

"Theengs ees not so good." Tony's face was rueful. "Theese Teepee ranch ees gone for hal, Meester Price. She's not good outfeet any more."

20

"Going to quit, Tony?" Price asked, watching the man narrowly.

Tony shook his head. "Not queet," he announced. "I theenk I'm goin' to make ride an' see theese Potheros. Then I cut hees nack an' we have good outfeet some more." Tony was very cheerful as he made the announcement, but Price knew what was said was meant exactly. Tony would cut a throat for the Teepee or steal for the Teepee or work from dawn to dark and on into the night for Will Thorn.

"Pothero bother you?" Price asked sharply.

"Hees cows," Tony explained. "They are all over the place. Now that you come back mebbe you an' me go see them, huh?"

"Maybe we will," Price agreed. "What horses do you have, Tony?"

"Een the corral," Tony answered.

"Let's look at them."

Tony walked ahead and Price, leading his bay followed. There were horses in the corral, twelve head. Four were young, unbroken. There were eight head of saddle horses and of these Price's knowing eyes picked out those that were being ridden. Tony watched the young boss with shrewd, beady eyes and spoke of the merits of each horse.

"Why don't you ride the dun?" Price asked sharply, his eyes singling out a big smoky dun horse that was close to the fence.

"Jefe?" Tony inquired.

"If that's what you call him."

Producing papers and tobacco Tony rolled a cigarette. "I tell eet to you, Meester Price," he answered. "That Jefe he's a beeg horse. He's bock lak hal weeth me. One mont' ago I start to ride heem an' I geeve a beeg jomp an' land on hees heeps. He bock weeth me an' t'row me off een the fence on my head an' hurt my ankle pretty bad." Tony's face was entirely serious as he put the cigarette in his mouth.

"I'll take him along, then," Price said, hiding his amusement. "You got anything else you don't want to ride?"

"That grulla," Tony gestured with the cigarette. "He's sono-fabeech. You want heem, Meester Price?"

"I'll take him," Price agreed. "I want to make a little ride with you, Tony. I think I'll take the dun horse."

"Seguro," Tony agreed, and opening the gate, went into the corral.

The dun horse, Jefe, humped his back and rolled his eyes when Price changed saddles. Aside from that he did nothing. Tony saddled a pinto and waited while Price rode the dun in the corral. When he was satisfied that the dun would not buck, Price rode the horse out and Tony turned the rest loose, keeping in the pen only the bay that Price had ridden to camp. Side by side the two men left the Mule Pen camp and Price grinned as Jefe struck a running walk that was easy as a rocking chair. The dun horse Jefe had run a bluff on Tony; that was all.

When they came back to the camp that afternoon, Price was scowling. There were X Bar and O Slash cattle all over the country. The cows had been

22

deliberately shoved into the Ranas. It was pretty evident that the X Bar and the O Slash were using the Rana hills for summer country, just as the Teepee had always used it. And, by range custom and by control of water, the country belonged to the Teepee.

"Damned hogs," Price snapped when he and Tony reached the camp. "We're goin' to do something about this, Tony."

"We talk weeth theese Potheros, huh?" Tony suggested brightly.

"Yeah," drawled Price, and with him a drawl was a sign of danger, "and if talking doesn't work we'll do a little something else."

Tony grunted and went in to cook dinner, and Price, squatting against the rock wall of the Mule Pen camp, smoked a cigarette and stared off into the distance.

He was quiet that evening when he returned to the Teepee headquarters, quiet and filled with ideas. He brought back the bay, which he had dubbed Doughboy, and the grulla that Tony, in all innocence, had named Judas. Price had very little to say at the supper table and after the meal, sitting on the stoop with Jim Harvie, he questioned the older man closely and filed away the answers for future reference.

"I'm going to town tomorrow," Price announced when he had finished his good-night cigarette. "I'll see Pearsall at the bank and see if we can't get a loan. We need about a thousand head of cows in here, Jim."

Harvie stared through the darkness that was made less dark by the lamp in the kitchen behind them. "Goin' to play a little, are you, Price?" he asked.

"I'm going to stock the range," Price said grimly. "I think it's time the Teepee ran cattle on our grass in place of somebody else using it."

Jim Harvie's cigarette made a little glowing arc in the dark as he gestured with it. "You'll have to talk to Will," he warned.

"I'll talk to Dad," Price agreed.

"Then," Harvie got up, "I'll go to bed. I'll want to get some stuff in town tomorrow, Price. I need a haircut anyhow."

Price Thorn grinned. He would not be alone when he rode to Coyuntura in the morning, "All right," he agreed, "and I'll talk to Dad now." He too got up, his shoulders bulking black against the lamplight that streamed through the door. Broad, square shoulders they were, capable of taking a load, Jim Harvie thought.

"Good night, Price," said Jim Harvie.

In the house Price Thorn found his father dozing in a chair. Will Thorn roused when his son entered the living room and rubbed a big, wrinkled hand across his eyes. "Just catchin' forty winks, son," he apologized.

Price sat down. "Dad," he began, "I want to take hold of the Teepee if you'll let me. I want . . ."

Will Thorn's hand made a little gesture. "I've held on for you," he said. "It's yours, you know that."

Price nodded. "I just wanted to ask," he said humbly. "That was all, Dad."

The big hand came out slowly and rested on Price's shoulder. "Whatever you want, boy," said Will Thorn. "Just whatever you want." It was a promise, but there was no force in the words.

Will Thorn released his grip on his son's shoulder, turned slowly and walked to his room. Price watched his father go and then turned to the table beside which he sat. He had watched an old, beaten man leave the room, a man that living had whipped. But he, Price Thorn, was young and strong and he was not beaten. The Texas men, blackleg, all the trouble and grief in the Rana, could not whip him! Price's jaw squared. He would do something about this trouble in the Rana. He would do it now.

Price drew an ink bottle and a tablet toward him. He had a letter to write. Back in the laboratories there were men who knew about blackleg, who had been learning how to handle it. Price knew some of those men. He would appeal to them for help. And as for the rest of the trouble on the Rana: When it came he would take care of that too! Dipping a pen into the ink, Price Thorn began to write.

When morning came Price did not immediately leave for Coyuntura as he had planned. At seven o'clock, having been up since five, he was in the corral saddling the bay Doughboy, when a grunt from Jim Harvie caused him to look up. There was a rider coming in from the south. Price finished pulling up his latigo, and then looping his reins on the saddle horn, walked out of the corral gate, his derby slightly tilted on his head.

The incoming rider halted by the corral and spoke without dismounting. "Where's Thorn?"

Price, sizing up the man, saw a big heavy fellow, full-bellied and with a clean-shaven face that was oddly thin. Head and body did not belong together, Price decided. A man with a paunch like that should have a full, fleshy face. "Mr. Thorn is in the house," Price answered. "I'm his son, Price."

Still the heavy man did not dismount. He grunted, looked Price over and spoke his name. "I'm Ed Pothero," he said, and there was the unmistakable twang of Texas in his voice. "I own the X Bar."

Price nodded and said nothing by way of acknowledgment, and Pothero spoke again. "I want to talk to Thorn," he demanded.

"I've sort of taken over since I came home," Price drawled. "What have you got on your mind, Mr. Pothero?"

"I came out of the Dobie camp this mornin' an' rode my drift fence," Pothero said heavily. "Somebody pulled down about half a mile of it. I want to tell Thorn that I won't stand for that. You or him or nobody else from this layout wants to monkey with my fence."

"I didn't monkey with it," Price's voice had dropped a tone and was deceptively gentle. "I pulled down that wire and this morning I'd planned to ride over and tell you to get the rest of it down. That's Teepee country you've got your fence on, Mr. Pothero."

"It's open range," Pothero snapped. "You'll put up the fence you tore down."

"No," Price Thorn shook his head, "You'll take it down. We own the Seco spring, Mr. Pothero. I think if you go to the courthouse, you'll find that we own most of the water south of here clear in to the Dobie camp. I'm glad that you showed up this morning. It saves me

26

a ride. You can get that fence down right away. We're going to be using the grass below it."

Pothero's scowl deepened. "Your father agreed to that fence," he snapped. "I talked it over with him before I ever put it in. I want to see him."

"It won't do you any good," Price said, shortly. "My father has turned the ranch over to me. I'm running it. The only reason I haven't taken a pair of pliers and cut that fence to pieces is because I judged you'd talked to Dad before you put it up. I try to get along with my neighbors, Mr. Pothero."

Ed Pothero digested that. He grunted and swung down from his saddle. "I'll go talk to Thorn," he announced.

"And I'll go with you," Price affirmed. "I think you're going to find things a little different in the Rana country, Mr. Pothero. You're new here, aren't you?"

"I've been here long enough," Pothero snapped, striding off toward the house.

Price followed the fat man, glancing back over his shoulder as he reached the stoop. Jim Harvie had come out of the corral and was grinning. As Price looked back Harvie heartily shook hands with himself. Price's lips twitched as he withheld a smile.

Will Thorn came to the door to meet the two men and held it open to let Pothero enter the kitchen. Price, following the fat man into the room was shocked at sight of his father's face. He had never seen that look on Will Thorn, the look of a man who was frightened and who wished to conciliate an enemy.

"See here, Thorn," Ed Pothero began without preamble, "this kid of yours admits that he pulled down a half mile of my fence. I want you to tell him what we agreed about that. I want you . . ."

"It doesn't make a damn what you want!" Price had completely lost his temper. The bullying tone of Pothero's voice was too much for him.

"Why, Price," Will Thorn began apologetically, "Mr. Pothero came up here and talked to me about putting up that fence. It seemed to me to be a good idea. It would keep my cattle from drifting an' . . ."

". . . and hold them off grass that belongs to you," Price snapped. "Am I going to run the Teepee or not, Dad? I've got to know right now!"

"Why, —" there was a plea in Will Thorn's eyes as he looked at his son, "— I said you were going to run the place, Price. I told you that, but I thought . . ." He paused, undecided.

"That's all I want to know," Price said swiftly. "You heard what my father said, Mr. Pothero. Now I tell you to get your fence down if you want to save it!"

"You touch that fence an' you'll be sorry!" Pothero rasped harshly. "I'm warnin' you, Thorn." The fat man's little eyes turned to Will Thorn. "You can save a heap of trouble if you'll tell this young jackass to stay clear of me. You know that!"

Price Thorn's broad hand shot out and settled on Ed Pothero's shoulder. The hand contracted and the fingers sank into the flesh. "Trouble?" Price snapped. "You don't know what the word means. Now get out, Pothero! I've told you about the fence. Get it down!

28

And don't come back here and try to run your bluff on the Teepee again. It won't stick!"

Ed Pothero was shrinking away under the grip of Price's hand. Now, with a jerk, Price turned the man, heading him toward the door.

"Get out!" Price Thorn commanded once more.

Ed Pothero got out. When he had slammed the door after him, Price turned to his father. Will Thorn's face was worried. "Price," Will Thorn began, "you shouldn't have acted like that. After all, I talked to Mr. Pothero before he put up that fence. This will only make trouble. I'm afraid . . ."

"Dad," Price's voice was very gentle, "Ed Pothero won't make any trouble that we can't handle. All he needs is to have his bluff called. I've called it!"

Unwittingly Price was cruel. He did not mean to be, but there was a contrast between his sureness and the uncertainty of his father, the never-ending contrast between youth and age.

"I don't know, Price," Will Thorn said. "I'm afraid you'll go too far."

Price hardly heard his father. He sat down and was quiet for a time, looking out the window to where the grass was green across the flats. "I'm going to town," Price said suddenly. "It's time we did a little stocking of our own grass. I think I can fix it up with Pearsall."

Will Thorn made no comment and Price, looking now at his father, saw the age lines on the old man's face; the lines of strength were strong upon Will Thorn but the driving force, the thing that had etched those

29

lines, was gone. Price got up and walked over to his father.

"Don't worry, Dad," he said. "You sent me to school to learn the scientific side of this business. You let me go to Argentina because you thought I could learn something there. Don't you think it's about time I came back and used some of the things I've learned? I've been laying out on you long enough." Price's words were light but there was soberness and consideration on his face. The main trouble with the Teepee was not the fact that the neighbors were hogging grass, not the fact that the ranch was run down and the cattle depleted. None of those things counted so much. The real difficulty was with Will Thorn.

"Don't worry, Dad," Price said again. "You've hired you a good manager now."

Will Thorn said nothing, and Price went out of the room.

Down at the corral he found Jim Harvie with a horse saddled. Harvie looked at Price and grunted. "Pothero pulled out talkin' to himself," the little man announced. "Acted like you'd put a tick in his ear. Did you, Price?"

"I told him he'd pull that fence," Price answered. "Jim, I'm not going to take you to town with me. I want you to stay here. See if you can get Dad to go out with you. We've got to do something about him. He's just letting himself go."

"I thought maybe when you came back he'd pick up," Harvie said wistfully. "He did for a little while. I can't figure Will out, Price."

30

"He needs to get his teeth into something," Price said. "See if you can't get him to go down to the vegas with you. He used to be mighty anxious to have a hay crop. He always wanted plenty of feed. Get him to go down and look them over."

Harvie nodded. "All right," he said dubiously. "But I don't think he'll go."

"I'll go on then," Price said.

Harvie held up his hand and the younger man stopped. "You had a round with Pothero, Price," Harvie said. "Better get dressed before you go to town."

"Get ..." Price stopped. He looked at the salt-and-pepper pants he wore, let his gaze wander on down to the tips of his old boots, and then, suddenly, he realized what Harvie meant. Lifting his eyes to meet Jim Harvie's, Price found them bright and sharp.

"Oh," said Price Thorn. "Yes. I'll get dressed, Jim."

"Just in case," said Jim Harvie.

Back in the house Price passed his father, still motionless in his chair. In his room he picked up his belt and holstered gun, looked at them and then looped the belt around his middle so that the scabbard was under his coat. With a glance at the mirror, he cocked the derby to a more rakish angle and then, leaving the bedroom, went out to where his father sat.

"I wish you'd go with Jim today, Dad," Price suggested.

Will Thorn shook his head. "I'm tired, Price," he answered. "I think I'll just stay in and read."

Price opened his mouth to expostulate, thought better of it and went on out.

31

CHAPTER
THREE

Additional Security

It was thirty-two miles in to Coyuntura from the Teepee. The road made it eleven miles longer, but by cutting across Price saved time and distance. He had left the Teepee at eight o'clock and it was eleven-thirty when he rode into Coyuntura's main street. Coming in from the ranch he had experimented with Doughboy and found his gaits. A man that works from a saddle must know his horses, just as he must know his other tools. Doughboy was handy and he had a little rack that made distance shrink and that caused the saddle to feel about as comfortable as an old shoe. Price was pleased with Doughboy, just as he was with Jefe. Jefe had proved his ability to handle cattle, for Price had worked and roped off the dun during his ride with Tony. Now if Doughboy proved to be as good a cow horse as he was a ground coverer, Price would have at least two real mounts in his string.

Coyuntura had been laid out by a drunk Mexican driving a burro on a dark night, and straggled over a considerable portion of the landscape. There was one straight street that ran from the depot to the courthouse and on which the business houses faced.

The First State Bank of Coyuntura was almost in the middle of this street, just across from Brumaker's General Store. On one side of the bank there was a vacant lot and an alley ran down the opposite side of the one-story brick building. Beyond the alley was Coyne's saddle shop and next to Coyne's was the Cliff saloon, the largest saloon in Coyuntura.

Price stopped briefly at the post office to mail the letter he had written and then rode Doughboy on to Brumaker's store, stopped, dismounted and tied the horse to the hitchrail. There were things he wanted to buy in Brumaker's but now he had business at the bank.

Crossing the wide street he entered the little brick building where he found Claude Pearsall in his office at the front of the bank, and the bookkeeper working behind the barred enclosure. Removing the derby, Price went into Pearsall's office. The banker did not at first recognize his visitor but when Price had made his identity known, Pearsall gestured toward a chair and invited Price to be seated.

"What do you have on your mind, Mr. Thorn?" the banker asked after Price sat down.

"I want a loan, Mr. Pearsall," Price answered. "I've come back to stay at the Teepee now and I want to increase the number of cattle we're running."

"So?" With cautious blue eyes Pearsall considered the man opposite him. Claude Pearsall was a good banker. He could say "no" to anyone, but he always heard a man through.

33

"Yes." Price nodded. "We have about four hundred head of cattle. They're clear and there was an eighty-five percent calf crop this spring. Cattle are cheap. It's a good time to buy. We control the water from the Ranas clear on down almost to the Dobie camp. I'd like to get a thousand two-year-old heifers."

Pearsall considered a moment and then spoke. "That would be twenty thousand dollars you'd need," he said slowly.

"A little more than that," Price answered. "I'll need some money for bulls, too, and I'm not sure I can get the heifers I want for twenty dollars. They might go to twenty-two or twenty-two fifty."

"And the security?" Pearsall suggested.

"You'll take a mortgage on the heifers and on the cattle we have," Price answered, "and on the new cattle."

Pearsall considered that answer. "And you'll pay off on your calf crop," he said. "Suppose that you don't have a calf crop? Suppose that the blackleg hits you like it hit last Fall?"

Price leaned forward eagerly. "There's ways of fighting blackleg," he said. "When I was in school I learned a good deal about that. I've friends back there that will help me. I tell you, Mr. Pearsall, I believe I can handle the blackleg if it hits. I . . ."

Pearsall interrupted. "Suppose we grant that?" he said. "Frankly, I'm doubtful that anything can be done to stop the blackleg: but suppose you can handle it? I still think . . ." He broke off, drumming the desk top with his fingers. There was a long silence. Price waited, and then: "Ed Pothero and his brother, and Merriman, all have cattle in that country," Pearsall said. "How is the grass?"

"Good," Price answered.

"And you'll give me a mortgage on all the cattle as security," Pearsall mused.

"Yes."

Again the banker lost himself in thought, then he shook his head. "I'm afraid we can't make the loan," he announced. "I'm afraid not."

"Not enough security?" Price suggested, rising.

"That's part of it." Pearsall also got up from his chair. "I'm sorry, Mr. Thorn."

Price was sure that the banker had not given all his reason for refusing the loan. There were other considerations in Pearsall's mind and Price knew some of them. The fact that Will Thorn had slipped, had let things go, had entered Pearsall's thoughts; and too, there was the fact that Price was an unknown quantity to the banker.

"It's your business to protect your depositors," Price said. "I wouldn't want you to make a bad loan. Good-bye, Mr. Pearsall."

Pearsall said good-bye, his eyes still studying Price. Price left the office and went out of the bank. As he stood for a moment on the sidewalk, he heard the key turn in the bank's door behind him. It was twelve o'clock and Pearsall was locking up.

Decision reached, Price crossed the street. He would get what he wanted at Brumaker's and then head out for the ranch and when he got home he would not speak of his failure. There were other banks besides the First State, and there were other bankers besides Pearsall. Price could try again. He reached Brumaker's walk, crossed it and went into the store.

Inside the store, where the light was not so bright, — for Brumaker's windows were shaded by a tin awning along the front — Price caught the peculiar scent of the place. Only a general merchandise store can have that particular odor, a mingling of the smells of oil cloth, rubber, woolen goods, groceries, coffee and spices, all intermingled to make a scent, pleasant and as individual as a man's name. Brumaker himself was in the front of the store and after staring at Price for a moment, came forward.

Again it was necessary for Price to speak his name to the storekeeper before recognition came to Brumaker's eyes. When that was done, however, there was nothing in the store that Price could not have. Will Thorn had done business with the little merchant when Brumaker had first come to Coyuntura, and they were friends of long standing. Accompanied by the merchant, Price went about outfitting himself. He bought a hat, Levi's, gloves, a neckerchief — the good, durable, useful clothing of the range man. Brumaker computed the prices and said that he would have the packages ready when Price came back for them, and Price, smiling, started for the front of the store, the merchant beside him. It was almost one o'clock now.

As they reached the door of the store the two men stopped for a final word together. Price had his back to the store front and Brumaker was facing the windows.

36

"It's good that you've come home," the merchant said. "I've . . ." He stopped and stared past Price.

Price asked a question swiftly. "What's the matter?"

"I don't know . . ." Brumaker began, and stopped.

Turning, Price could see a man standing just beside the door of the bank. The loafer had his back toward them and they could not see his face. Looking to the left Price saw another man standing in the alley between Coyne's saddle shop and the bank. There were four horses in the alley and the man there held their reins.

"It looks queer!" Brumaker said suddenly, and moving away from Price, went behind the counter and reached under it. Even as the merchant moved, a cowpuncher, loafing on the bench under the tin awning of the saddle shop, raised himself to his feet and turned to stare toward the bank. The loafer before the bank also moved as the cowboy arose. He half turned so that Price could see that a blue bandanna was raised to cover chin and mouth and nose, much as a man might wear his neckerchief when riding in the dust of a herd. There was a sharp explosion in the street. Billy Wayant, the cowboy in front of the saddle shop, sat down abruptly on the bench and then began to fold over. Price saw smoke trail up from the hand of the man with the blue bandanna. Then with a long step, Price reached the door, jerked it open and was out on the sidewalk, the thirty-eight Smith & Wesson in his hand.

Glass tinkled down from the door behind Price as he reached the walk. Indistinctly he understood that the man in front of the bank was shooting at him. He did not return the fire for the horses at Brumaker's hitch rail were frightened and bay Doughboy reared high, jerking the rein that tied him. In the alley beside the bank the man who held the horses was also shooting. A man thrust his head out of Coyne's shop and hastily ducked back in. Price, ducking under the hitchrail, dodging a flying hoof, reached the street. From the door of the bank two men came running, one carrying a heavy canvas sack. Both men were armed and they paused to whirl and shoot at someone that Price could not see. The whole thing was happening in split seconds. It seemed to Price Thorn, running toward the middle of the street, that it was unreal, that he was looking through the eye piece of some machine in a nickleodeon, and watching a drama unfold as the little pictures flashed.

The men who had come from the bank were at the horses now, mounting, fighting down the frightened animals. The man with the blue bandanna was already up and had turned in his saddle. Now the horses were running, churning up dust from Coyuntura's street as they headed toward the depot. The riders, half turned in their saddles, were looking back and shooting as they pounded out of town. Something kicked up the dirt at Price's feet. Something smacked into the air beside his head. Then Price Thorn's long arm was deliberately lifted and over the sights of the blue thirty-eight he caught a bobbing figure. His finger contracted just as slowly and surely as ever, back in the East on the pistol range, he had sighted at a target and pulled the trigger. The thirty-eight bounced, dropped level, bounced sharply again, and instead of four men fleeing wildly up Coyuntura's street there were now three men and a riderless horse. A huddled figure lay in the dust, and beside the figure there was a canvas sack. Price walked slowly forward, hardly conscious of Howard Brumaker coming from the store, not heeding the men that came from Coyne's and from the Cliff saloon, not noting the hatless, gray-haired man that ran, shouting, out of the bank. Beyond the depot were running horses, their riders bent low in their saddles. The horsemen rose as they topped the long swell beyond the depot and then dropped out of sight. Price stopped beside the huddled figure in the street, his gun lowered, pointed down. The man on the ground moaned softly and then was still, and Brumaker, stopping beside Price, lowered the rifle he held, so that the butt rested in the dust, and spoke.

"And that's that," Brumaker said.

The crowd closed around Price then, the men from the Cliff, from Coyne's, from the business houses and from the other three of Coyuntura's four saloons. Price found himself elbowed away, pushed back. He was glad enough. He did not wish to stand looking down at the body of the man he had killed.

From the courthouse at the far end of the street Enrique Lucero, the sheriff, arrived with Donancio Lucero, Enrique's brother and under-sheriff. The two officers were middle-aged, hard-bitten men who held office because they were efficient, and also because they were the head of the clan of Lucero, the clan that dominated the native population of Buhera county. It was Enrique who picked up the canvas sack, and it was

Donancio who worked through the crowd until he reached Price Thorn's side.

Enrique took the sack and accompanied by Claude Pearsall went into the bank. Donancio gave orders that the bandit's body be brought to the courthouse and with Price and Howard Brumaker, together with some others who had seen the shooting, walked back along Coyuntura's street. The cowboy who had been on the bench in front of Coyne's saddle shop, was Billy Wayant, an old-timer in the country. He had been hit through the belly and Doctor Cirlot was attending him in the saddle shop where they had carried the wounded man. Donancio Lucero stopped to question the doctor and when he rejoined the group his face was grave. Wayant was badly hurt and he had not recognized either the man who had shot him or the man in the alley. When the other two men had come running out of the bank Wayant was lying on the sidewalk and had not seen them.

In the sheriff's office, Price, Brumaker, and three others who had seen part of the activity at the bank, seated themselves, and Donancio walked over to the sheriff's desk and drew out a chair. Within minutes the shuffling of feet spoke of the arrival of the bandit's body. The body was brought into the office and placed on a bench. Someone had thrown a blanket over the dead man and one corner of the blanket trailed down to the floor. Donancio, pulling back the covering, exposed the dead man's face, looked at it for a long minute and then shook his head.

"No sé," Donancio announced. "I don't know him."

40

In turn others looked at the face, pale with death under the tan, and shook their heads. The dead man was a stranger in Coyuntura. Donancio, replacing the fold of blanket, went back to the desk and, sitting down, began to ask questions. Price and Brumaker told what they had seen and done. The other three spectators also told their stories. In the midst of the interrogation Enrique and Claude Pearsall came into the office.

Enrique reported briefly that all the money stolen from the bank had been in the canvas sack. For the sheriff's benefit the stories of Price and Brumaker were repeated, and Pearsall gave his evidence.

He had just opened the bank, Pearsall said, having come back from his dinner, and was engaged in unlocking the safe. The bookkeeper had not yet returned. Pearsall had the combination worked on the safe and had just thrown the bolts when the back door of the bank, left unlocked for the bookkeeper, was opened and two men, both masked, walked in. One of them had covered Pearsall with a gun and ordered him to lie down on the floor. The other had opened the door of the safe and was stuffing currency into a canvas sack, when the first shot sounded. Neither man had spoken after the first gruff commands to Pearsall. The banker had taken a chance and rolled over so that he could look at the men. They had paid no attention to him but continued with the looting of the safe. Then, with the sack full of currency, they had run out through the front door. Pearsall had scrambled up and followed to give the alarm, and had been in time to see the men riding down the street and to see Price step out and shoot. Brumaker had also been shooting from the porch of his store. Pearsall had seen one man fall.

Enrique Lucero did not wait for the end of Pearsall's story. He had already formed a posse and now, before the banker had finished talking, the sheriff, apprised that the posse was ready to go, left the office. Donancio remained in charge and the men in the courthouse heard the riders pound away as they followed the fleeing bandits out of town. When Pearsall finished talking, Brumaker turned to Price Thorn.

"It was you, Price," he said. "You dropped him. I was shooting high. I could see where my shots were going, and I didn't touch a man."

Price nodded glumly. He was not feeling good. There was a squeamish feeling in the pit of his belly. It is not nice to kill a man and it is worse when you must recount the happenings and sit in the same room with the corpse.

Donancio, looking keenly at Price, made a suggestion. "Why don't you go home with Howard?" he asked. "I've got to get a coroner's jury together and hold an inquest. I'll send for you, Price."

Price readily agreed and, leaving the sheriff's office with Howard Brumaker, got out before Pearsall could speak to him. He did not want to talk any more and he did not want to be praised for killing a man, even a bank robber. His actions there in the street had been instinctive, and as he walked along beside Brumaker he thought that if he had it to do over, the bandits could have gotten dear away, for all of him. Brumaker seemed

42

to sense something of his thoughts. The little storekeeper talked cheerfully and when the two men reached the merchant's house, Brumaker drew his wife aside and talked low-voiced and earnestly to her for a moment. Mrs. Brumaker nodded understandingly and went to the kitchen, while Brumaker took Price to the living room, found a decanter and gave his guest a stiff drink.

The whisky and the food that Mrs. Brumaker prepared warmed and steadied Price. He was himself once more when word came from Donancio that the inquest was to be held at once and, accompanied by Howard Brumaker, Price walked back through Coyuntura's busy streets to the courthouse, not heeding the curious glances and the comments of the people he passed.

The six-man jury, meeting in the sheriff's office at the courthouse, heard the evidence of Brumaker, of Pearsall, and of Price Thorn. The foreman consulted with the others and informed the justice of the peace of their decision. The bandit, unknown to the jury, had met his death at the hands of Price Thorn while engaged in robbing the First State Bank of Coyuntura and, so the foreman said, the jury wanted to compliment Mr. Thorn on good, straight shooting. Price knew the black-smith who was acting as foreman, and the smith grinned a little as he finished his announcement.

With the inquest over, Pearsall came to Price's side and said that he wanted to see him before he left town, and assured that Price would come to the bank, the banker left the room. Brumaker also went out, going to the store, and Donancio Lucero, taking Price aside, spoke briefly to him.

"How come you had a gun, Price?" Donancio asked. In contrast to his older brother, the sheriff, Donancio spoke good English. The undersheriff had been in school in the adjoining state of Colorado, while Enrique had never left the Rana Hills country.

"Why, I was just carrying it," Price answered the sheriff's question. "What's wrong with that, Donancio?"

The undersheriff shrugged. "Law in town that you can't carry a gun," he said. "It's all right and nothing will be said about it, but that's the law. You weren't expectin' any trouble, were you, Price?"

Price Thorn had known Donancio Lucero since boyhood. Enrique Lucero had worked as a rider for the Teepee when he was a young man and Price had grown up side by side with Donancio. Now he looked at his questioner for a long minute and then shrugged. "Maybe," he answered.

"Tony is a cousin of ours," Donancio announced. "Enrique had to talk pretty straight to Tony to keep him out of trouble with some X Bar riders here in town a year ago. I wouldn't push things too far, Price."

"You wouldn't stand around and be pushed either," Price answered.

Donancio grunted. "You got to remember that Enrique is the sheriff," he said. "It would hurt Enrique, and it would hurt me, to have to arrest you, Price."

"Maybe you won't have to," Price answered. "I'm a peaceful cuss, Donancio, and I'm mighty careful."

"Until you're crowded," Donancio concluded. "All right, Price. Try to get along. And remember that Enrique and I are friends of yours, but we're officers."

44

Price grinned suddenly and shook hands with Donancio. "I'll remember," he promised. "Come out and see me, Donancio. Tell Enrique to come out."

Donancio, returning the smile, promised that he would sample the hospitality of the Teepee within a short time, and Price, bidding the officer good-bye, left the office and the courthouse. Walking along the street toward the bank he thought of what Donancio had told him. Both Donancio Lucero and Enrique were square as a die and would help a friend when they could. Price knew that he could borrow a horse or money or anything either of the brothers had. He also knew that if he stepped over the line, if he broke the law and Donancio or Enrique found it out, they would trail him down and bring him to justice as surely as any of their Indian forebears would trail and kill a deer, and do it with as little compunction. Good officers, the Luceros, good men, good friends, and hell on wheels when it came to enforcing the law.

When he reached the bank Price found it closed. Going to the back door he knocked and presently the door was cautiously opened. Seeing who was there, Pearsall stepped back and, inviting Price to enter, led the way to his office. For the second time that day Price Thorn sat down in a chair across the desk from the banker.

"I asked you to come back," Pearsall said. "I thought that you were entitled to a reward, Mr. Thorn. You saved the bank a good deal of money and . . ."

"I don't need a reward and won't take one," Price said quietly.

"But . . ." Pearsall began.

Price rose to his feet. "I do business with banks," he said. "It's just business with me. Thanks, Mr. Pearsall, but I don't want any money for killing a man. I've got a bad enough taste in my mouth the way it is."

Pearsall rose with his visitor, his eyes searching Price's face. "I turned you down for a loan this morning," he said slowly. "Did you think of that when you were in the street, Mr Thorn?"

"No," Price answered honestly, "I didn't."

"I thought you were a *young* man, too young," Pearsall said. "That was part of my consideration. And I know the kind of neighbors you have. It would be a difficult thing to put another thousand head of cattle into the Rana flats, Mr. Thorn."

An idea formed in Price's mind. Pearsall was inviting him to reapply for the loan, not in so many words, but by innuendo. Suddenly the stern mask of Price's face broke into a grin. "You were talking about additional security for a loan, Mr. Pearsall," he said suddenly. "Maybe I can furnish it."

Reseating himself Price slid the Smith & Wesson from his holster, broke the gun and, punching the ejector, lifted out the shells. From the brass rimmed cylinder he selected one, a spent cartridge, and closing the gun, replaced it in the holster. Then, reaching out to the banker who was again seated at the desk, he carefully placed the empty brass case, upright.

"Would that do?" Price Thorn asked. "For additional security, I mean?"

46

Pearsall's lips twitched convulsively as though he suppressed a smile. His eyes were expressionless as he replied. "I believe it will," he said, no inflection in his voice. "I believe it will. I'll have a man come to inspect your cattle. If his report is favorable you can come in and we'll fix up the papers for your loan. Good-bye, Mr. Thorn."

Price stood up. "Good-bye, Mr. Pearsall," he answered, "and . . . thanks."

CHAPTER
FOUR

Tough Hand

Claude Pearsall had several qualifications that made him a good banker. He was not subject to cold feet, and he acted promptly. If Pearsall made a loan to a man he stayed with him until he knew that he was wrong, and it took a lot to prove that. Price knew that Pearsall would back him a long way, and within three days following the attempted bank robbery, a grizzled veteran named Charlie Rainbo, turned up at the Teepee and announced that he had come to inspect for the loan Price had requested.

Rainbo was a welcome visitor. Price rode with him while Rainbo looked at the cattle and while they took a count. Rainbo had but little to say. He asked one question, however. "Pearsall says that you think you can lick the blackleg, Thorn. How about it?" the grizzled man asked.

"I can," Price said confidently. "Right now they're experimenting with a way to vaccinate cattle against the disease. I've written back to a friend of mine to give me the latest reports on what they've done. As soon as I hear from him I'll know what to do. You tell Mr. Pearsall he needn't worry about blackleg cleaning us out."

Price spoke confidently. He wanted this loan; wanted it badly. He did not feel as confident as he seemed.

Rainbo grunted skeptically. "Well . . . mebbe you can do it," he agreed. "I'll tell Pearsall what you say anyhow."

Rainbo spent two days at the Teepee then left for town, deliberately chewing his tobacco and making no statements as to how he had found the outfit. Before the end of the week, however, there was word brought out that Pearsall wanted to see Price, and when Price rode in to Coyuntura and visited the banker he found not only that Pearsall was ready to make the loan, but that the banker had done some looking around and had cattle located. Accordingly Price left for Midlands, where Pearsall had learned there were cattle to be bought.

Price was gone for two weeks. During those two weeks Jim Harvie ran the Teepee, doing his best to bring Will Thorn out of his lethargy, and not succeeding. It was Jim Harvie who got the fences around the vegas in shape. It was Jim Harvie who hired Duke Wayant to come to the ranch and snap broncs. Duke was just a youngster, Billy Wayant's nephew, and a good rider. Billy Wayant, after lingering on for two weeks, died of his wound and the bank bandits were now wanted for murder as well as armed robbery. Duke had been very close to his uncle and Billy's death had been a shock to the boy.

When Harvie received Price's telegram from Midlands, he got things together at the ranch, organized the crew, stocked the wagon and brought

Tony Troncoso down from the Mule Pen camp. Then, with the outfit in readiness, Jim Harvie confronted Will Thorn.

"Price is comin' in with some cattle he's bought," Harvie announced. "We're goin' in to meet him. Are you comin', Will?"

"Can't you get along without me, Jim?" Will Thorn asked.

"No," Harvie answered shortly. "We're goin' to need everybody. You can't let your own kid down, Will. You can ride in the wagon with Granny, but I've throwed in yore saddle an' we're goin' to need yore help. Come on an' I'll help you roll yore bed."

Reluctantly Thorn accompanied the little man, helping Harvie drag out an old camp bed that Will had not used for five years, roll it, and put it on the wagon.

Price came back on a train that hauled fifteen cars of cattle and a car of horses, and with him was a gaunt, hard twisted stranger whom Price introduced as Ben Utt. The whole Teepee was in Coyuntura that day: Will Thorn, Duke Wayant, Jim Harvie, Tony Troncoso from the camp; even old Granny Davis with two mules hitched to a chuck wagon.

"Ben, here, is going to stay with us," Price announced when he had climbed down out of the caboose, shaken hands all around and introduced his companion. "Texas wasn't just suiting him and when I told him about this country, he decided that he'd try it awhile."

Utt, his face looking a good deal like a twisted pine knot, spat gravely and seconded Price's words. "He done sold it to me," Utt said mournfully. "I got tired workin' around on the flat country an' when I seen this whole ranch movin' west, I thought I'd better come along an' find out where he was takin' it."

Price laughed and walked off toward the depot. When he returned the conductor of the freight was with him and the business of spotting cars at the stockyard chutes and of unloading cattle began. Price had bought not only heifers but also a carload of bulls and a car of horses.

"I wanted a thousand head," Price told Jim Harvie as they stood waiting for cars to be spotted. "I didn't get them. We've got seven-hundred and seventy here, and thirty bulls. I knew that we were short on broke horses so I bought a carload. How did you get along with Dad, Jim?"

Harvie shrugged. "Not so good," he said. "I pretty near had to pull him out of the house to get him to come along with us. What'd you give for the horses, Price?"

"Thirty a round," Price answered. "That sorrel cost me sixty."

The horse car had been the first unloaded and Jim had seen the horses go into the pen. He looked them over with wise old eyes and was pleased. The horses were all solid colors, bays, blacks and sorrels, and there was one sorrel horse in the bunch that was outstanding. "I like that big sorrel," Jim commented.

"Name's Nugget," Price announced. "I bought him for Dad. He's quite a horse."

At that moment Tony yelled from the chute and Price and Jim moved off to attend to the work.

It was late when the unloading was finished and Price decided to hold in the stockyards over night. Hay was brought and put in the horse pen, and the few mounts that the Teepee men had brought to town with them were turned in with the newly purchased animals. There was a windmill by the yards and troughs in the pens and Price did not think it necessary to throw the cattle on grass immediately. The Teepee finished work about six o'clock and Granny had supper ready.

When the meal was finished Price, Jim, Will Thorn and Ben Utt remained in the camp by the stockyards while Duke and Tony announced that they were going to town. Accordingly the younger element pulled out for what bright lights Coyuntura afforded. The older men spread down their beds and loafed.

Price was full of his trip. He talked about the cattle he had seen, the men he had met, the condition of the country, and he had one item of exceptional interest.

"I wrote back to an old professor of mine before I left," he said. "I told him about the trouble we'd had with blackleg out here. He seems to have taken an interest in what I wrote him. Anyhow, in Midlands, a fellow I went to school with looked me up. He'd heard from Professor Barnes. This fellow's name is John McCready and he's working for a company that is putting out a vaccine for blackleg."

"We had blackleg in the Rana last year an' it about cleaned us," Harvie announced. "There's nothin' that will stop blackleg. I've seen it all tried: dockin' their tails, puttin' a piece of rope through their dewlaps, puttin' a piece of garlic or onion under their hides, runnin' 'em. Everything! What's this here vaccine you're talkin' about?"

"It's an injection that's put under the skin," Price answered. "It's a new thing."

"A couple of years ago there was a fellow down by Secorro that tried somethin' new," Harvie drawled. "He had some little pills that he shot into the calves. They died anyhow. There ain't nothin' that will stop blackleg, Price."

"McCready says that they've got something," Price maintained stubbornly. "They stop smallpox and diphtheria in humans and there's no reason why they can't stop blackleg in cattle. I've made arrangements for McCready to come to the ranch and give us a hand. It's an experiment, but I feel sure it will work. Anyhow McCready's coming!"

"He'll no doubt make an interestin' visitor," Harvie said dryly.

It was full dark two hours after supper. The talk around the Teepee's fire had died away into drawling comments, for the men were tired. It was almost time for the visitors to town to return. Away to the north a whistle sounded; presently the rails began to hum and the horses and cattle in the stock pens lifted their heads to listen.

The approaching freight slowed as it came nearer, the headlights boring into the night, stopped beyond the yards and a brakeman, coming from the engine, threw a switch. The train, engine snorting laboriously, pulled into the siding and stopped again so that the caboose was below the yards.

"Goin' to meet a passenger," Granny said wisely. "The east-bound is about due."

No one replied to Granny's comment and the fat cook relaxed again on his bed. Beside the freight, feet crunched the cinders of the right-of-way, a lantern bobbed, and a hoarse voice came through the night. "Come offen there you young devil!"

"Hobo," Granny said, airing his wisdom once more.

There was a scramble beside the train, the hoarse voice was raised in a curse and there came the thud of a blow and a shrill yelp of pain. Price Thorn, getting to his feet, peered through the darkness. A man carrying a lantern was coming from the caboose. The lantern bearer stopped and in the light the men at the fire could see a burly figure holding a lesser one by the collar.

"Nothin' but a kid," Price commented.

The big man moved suddenly, again a blow thudded and again there was a whimper of pain. Price started toward the right-of-way, the others at the fire scrambling to their feet to follow.

Price reached the scene of action before his companions. A brakeman, burly and scowling, was holding a wisp of a boy by the collar of his ragged jacket and even as Price arrived the brakeman swung his fist again.

"Don't hit him, Gus," the lantern holder remonstrated.

"Lay off the kid!" Price snapped.

54

The brakeman let go the ragged collar and wheeled. He was just as peaceful as a sucking sow whose pigs are menaced. "Who in hell says so?" demanded the brakeman.

"I do," Price answered, and ducked.

The railroader's roundhouse right removed Price's hat and he wheeled, following the blow, just in time to receive a swiftly moving left hand. The conductor wailed: "Now stop that!" and on the far side of the freight the passenger rushed by, noise beating back from the box cars.

One left-handed jolt did not stop the brakeman. He came back for more, scooping up his lantern from where he had placed it when he hauled the kid out of the box car. The lantern circled and came down, and Price, dodging back and then leaping in, grappled and twisted. The brakeman released the lantern which dropped with a crash of breaking chimney and then went out. There was a thud . . . thud . . . thud . . . of fists, the brakeman sat down and stared at Price Thorn and the conductor complained, "Now you went an' broke the lantern."

From the engine there came a questioning, "boot . . . boot . . ." as the engineer asked about getting out of there.

"We got to go, Gus," the conductor cajoled his brakeman. "We got to make Tyban for Number Twenty-four."

Somewhat bewildered, Brakeman Gus got to his feet. Jim Harvie gravely handed over the broken lantern which he had retrieved.

"Here's yore lamp," Jim announced. The brakeman took it.

"Come on, Gus," the conductor commanded once more. "Come on." He pushed Harvie aside and made little circles with his own lantern. Again the engine whistled. Gus looked at his broken lantern, examining it as though he had never seen it before. Gus had a lump forming on his jaw and there was still bewilderment in his brain. Again there came a whistle from the engine, then the long rumbling noise of slack coming out of the train, and with a creak the wheels began to turn. The conductor waddled back toward the caboose and Gus, turning, possessed himself of a grab iron and stepped up on the side of the moving car.

"So long," Jim Harvie called.

When the rear markers of the caboose were passing the depot, Price turned. "Where's the kid?" he demanded. "Did he hop the train?"

Old Granny Davis answered, "I've got the kid."

"Let's go to camp," Price said.

Back at the fire the Teepee men inspected their acquisition. The boy was barely in his teens. He was dirty, ragged and disheveled, and his face was gaunt. With no word, old Granny set about certain preparations, while Price, his hand on the youngster's shoulder, looked over the boy.

"What's your name, sonny?" Price asked.

The boy made no answer and Price gently shook the shoulder he held. "What's your name?" he asked again.

"Neil Redwine." The voice was sullen.

"Kind of young to be ridin' freights," Price said. "Where's your home?"

"I've got no home."

"And your folks?" Price was insistent.

"I've got no folks neither."

Granny came back from the wagon carrying a plate. He put down the plate beside the fire, poured a cup of coffee from the pot that stood close to the blaze and stood back. "Throw that into you, kid," Granny commanded.

Neil Redwine looked from the fat cook to Price. Price nodded. The boy took a slow step, another was more hasty, and then, squatting down, began to wolf the bread and cold beans that Granny had set out.

"Little devil's hungry," Price said.

The boy, Neil, cleaned the plate that Granny had brought, and looked up. Granny watched him, a friendly grin on his face. "Plenty more, kid," he said. "Want another load?"

"I . . . yes," the youngster answered.

"Fetch yore plate," Granny ordered, and walked toward the wagon. Carrying the plate, the boy followed him and Price said, "He's about starved. I hate to see a kid hungry. It's bad enough for a man to go without grub, but a kid . . ."

"Somebody comin' out from town," Harvie interrupted. "Headed here."

Duke Wayant and Tony had, naturally, taken horses when they went to town. The distance was all of half a mile and who ever heard of a man walking all of half a mile when there were horses handy? This was a single rider coming out to camp and he was coming fast. Price and his companions faced toward the sound.

The rider, Wayant, stopped, threw himself from his saddle and hurried toward the fire. "Tony's in the Cliff," Duke said, "an' he's tangled up with Jule Pothero and Hank Kuhler. Tony's about half crocked."

Price swore. He knew Tony and he knew that when Tony had a small load of liquor aboard he was a pugnacious little pest.

"I thought I'd better come out an' tell you," Wayant said, worriedly.

"I'll go in and get him," Price decided. "I think you'd better stay here, Duke. You stay too, Dad, and you Jim."

Jim Harvie, excitable and combative as a bantam cock, swore that he was going along. Will Thorn's deep voice stopped the declaration. "We'll stay here, Price. Don't get into trouble."

Price had already hurried away toward the stockyard fence. He had a night horse tied there, Doughboy, who had been brought in from the Teepee for him. As he led Doughboy back and began to saddle, Ben Utt appeared from the wagon, stuffing something inside the bosom of his shirt. "Guess I'll just go along," Utt announced.

"Near as I heard from the talk," Duke Wayant announced, "Jule Pothero an' Kuhler just got back from someplace. Seems like they heard about your tellin' Ed to take down his drift fence, Price, an' they jumped the first Teepee men they seen. Hank Kuhler got pretty tough with me an' I kept my mouth shut."

"An' that was right, kid," Ben Utt affirmed. "You don't have no business mixin' with anybody like Kuhler."

"You know him?" Price asked, finishing with his saddle.

"I heard of him," Utt agreed, also completing his saddling.

Price mounted. Ben Utt also stepped up on his horse. "We'll be back as soon as we can get Tony out of there," Price said.

There was a slight tremor in Will Thorn's voice. "Don't have trouble, Price," he warned.

Price did not answer. The horses were pounding away from camp. Momentarily Price wished that he had taken Jim Harvie along. He did not know a great deal about Ben Utt, did not know just how Utt would stand up in a hard spot. He thought, grimly, that he was likely to find out before this was over.

There were plenty of horses at the hitchrail in front of the Cliff saloon. Price and Ben Utt, reining in, dismounted and tied their horses where they could find room, then ducking under the rail they crossed the sidewalk and pushed back the swinging shutters that were the Cliff saloon's front door.

Their entrance was noted by three men near the front of the long room. The rest of the dozen men in the room paid no attention to the arrival of Price and Ben. Away toward the back of the room Tony Troncoso was sitting at a card table, a bottle in front of him and no one in the other chairs. As Price pushed his way toward the table where Tony sat, he noted that there were two men leaning against the bar. One of these had his back to Price and the other was half-facing him. Price was struck by something oddly familiar in the shape of the back of the head turned toward him. He had seen that silhouette someplace, but did not know where. It was not a time to stop and consider. At his elbow Price heard a man say, "Harrison's sent for Donancio," and then he was in the clear space between the men at the bar and Tony's table.

"Goin' to drink all that bottle?" Price asked Tony cheerfully, "or have you got enough to spare a couple of friends a drink?"

Tony, face enigmatic, turned to look at Price. The mask-like face broke into a smile and he gestured with his left hand. His right hand was hidden under the table top. "Plenty to dreenk, Price," Tony announced.

"What white man'ud drink with a messican?" one of the men at the bar rasped harshly.

Price turned so that he could see the speaker. It was the man with the vaguely familiar head. The Pothero mark was strong in his face. It was lean and bony, but the man's body was not fat as was Ed Pothero's. This man's head and body belonged together.

Tony shifted in his chair. *"Flaco!"* he said distinctly, *"Cabrone!"*

In that tone of voice, those words meant fight to a man that understood them. Price said, "Sit down, Tony," and then coolly seating himself, stared at the man who had spoken. "I'll drink with Tony anytime," he announced. "He's a damn sight whiter than you are, Pothero!"

Price was not armed. He had not carried a gun to town; did not consider that he needed one, and in the haste of leaving camp he had neglected to equip

60

himself. To all appearances neither Pothero nor Hank Kuhler carried weapons. But now Pothero's hand slid up into the opening of his shirt and Kuhler was brushing aside the skirt of the coat he wore. Pothero had a shoulder holster under his shirt and Kuhler was packing an iron in his hip pocket. Price knew it!

The two men moved apart a little and Price tensed himself. He hadn't a chance, he realized, but still he would try. If Pothero pulled his gun, if Kuhler's hand came from behind his back, then Price would jump. What good he could do he didn't know, but his eyes fixed on Jule Pothero's neck, settling on the place where his hands would fasten if, in mid-leap, he was not knocked down by a slug.

"You want to be sure a man hasn't got friends with him," Price rasped at Pothero. "Make sure of that before you jump him, you and the rest of your lice!"

That was fighting talk, no less. Jule Pothero's hand stirred beneath his shirt, the back appearing. And then Pothero stopped and Kuhler likewise checked his motion. A cold voice, contained, level, came from the bar.

"No, Hank!"

Both men turned a trifle. Looking toward the voice, Price saw Ben Utt, knobby face expressionless, hands hanging limpy at his sides. And yet there was that about Ben Utt that spoke of danger, of readiness and of waiting.

"You want me to chip in, Hank?" Utt drawled.

Hank Kuhler gulped. Pothero checked his motion. "That's . . ." Kuhler began.

A disturbance at the door and a ripple along the bar checked Kuhler's utterance. Donancio Lucero, his face as mild as a monk's, stopped just at the edge of the open space.

"Hello, Price," Donancio greeted. "Hello, Tony." The gold shield at the pocket of Lucero's vest caught and reflected light from the chandelier. Donancio slumped on one foot. The big gun at his hip swelled a lump under his coat and, gently, Donancio pushed the coat aside.

"You get your cattle all right, Thorn?" Donancio asked.

"All right," Price answered.

"I'd like to see them," Donancio drawled. "I'll go out with you as soon as you can spare the time."

Price looked for Ben Utt. Utt had disappeared.

"You can't see much tonight," Price said to Donancio.

"You'd be surprised what I can see at night," Donancio drawled. His little beady black eyes moved slowly about the room, shifting from face to face. "Lots of *cucarachas* out at night, Price," Donancio said softly.

"If you want to see the cattle tonight I'll take you out," Price offered. "Come on, Tony."

He got up, Tony rising uncertainly with him. There was a rattle on the floor and a bottle, the bottom broken so that jagged edges remained, rolled out from under the table where Tony had been holding it. The chairs made a scuffling noise and Jule Pothero spoke.

"There's a man wanted in Texas, here, Sheriff. His name's Utt. He killed a man in Marfa an' . . ."

62

"We'll go look at your cows, Price," Donancio said softly, paying no attention to Jule Pothero. "Come on, *primo.*"

"*Seguro,*" Tony agreed amiably. "I am comeeng."

Donancio stepped back, opening a passageway. Tony and then Price walked through it, Donancio following along behind. Outside the Cliff saloon all three of the men stopped. Donancio grinned.

"I think I'll look at your heifers tomorrow, Price," he said. "Maybe I *couldn't* see them so well at night."

"I'm sure obliged to you," Price announced in a relieved voice. "That . . ."

"*Por nada,*" Donancio interrupted. "If I was you, Price, I wouldn't pay too much attention to the law in town. If a man had a gun under his coat or under his shirt . . ." Donancio shrugged. "Maybe Enrique or me would not see it," he completed. "Tony, you damned fool, don't you know enough not to get drunk?"

Tony was crestfallen. "Me, I take wan leetle dreenk," he said. "I have jus' wan . . ."

"You drank a pint!" Donancio snapped. "Keep him in camp, Price. He makes trouble."

"I'll try to," Price promised. "Donancio, you sure pulled us out of that. Someday maybe I can do . . ."

"Sure, sure," Donancio waved the thanks aside. "You go along now. I'll stay here an' watch this pot awhile."

"Come on, Tony," Price ordered.

They took their horses and mounting, rode to the center of the street.

Ben Utt's horse was not at the hitchrail. Price could see nothing of the man who had come to town with him. Donancio waved to the mounted men from where he leaned against the front of the Cliff, and Price and Tony, starting their horses, rode slowly along the street.

They were out of town and in the starlit dark when they heard a horse coming up. Both riders stopped and Price spoke sharply. "Who is it?"

Ben Utt's slow drawl answered from the darkness. "Jus' me." Horse and rider loomed suddenly beside Price and Utt chuckled in the night. "That fellow sure thought he knowed me," he said.

"Mebbe he did," Price commented.

"Mebbe he did at that," Utt drawled. "What about it, Thorn?"

"I didn't hire you for a tough hand," Price said levelly.

"But you ain't goin' to fire me if I turn out to be one," Utt suggested.

"And I pay forty a month and chuck," Price continued.

"An' that's what I'm workin' for." Utt's voice was placid.

"Then let's go to camp," said Price.

When the three reached the fire Will Thorn, Granny, Duke Wayant and Harvie sprang up from about it. It was Will Thorn's booming voice that asked the question. "Did you get Tony?"

"Yes," Price said.

"Have any trouble?"

"None to mention," Utt made answer.

Ben Utt and Price dismounted. Tony Troncoso, a much chastened Tony and feeling somewhat rocky from his liquor, also got down. Leather creaked as Utt pulled on his latigo. "You know," drawled Utt, "I'm beginnin' to like it here."

"What happened?" Will Thorn demanded.

"Donancio showed up," said Price, his voice weary, "and we rode on out to camp. What did you do with the kid?"

"Put him to bed," Granny said. "He's sleepin' under the wagon."

"I'm going to bed too," Price Thorn stated.

CHAPTER
FIVE

There Won't Be Any Fence

The Teepee moved their cattle the next morning. Duke Wayant took the remuda, and the rest of the men went with the herd. Somehow it was natural for Granny Davis to take the kid, Neil Redwine, on the wagon with him. No one said anything about it. Granny, when the beds were loaded and the wagon ready to go, said, "Come on, kid," and Neil eagerly climbed up on the wagon seat and waited for the puffing Granny to join him and start the team.

They went eight miles of the thirty-two that lay between the ranch and Coyuntura that day, for they made a late start and did not push. Jim Harvie and Will Thorn rode behind and in the swing. Price and Ben Utt cleaned out the country as the cattle moved, driving off the local cattle so that they would not join the slowly moving herd. That night when camp was made beside Big Willow spring, just at the edge of the trickle of water that was called Arroyo Grande, Price made his dispositions. There was a cabin beside Big Willow spring, and a horse trap. The remuda was put into the trap so that it need not be night guarded, and Price split up the crew to take regular guards on the herd.

Price was worried. He had to get the cattle to the Teepee and get them branded. He wanted to get them into the Teepee iron as soon as possible and he wanted to do it without trouble. And there was every chance for trouble. The cattle were not trail broken, anything would stampede them, and there was every chance that something would. The Potheros, Merriman, any of the cowmen running cattle on what had once been Teepee range, would resent this influx of cattle. What they might do about it was problematical.

Will Thorn and Jim Harvie took over the first watch after supper, relieving Price and Ben Utt. They would stand a three-hour guard and be relieved by Tony and Duke. Then, in the morning hours when anything might happen, if it happened at all, Price and Utt would be on the job.

Price and Utt, coming in, unsaddled and turned their horses into the pen. Both had night horses tied to the fence, Price the big dun Jefe and Utt a likely black from the bunch that Price had shipped in from Texas. Squatting beside the fire with loaded plates, they were joined by Tony, Duke, Granny and Neil Redwine.

The talk, while the meal was eaten, concerned the happenings in Coyuntura the night before. Utt did no talking and Price did not dwell on Utt's part in the affair. Tony bragged a little about his cousin Donancio and his cousin Enrique. Duke, being young, was inclined to be loquacious. Granny put in a word here and there and Price said as little as he could. It was Duke, therefore, who did most of the talking about Jule Pothero and Hank Kuhler. Duke had not been at the

Teepee very long. He had met some friends in town before he ran into the trouble at the Cliff saloon, and he had considerable information.

Most of the things Duke retailed, Price knew already. He knew that the Pothero brothers had come into the Rana country five years before. He knew that they had brought a sizeable herd with them, that they had at first used a wagon for headquarters and that later they had paid Oscar Schuster a small sum for his Double Loop headquarters and iron. Price knew too that Merriman had closely followed the Potheros. Merriman, however, had bought out a small rancher immediately after his arrival and Merriman did not run as many O Slash cattle as Pothero ran X Bar. From what Price had heard, and from what Duke now said, Merriman was a pretty good sort of fellow except that he was friendly with the Potheros.

No one, Duke said, had much use for the two Pothero brothers and most people were afraid of them. The Potheros had a way of riding rough-shod over their neighbors. While they were not actually law breakers they gave an impression of being bad men to fool with, and the men they hired were salty. All these things Duke related at the fire while Price cleared his loaded plate. Jule Pothero and Hank Kuhler, so said Duke, had been gone for some little time. They had just returned. They were the toughest two of the outfit, but Ed Pothero was the brains. That was the opinion of the Rana country, as retailed by young Duke Wayant.

Price, getting up with his empty plate in the midst of the talk, looked across the fire to where Neil Redwine

68

sat. The kid's eyes were wide as he listened to Duke. Price grinned, dumped his plate in the wreck pan and walked around and stood beside Neil.

"You said that you had no home," Price spoke abruptly, "and that you hadn't any folks. What are you aiming to do, kid?"

Neil, startled, looked at his interrogator. "Why . . ." he said, "I don't know . . ."

"Whereabouts in the country are you from?" Price asked.

"I came from Iowa," Neil said reluctantly.

"Came west to be a cowboy?"

The boy nodded.

Price grinned. "All right," he announced. "I'll give you a chance to be one. You've come this far with us, how'd you like to stick on with this outfit?"

A light began to dawn on Neil Redwine's face. The face was clean scrubbed, Price noticed, and some of the hang-dog look that had been there the night before was gone. "Do you mean it, mister?" Neil asked eagerly.

"I'll start you helping Granny," Price said. "If you make good with that I'll pay you ten dollars a month."

The boy's face fell. "But that's cookin'," he objected. "I want . . ."

"You want to be a rider," Price completed. "That's right. But you got to learn to walk first in this country, before you get promoted. You make a job of helping Granny and I'll see that you get a chance to do what you want. How about it?"

All the light was back in the boy's eyes. "I'll do it, mister," he promised.

"Good," Price spoke shortly. "Granny fixed you a bed last night. You keep on using it. Has he been helping you, Granny?"

"He rustled wood an' water, an' he's goin' to help with the dishes," Granny answered.

Price nodded to the boy. "Stay with it and you'll make a hand," he said, and that was all, but as he walked away toward his bed Neil Redwine's eyes followed him with a doglike devotion.

Nothing happened during that first night. Twice during the guards that preceded his own, Price got up, took the saddled Jefe from where the horse was wagon-wheeled, and rode out to the cattle. Both times he met with a low-voiced challenge before he reached the cattle, and both times he found things peaceful and quiet.

The second day was a repetition of the first, but the second night was not so peaceful. Ben Utt, coming to Price after supper, sat down beside his boss and indulged in a long and meditative clearing of the throat.

"If I was holdin' down a country," Ben announced, "an' somebody was movin' into it, goin' to crowd the grass, I'd let him get strung out an' then when he was away off from town or anyplace, I'd figure to make it tough for him."

"Speaking from experience?" Price chuckled.

"Mebbe," returned Utt. "Anyhow, that's what I'd do."

"And if you were the fellow moving into the country?" Price suggested.

70

Utt scratched his head. "That depends," he said. "I might look the other folks up first." He looked shrewdly at Price.

Price shook his head. "I may be a damned fool," he said shortly, "likely I am, but I won't make a move until somebody crowds me."

Utt sighed. "That's the trouble with a law-livin' fellow," he complained. "Well, then, if I was lookin' for trouble I'd think it might be a stampede. I'd try to make sure that the run went in the right direction an' I'd make damned sure that the heifers didn't pile up against a fence or nothin'."

"That's an idea," Price said. "Are you sleepy?"

"I'm a regular owl," Utt assured.

"Then we'll take a ride and hear you hoot," Price announced. "Come on."

Utt got up, and Price rising with him, went to the wagon where the night horses were already saddled and tied to the wheels and tongue. Price came back carrying a pair of fence pliers in either hand. Utt received his pair of pliers, clicked them open and shut, and grunted. Price, standing beside the fire, spoke to Duke and Tony.

"We're having to hold everything together tonight," he said. "It makes it kind of tough. I wish we had a pen for the horses, but we've got a bunch of them hobbled and they ought to be all right."

"I'm not sleepy," Duke announced.

"Then suppose you go out and night jingle," Price said. "Take over the job from Jim and move the horses out pretty well. Think you can do that, Duke?"

Duke said that he could.

"How about you, Tony?" Price asked. "Are you sleepy?"

Tony shook his head. "I'm not needeeng sleep," he answered.

"Then how would you like to stand guard all night?" Price asked.

"Bien!" Tony said.

Granny spoke up from where he sat. "The kid an' me'll keep the coffee hot," he announced. "We'll be ready to move, too, Price."

"Good," said Price. "Tony, I don't think Dad can stand it all night. You let him come in when he wants to, and Tony, keep on this side of the heifers. Keep east and south of them. If they start, do what you can to make them run west or north."

Tony nodded his understanding and Price, tightening Jefe's cinch, mounted and rode out to the cattle, Ben Utt following him.

At the herd he talked briefly with Jim Harvie and with Will Thorn. Thorn was anxious but seemingly he had braced up. Perhaps it was the work he had done, albeit the others of the crew had kept him from taking any great part in handling the cattle; perhaps it was the fact that he was proud of Price and did not want to let his boy down. But whatever the cause, Will Thorn was more like his old self than he had been for years. Price saw the change and was glad.

Jim was frankly pessimistic. "If they want to run this bunch they can," he said. "We can't do nothin' to stop 'em."

72

"That's right," Price agreed, "and maybe they won't try. But if they do, all we can do is to try to make it go in the right direction. Try to make it go north or west."

"An' pile up against the drift fence," Harvie said.

"There won't be any fence," Price answered sharply. "Do what you can, Jim. Tony will be out in a minute. Don't let Dad hang on too long. He's got to have some rest. He can't stand the gaff like the rest of us."

Harvie grunted an affirmative and Price and Ben Utt rode off toward the northwest. When they were a short distance out from the cattle, Utt said, "I talked out of turn back at camp, didn't I?"

"How do you mean?" Price asked.

"You figured on makin' this ride anyhow," Utt said. "You had it all planned. You'd even brought the fence pliers along. You threw the herd down into that bend of the wash so that the only way they could run would be northwest."

"Well?" said Price.

Utt grunted. "I didn't figure you for a pilgrim down in Midlands," he commented. "Now I'm damned sure you ain't no child."

"That fence is just a little ways ahead," Price said. "You got out of kindergarten awhile back yourself."

"Yeah," Utt drawled. "I graduated."

When the two Teepee riders struck the drift fence they fell to work. The fence was a three wire affair and the posts were twenty feet apart. It was not put up like a pasture fence but simply stretched as a long line of posts and wire to turn back drifting cattle. Still, if a run struck it, that fence could do plenty of damage. It might not turn back the run but it would cut to pieces the first cattle that struck it.

Ben Utt and Price worked thoroughly. They cut the wire on either side of the posts, letting it fall. They pulled the strands, tangling with each other, away from the fence, and scattered them. They worked by sense of touch and by the starlight that made the night less black and caused men and horses to loom darkly against the skyline. And they worked rapidly. Once, when Price passed Utt, the toll rider spat and grunted: "I'll sleep a week tomorrow." And once, when Utt passed Price, the younger Thorn said: "You act like you were used to this, Utt."

"You kind of show experience yorese'f," Ben Utt retorted.

There was ten miles of the drift fence. When morning broke, gray and a line of pink against the eastern horizon, there was not a great deal of fence left standing. Price and Ben Utt, leaving their labors, rode toward the north. They had, during the night, heard a faint popping of hoofs, a rumble that told of running cattle. They knew that the expected had happened and they knew that the herd had run north. Now they headed across country, away from the fence which was a fence no longer, but just a line of posts.

"Wonder how far they run?" Utt said.

Price shrugged. "I don't know," he answered. "They were tired. We took them a long ways yesterday."

"It ain't so far to the ranch?" Utt suggested.

"About eight miles over west," Price said.

74

"Ought to be findin' somethin' pretty soon," Ben Utt announced.

Some three miles beyond the fence the two riders found and picked up a little bunch of the JV heifers. Further along they encountered Jim Harvie with a gather ahead of him. Jim was filled with news.

"They started about midnight," Jim announced. "Don't know what spooked 'em, an' it don't matter. They got up an' lit out an' went from there. That cut bank was right behind 'em an' Tony an' me was over east. We yelled an' shot an' turned 'em north an' they sure went places. They passed right through where that fence was an' never stopped. Seemed like the fence musta been down." He grinned appreciatively at Price and Utt.

"Where's Dad?" Price asked.

"He was at the wagon, on top of the bank," Harvie answered. "Tony an' me hung an' rattled with the heifers, but I seen Will awhile ago an' told him we'd throw these together down below the vegas."

Relief showed on Price's face as he asked another question. "Where are the horses?"

"Duke had 'em," Harvie answered. "I run into him just before I found this little wad of cattle. I told him to take 'em to the lower vega an' throw 'em behind that fence. I changed horses an' he took 'em on. What do we do now, Price?"

"Ben and I will change horses," Price decided. "Then we'll pick up what we can easy and take them to the place and throw them in the upper vega. It oughtn't to take long to gather the country, Jim. They were tired and they can't have scattered very much."

"Just little bunches splittin' off," Harvie agreed. "All right, Price, we'll take these I've got an' what you picked up an' throw 'em down there below the vega. You boys can change saddles an' we'll make a circle or two."

And that was the program. Tony had a bunch of cattle below the lower vega fence, about four hundred head. Duke had just thrown the horses into the vega and held them in a corner of the fence while Price and Ben roped out fresh mounts and changed saddles. With Duke accompanying them, and leaving Tony to hold the bunch, Price and Ben rode back toward the southeast and within a mile encountered Will Thorn bringing the drive along, and stopped to speak to him. Will thought that they had better take what cattle they had to the upper vega, and Price was pleased for his father seemed keen and alert. Price outlined the ride he wanted Will to make, really just suggesting what he wanted and letting Will select his own route. They separated then and went on, and shortly saw the wagon coming.

Granny and Neil Redwine were on the wagon and everything was shipshape. Granny had been awake when the run started and he had his ideas as to the cause of the stampede. Granny had seen a man on the cut bank between the herd and the camp, and he thought that the nocturnal visitor had spooked the heifers. Price and Ben did not disagree with him, but told Granny to go on to the ranch, that they were coming in when they had finished their circle.

Price and his companion went clear down below the fence, back to the bedground. They made a little circle around the bedground and found an old cowhide and plenty of horse tracks. Neither spoke of their finds. There seemed to be a mutual understanding between the two that did not require speech. It was only when riding away from the bedground that Utt asked a question.

"You figured to cut that fence," he said. "Why didn't you just keep agoin' yesterday? We had about twelve miles to go. Why didn't you keep a travelin'?"

"The heifers were tired," Price answered. "We'd come fourteen miles since sun-up. We don't have a big crew and we'd have lost some from dropping off in the night."

"An'," Utt said pointedly, "you wanted to know if they were goin' to start anything, an' you kind of hoped they would."

"No," Price said, "it wasn't that."

"You law-abidin' guys!" Utt said, and grinned. "You go all around the barn before you go in. I reckon you think now that they've started it, you can do your own share of the chousin'."

"Who do you mean 'they'?" Price asked.

"The Potheros," Ben Utt answered. "An' don't look so damned innocent."

Price laughed. "You swing over west," he said. "Go up the arroyo about a mile and then turn north and pick up any of the JV's you see. I'll go straight north from here and meet you below the vega."

Utt nodded and moved away, and Price set his course toward the north.

By noon, with Will Thorn, Price, Jim Harvie, Utt and Wayant all riding, they had five-hundred of the heifers gathered. There were two-hundred odd left to pick up but Price knew approximately where he would find them. He knew the country, knew what part of it had been covered, and what remained to ride. The crew was tired, bone weary. Price announced that they would take what they had, on to the upper vega, and so again the heifers were strung out.

The cattle were as weary as the riders. It was a task to keep them moving the way they should and the movement was slow. By two-thirty the last of the bunch had been counted through the gate into the vega and the riders went to the ranch. In the morning, all through the next day, they would cover country, picking up the rest of the heifers they had lost, but now they were going to hit the hay until old Granny should call them to supper, and then when that meal was eaten they would go right back to bed again.

At four o'clock the morning after the run, Granny Davis' battered alarm clock jerked the Teepee awake. Unwashed and yawning, Duke departed to wrangle horses. Neil built a fire. Granny stirred up flapjacks. Harvie went out for water, carrying two buckets. Ben Utt, down in the corral with Price, fed two orphaned colts. Will Thorn, rolling up his shirt sleeves, milked away at two old range cows, getting a scanty measure,

78

and then turned the calves out of the pen and let them suck.

"Down where I come from," Ben Utt remarked, "the milk comes outen cans."

"Up here," Will Thorn answered dryly, "it comes out of a cow."

"Easier to get from a can," Utt pointed out. "All you need is a knife."

"Breakfast!" Granny yelled from the kitchen door.

With healthy outdoorsman-stomachs stoked full of flapjacks, salt pork, gravy, molasses, and black coffee, the Teepee started out that day. Tony went to the Mule Pen camp to look after things there. The rest of them, as Price told them off, combed the country for JV heifers. That night there were still a hundred of the heifers gone. For two more days the men rode, and then Price called a halt. There were only eight head of heifers missing. These would be hard to find and it was necessary now that they get the cattle off the vega and out on the grass. Already the upper vega was showing signs of wear.

And so the branding started, with all hands at work. Will Thorn could not, because of his age, take a full part, but he was there and helping as much as he could. Price did the roping. Handling two-year-old heifers and bulls is different from working calves, but still the Teepee crew made good time. They were not molested, and when the last of the heifers had been branded to the Teepee, and had been moved out and located, Price felt satisfied and content. It looked as though the Teepee was back in the cow business once more.

"And now what?" Jim Harvie asked on that last day of the branding. "What's next, Price."

"Ride the country," Price directed. "Put down salt at the water holes. You know what we've got to do, Jim, just as well as I do. You know what we got to do if we want a calf crop next spring."

"Them young bulls is active," Ben Utt said, pensively rolling a smoke. "They'll get around. You got heifers all over the world, Price. Think the bulls will find 'em all?"

Price grinned at the speaker. Somehow he felt more akin to Ben Utt than he did to any of the others. Jim Harvie was too old; so was Granny. Tony, despite his long connection with the Teepee, lived pretty much to himself. Will Thorn, relapsing from his spurt of activity, was showing his age, having long spells of silence when to all appearances he did nothing but daydream. Duke Wayant was too young and, as for Neil Redwine, a man cannot be too familiar with a kid who follows around at his heels and who mimics his slightest action. Neil Redwine was embarrassing to Price. The boy was so open in his devotion, stayed so close to Price when he was at the ranch, that Price felt ill at ease. Price had started the kid doing a little work. Neil, proud in his old saddle, was now entrusted with the morning wrangling. Neil fed the colts and was getting them so gentle that they walked on his heels in the corral. Neil was coming along, but his admiration for the young boss of the Teepee was so great as to be almost an obstacle.

Thinking about Neil Redwine Price finally struck upon an idea. All during the drive, all during the gather after the run, and throughout the branding, Will Thorn had been active and interested. He had slipped at the end of the branding, true enough. It seemed to Price that nothing could hold Will very long, but Will Thorn liked Neil Redwine. The kid's awkwardness, his eagerness, amused the old man. And so, wanting to interest his father, and embarrassed by Neil's constant attendance, Price put the two together. He drew the boy aside and talked to him, telling Neil that Will was an old man, that Will must have someone with him; in short, making Will Thorn Neil's particular responsibility. And having done that, Price talked to his father.

"We've got this kid on our hands, Dad," he said. "He's an orphan and he's never had a chance. If you'd kind of take him in hand I think you could make something of him."

"You think so?" Will Thorn asked.

"I know it," Price returned. "You kind of owe it to the kid, Dad."

Will made no comment but the morning following that conversation Price saw Will and Neil down in the corral and Will was giving the youngster directions. That day Price rode off with a grin on his lips and in his eyes. It looked as though he had been successful and that his idea was going to work.

And so the Teepee men rode the country and Duke Wayant went back to work on his young horses and Neil Redwine grew plump and round-cheeked, and practiced surreptitiously with a rope. Will Thorn, with interest in his eyes once more, kept the boy in hand, and then one day Ben Utt came riding in from the Seco springs and found Price already at the ranch, standing beside the corral and looking over the bars to where Duke Wayant was riding the second saddle on a young horse.

"There's cattle at the Seco, Price," Ben said. "A whole heap of cows."

"And along the Salado," Price amplified. "I wonder if Jim will have found them over by the west side?"

"Likely," Utt drawled. "What I saw was X Bars an' O Slashes."

"X Bars and O Slashes at the Salado, too," Price said. "And a funny thing, Ben, I didn't see any bulls but ours."

"Me neither."

"Now what do you think of that?" Price's drawl matched Utt's own.

"I think we'll have a short calf crop next spring," Ben Utt answered soberly.

"I don't," Price said slowly. "Here comes Jim. Let's hear what he's got to say."

Jim Harvie rode in, dismounted and walked up to Price: "The Potheros have got a wagon west of Muralla Butte," he announced. "They're shovin' cattle into that country."

"How many men?" Price asked.

"I don't know. I seen the remuda an' there were fifty-sixty horses in it."

A little frown creased Price's forehead. "The remuda, huh?" he drawled. "Now what do you think about that, Ben? Here the X Bars are, remuda and all. A man isn't much good afoot in this country, is he, Ben?"

82

A grin slowly spread across Ben Utt's gnarled face. "He shorely ain't," Ben Utt agreed. "Unless he's mounted he ain't but half a hand."

"And so," Price. Thorn. said slowly, "a half a man can't punch cattle. Maybe Ben . . ."

"I'm away ahead of you," grinned Ben Utt.

"Me too," Jim Harvie was grinning, and his voice was shrill with excitement.

"Just wait till dark," drawled Price Thorn, "and I'll see if I can't catch up."

CHAPTER
SIX

Horse Thief

The dusk was deep when the Teepee finished eating supper. Granny made a clatter with the dishwashing, Neil helping him. Will Thorn sat on the steps and smoked, and down at the corral Price talked with Jim Harvie and Ben Utt. From the bunkhouse came the soft strumming of Duke Wayant's guitar.

"We goin' to take Duke along?" Harvie asked.

Price shook his head. "Too young," he responded. "He'd do something we didn't want done. I trust the kid, but he needs some age."

Ben Utt's grin was infectious. "Too high sperets," Utt commented. "I left the remuda in, Price. Thought you'd want 'em."

"Wish I hadn't ridden Jefe today," Price said. "I'll take that bay Poco horse. You boys get good mounts."

Harvie and Utt nodded and Harvie opened the corral gate. "I'll saddle for you, Price," he offered. "You go on up to the house an' talk to Will awhile."

Price strolled off and Harvie and Utt went into the corral.

At the porch Price found his father and Neil Redwine. Will Thorn was talking to the boy, his voice deep and soft as he recounted a tale of the early days. Neil was all ears. He hardly turned his head when Price approached, so intent was he on Will's tale. The boy had a wood fork in his hand, rubbers attached to the prongs of the fork and a leather pouch fastened between the rubbers. Price, recognizing the weapon, smiled. There was a lot of kid in Neil Redwine, despite the fact that the boy was sixteen and wanting to be a man. Price sat down on the step, reached out a hand and possessing himself of Neil's weapon, picked up a pebble and flipped it off into the gloom.

"And so we rode back," Will Thorn continued. "We'd worked the country and never found a thing. And right back at the Seco springs there were our horses."

The old man laughed deep in his throat and Neil Redwine asked: "Had they been there all the time?"

"No," Will Thorn answered. "They'd pulled out all right. There's a hardpan flat over back of Muralla Butte and we'd lost their tracks there. They had just circled around the butte and come back to the spring. Did you want something, Price?"

Price shook his head. "Nothing," he answered.

Will got up. "Pretty near bedtime, Neil," he suggested. "Got a big day on our hands tomorrow."

Obediently Neil moved from the stoop. He held out his hand toward Price for his slingshot, but Price, apparently, did not see the extended hand. The boy waited a moment and then walked off toward the bunkhouse, and Will Thorn said, "I think I'll move him up with us, Price."

"All right," Price agreed. "He can have the little room off the kitchen."

The older man went into the house and Price, waiting a moment more, stuffed the slingshot into his hip pocket and went on down to the corral.

Harvie and Ben Utt were all ready to go. Still they waited until the light in Will Thorn's room went out and until the guitar had ceased in the bunkhouse, then mounting, they rode off toward the west.

Harvie and Price knew the country intimately. Ben Utt was learning it rapidly, as a cowman does. Harvie told his two companions just where the X Bar wagon was located and they went directly toward it despite the darkness. A good two hours after the three left the Teepee they saw a glow that, marked the fire at the wagon and simultaneously they stopped.

"What's the plan?" Harvie asked.

"They'll have a night jingler," Price said, "and some of the horses will be hobbled. We've got to get rid of the nighthawk and drift the horses off. When we get far enough with them we'll move them over the hard pan behind the Butte and take them on to the Mule Pens." The story that Will Thorn had told was bearing fruit.

Utt made a criticism. "It won't do to take those horses to your own camp," he said.

"What do you think Tony will do tomorrow?" Price demanded.

Utt grunted, his criticism answered, and Price said, "You two stay here. I'll move up a piece and locate the remuda."

86

He did not stop to see that his order was obeyed, but rode off, looking back so that he could definitely mark where he had left his friends by the skyline. Ben Utt chewed tobacco and Jim Harvie said uneasily, "You think we ought to of gone with him, Ben?"

"Naw," Utt responded, "he's all right. We're goin' to have some moon in an hour or so."

They waited, both wishing that they could smoke, both repressing the desire. It seemed like a long time that they waited, but in reality it was perhaps twenty minutes. Then Price came riding back, finding his companions as surely as he might have found a numbered house on a well marked city street. "The remuda is about a quarter of a mile below the wagon," he announced. "Come on, let's go."

It was not necessary to caution these two to silence. They followed after Price, not a spur jingle, not a squeak of a saddle marking their progress. The way wound among folds of the ground until finally Price led them out of a depression and toward a rim. Just beyond the top of the rise he halted and their eyes accustomed to the starlit night, the men with him could see the black bulk of the X Bar remuda below them.

"Nighthawk is on this side," Price said. "I'm goin' to slip down and get him started. You wait here."

"What are you goin' to do, Price?" Harvie whispered. "Slug him?"

Price chuckled. "No. Here, hold Poco." Price dismounted and tendered Jim his reins. Harvie took them and Price slipped away into the night. Just below the crest of the rise, Utt and Harvie waited, almost breathlessly.

Price, working down hill, stealthy as any savage, had a plan. Neil's slingshot was in his pocket, a soundless weapon and, if Price had not lost his cunning, an efficient one for his purpose. Close by the horses Price stopped and, lifting his head stared into the night. The X Bar nighthawk, lulled by the peace of the night, was sitting against a stone, holding the reins of his bridle loosely in his hand. Price could see the man and the horse as black splotches against the lesser black of the grass and the dark sky. Carefully he searched about until he had found three small rocks, then removing the slingshot from his pocket he unwound the rubbers, fitted a stone into the leather pocket and, pulling back the rubbers, sent a stone whirling off into the dark.

In front of the X Bar nighthawk there was activity. His horse, gentle enough but not used to being struck in the head with a stone, the occurrence being particularly frightening because of the dark, jerked on the reins and pulled them out of the night guard's lax hand. Another stone, arriving on the heels of the first and striking the horse's flank, moved the animal further away and the nighthawk, coming to his feet with a rasping curse, did nothing to pacify his mount.

"Whoa! Damn you, whoa!" the nighthawk swore.

The horse, free, moved off, holding his head to one side so that he would not step on the dragging reins. The X Bar man ran after his horse and the animal's walk became a trot. Price, choking back his laughter, slipped up the slope. When he reached his friends he took Poco's reins from Jim and mounted.

"Let's move a remuda," he said. Down below they could hear the X Bar man still running after his horse, cursing all the way.

The X Bar nighthawk was proficient at swearing. He needed all his oaths when, at the end of a fruitless half hour, he walked back to where he had left his remuda. Pride, and the hope that his escaping horse would step on trailing bridle reins and thus anchor himself, had kept the X Bar nighthawk following his escaping mount. Now, returning to the little pocket in which he had left his charges, he found it empty of horses. This was serious and the nighthawk repaired to camp for help.

Price Thorn, Jim Harvie and Ben Utt, driving the X Bar remuda along, not hurrying it, were filled with glee. Price had to brag a little about his prowess with a slingshot, and Utt and Harvie laughed at the story. They were five or six miles away from where they had picked up the horses when the moon came up. They went a little further and then in a convenient little rincon in the side of Muralla Butte, Price and Harvie held the horses while Ben Utt cut a few pairs of hobbles. There were only four hobbled horses in the whole remuda and Utt made short work of freeing them.

Now, unhampered, they could take a faster pace. Across the hard-pan went the remuda and riders, around the northern edge of Muralla Butte and on toward the east. Tony Troncoso, awakened in his camp by voices and a pounding on the door, answered that summons, Winchester in hand. When he found who was visiting, Tony built a fire and made coffee. As he worked he listened to Price.

"Sure," Tony said finally, "*seguro*. Me, I'm take theese *caballos* up Juniper canyon an' across the gap. Then I put up the gate een that ol' fence at the gap an' come home, an' I'm not knoweeng a theeng."

Price set down his coffee cup. "That's right, Tony," he said. "We'll pull out now. We've got to be home when somebody from the X Bar walks in and wants a horse."

In the lamp light Tony's teeth flashed. "You geeve eet to heem that Judas horse," suggested Tony.

Price and his two companions were back at the Teepee by three o'clock. Granny could not get them up at four when his alarm clock went off and it was six o'clock before Price and Jim and Ben Utt sat down at the breakfast table. Will Thorn, Duke, and Neil Redwine had done the chores and Neil had wrangled horses. When Price went to the corral after breakfast, he saw that all the remuda was in, including the three mounts that had been used on the expedition after the X Bar remuda. These he hastened to turn out. Duke Wayant already was out riding a green horse. Jim and Ben Utt saddled when Price did and let their horses soak in the corral. Price was worried about Will and Neil staying at the ranch but that worry was relieved when Will announced that he was going to take Neil to Pichon, the little store and post office southwest of the Teepee. Will Thorn wanted to get the boy some clothes

90

and thought that he could outfit his young charge at the store, and Granny was in need of some staple groceries. When Neil and Will Thorn had saddled up and ridden away, Price turned out the horses, leaving only the grulla Judas in the corral along with the three animals that were already under saddle.

About eight o'clock Joe Nixon, the Merriman rider, came walking into the ranch. He was tired and he sat down beside the corral and pulled off his boots while he explained his wants.

"The nighthawk let the remuda get away from him last night," Joe explained. "His horse jerked loose from him an' went home, I reckon. There ain't a horse at the wagon. Ed Pothero sent me over to see if I could borrow a horse an' saddle."

Price, face expressionless, said that certainly Nixon could have a horse. He roped Judas, and Granny, coming from the house, donated his old saddle.

"Keep the outfit as long as you want to," Price said. "Sure too bad about your horses gettin' away. What did Pothero say to the nighthawk?"

"He fired him," Nixon answered. "I'll just go back an' we'll pick up them horses an' be all right. I'll bring your horse back this evening'."

"Keep him as long as you need him," Price said, and Nixon, pulling on his boots with sundry curses because of the soreness of his swollen feet, mounted Judas and rode away. Judas, the grulla, acted all right. Judas never gave any trouble except when it was least expected; then with a rider completely off guard, Judas would come unhooked. When Nixon had disappeared Price turned to Harvie and Utt.

"Now I think we'll chouse some cattle," he announced.

"Then you ain't goin' to move 'em?" Utt asked.

Price shook his head. "No," he answered. "We aren't going to move them much. This has always been summer country. If the X Bar and the Key want to use this grass this summer I can't stop them. It's open range. They oughtn't to object if the Teepee stuff uses down below along Arroyo Seco and Arroyo Grande this fall."

"But they've got no bulls with their cows," Harvie objected. "Price, you've got the thirty head of bulls you bought and we've got thirty-six more. That ain't near enough. It's enough for our little bunch, but with all the cows that they've shoved in here . . ."

"We've got salt at every waterhole," Price interrupted swiftly. "The bulls I bought are tired and they aren't going to move much from the salt and the water. The other bulls we have are old and they'll lay around a waterhole anyhow. Maybe, if we ride real good, we three can see that not many of the X Bar and the Key cows come in to water. If we don't take them out, the bulls aren't going to leave. What's your idea on it, Ben?"

Ben Utt nodded thoughtfully. "If we work at the job, we can have them X Bar an' Key cattle so damned wild they'll run every time they see a man on a horse," he said. "Even their own boys ridin' the water will spook 'em. Me, I'm goin' to keep my rope down an' I'll beat

92

the hell outen any X Bar or Key that don't move fast enough to suit me. I'm goin' to forefoot some of 'em an' spit a little tobacco juice in their eyes, too. I aim to see that the only gentle cattle in this country are Teepees."

"They can do the same thing," Harvie warned.

"Not afoot they can't," Price said. "They're going to be looking for horses for awhile. They won't have enough of a mount even if they go to the ranch for what horses they've left there. The chances are that they had everything but the young horses and some pensioners in that remuda. We've got awhile to work on this job."

"We got to be careful," Harvie warned.

"I'm carrying a thirty-thirty on the saddle," Utt said. "I notice that you got that ol' Springfield tied to yores, Jim. How you fixed for a gun, Price?"

"I've got one," Price said. "You two work east this morning. I'm going to see Tony and tell him what we're doing. So long."

He nodded cheerfully to Harvie and Utt, and reining his horse around, rode off toward the north. When he was gone, Jim Harvie, the confirmed pessimist, spoke up.

"It ain't goin' to work," Jim predicted.

"Mebbe not," Ben Utt drawled, "but he's got it figgered out an' it's sure goin' to be a hell of a lot of fun. So long, Jim."

Utt also rode away and Jim Harvie, grumbling, started toward the east. A mile out from the ranch, Harvie encountered Duke Wayant, coming in on a green horse. Harvie stopped and Wayant rode over, holding down the sweating bronc.

"Want to have a good time?" Harvie asked Duke.

"Sure," Duke said.

"Then leave any Teepee cattle you see on water, an' fog any X Bars or Keys you see to hell an' gone," Jim ordered. "That's straight from the boss. An' you ought to have a hell of a time doin' it. It'll educate them green horses yo're ridin'."

Duke Wayant grinned, lifted a hand in salutation and loped off toward the ranch. Duke was riding about eight horses a day now, bringing his charges along in the process of their education. The orders that Jim Harvie had relayed to Duke were just the same as apple pie to the youngster. As Harvie had said, Duke was going to have a hell of a time.

For the next three days the Teepee rode hard. Two or three horses a day were used for mounts and the men covered country: They gaunted under the riding they were doing, but they took care of their horses and the remuda stayed up and in shape. Ben Utt, true to his word, was using a plug of chewing tobacco a day. Jim Harvie, elaborating a little on Price's plan, picked up thirty head of mixed X Bar and Key cattle and took them twenty miles into the roughs before he dropped them. Tony, coming down from camp to see how things progressed, spoke of cattle that he had shoved up rough canyons.

On the fourth day, riding out from the ranch, Price headed toward the Seco springs. As he rode across country he spotted a little bunch of cattle and turned

94

toward them. They saw him coming. Up went their tails and with a rattle of split hoofs on rock they went from there. Price laughed. The X Bars and the Keys were getting an education all right.

Going on toward the spring he saw two men riding toward him. Price could not be sure at the distance, who they were, and so made minor preparations, shifting the Smith & Wesson forward from where it rode high on his hip, until it was under his hand. As the riders came on he relaxed, recognizing Donancio Lucero and his brother Enrique, the sheriff. The three men converged, stopped, forming a little group, and Price grinned at the brothers.

"Headed for the ranch?" he asked.

Donancio was smiling but Enrique kept a poker face. "We were goin' to Pichon," Donancio explained, "then we saw you comin' an' rode over to meet you."

"Better come on over to the ranch and have dinner," Price invited. "I was headed for Seco springs, but I can go there this afternoon."

"No," Enrique said, "we got to go to Pichon. You know, Price, there ees horse thieves in the country."

"No!" Price voiced his astonishment.

Enrique and Donancio nodded solemnly. "That's right," Donancio agreed. "Ed Pothero came in an' reported it."

"You don't say?" Price was still astonished. His eyes were twinkling, and in Donancio's eyes was an answering gleam.

"Sure enough," Donancio said. "Pothero an' his whole crew came to town yesterday. The crew was ridin' on the wagon. They'd borrowed a team from the storekeeper at Pichon to bring their wagon in. Pothero was ridin' a grulla Teepee horse."

"Judas," Price explained. "Three, four days ago Joe Nixon came over to the ranch afoot. He said that the remuda had got away from the nighthawk and that they were all afoot. I loaned him a horse. I never did ask what they had a wagon out for, this time of year."

"They didn't find their horses," Donancio elaborated. "Pothero thinks somebody stole them. There were some horses hobbled in the bunch an' they couldn't have gone very far. Pothero was ridin' that grulla you loaned him an' the horse threw him right in the middle of the main street."

"I'm surprised," Price said. "That horse never bucked with me." Price was telling the exact truth. Judas had never bucked with Price.

"Pothero," Enrique announced, "ees haveeng a lot of trouble. He loses hees horses an' somebody cut the drift fence he put up, all to pieces. He says you cut the fence."

"He might have a hard time proving that." The muscles at the corners of Price's jaw bunched.

"I told heem so," Enrique said quietly. "I told heem that the fence was on public land an' that he had no right to put eet there. He deed not like eet."

"An' he shot off his head," Donancio added. "Price, why don't you ride over to Pichon with us. We can eat dinner there at the store."

"I think I will," Price agreed.

All three started their horses and with Price riding between the brothers, they headed on toward the southwest.

During the ride Price asked Enrique what had been done concerning the bank bandits. Entique said that very little had been accomplished. The man Price had shot had not been identified and the county had buried him in Coyuntura's little cemetery. As for the others, they had changed horses somewhere to the west of town, and completely disappeared.

"They had horses staked out," Enrique explained. "We peeked up the ones they rode out of town."

Continuing, the sheriff said that the horses which had been picked up wore northern brands. He had written, Enrique said, to the sheriff of the country from which those horses came. So far he had had no reply to his letter. As for the bandits themselves, they had circled toward the north and struck the railroad. At that point all trace of them was lost. Whether they had turned their horses loose and hopped a freight, whether they had ridden along the railroad and then dropped off into some little draw, just what they had done, Enrique could not say. He had no adequate description of the men, excepting only the bandit killed in getting away. The description of that individual and a general description of the others had been relayed over the state.

"We got wanted notices out on them," Donancio said, "but everybody we asked had a different story. To hear some of 'em tell it those fello's was eight feet high. The photographer in town took a picture of the man you downed, Price. Would you like to have one of them?"

Price shook his head. "I don't want it," he said, shortly.

"I didn't think you would," Donancio answered. He looked at Price, understandingly. "Kind of makes a man sick to his stomach."

"The bank should have geeven you a reward, Price," Enrique stated.

"I didn't want a reward," Price said shortly. "Then the way things stand, there's not much chance of catching those fellows. It was that one in the blue bandanna that killed Billy Wayant."

Enrique nodded. Donancio swore softly. "I liked Billy," he said.

At Pichon, when they reached the little settlement, the two officers drew the owner, Art Bacon, into his office, and Price loafed at the counter visiting with Mrs. Bacon, a plump, motherly little woman who asked about Will Thorn and Jim Harvie, whom she knew well. Presently the woman lifted her hands in a hopeless gesture.

"I clear forgot," she apologized. "There's a letter here for you, Price. Came in the day after your father brought that boy over. I'll get it."

She bustled away, returning presently from the little walled-in cubbyhole that served for a post office, a letter in her fat hand. This she gave to Price and Price, excusing himself, opened and read it. His face changed expression as he followed through the letter and when he looked up he was smiling.

98

"Good news?" Mrs. Bacon asked.

"I think so," Price said. "Yes, I believe it's good news."

CHAPTER
SEVEN

Three Men on a Dime

Enrique and Donancio Lucero would not accompany Price back to the Teepee. They had to return to Coyuntura, they said. Price was puzzled concerning the mission of the officers to Bacon's store but neither Enrique nor Donancio offered an explanation and Price did not ask for any. As the three separated, Price, looking after the two brothers, saw something blue that protruded from Enrique's hip pocket and showed above the cantle of the sheriff's saddle.

Price rode back to the ranch. When he reached headquarters he did not go out again but sat with Will Thorn talking over the letter he had received. Thorn was reluctant to fall in with the idea that Price proposed and when Jim Harvie came in he announced that Price was downright crazy. Ben Utt said nothing, and Duke, Granny and Neil were not consulted.

The letter Price had received advanced a proposition from John McCready who was working for the Flag Company. The Flag people had perfected a vaccine against blackleg, or so they believed. It had stood up under laboratory tests but now the company wished to test their product under field conditions. McCready proposed that Price vaccinate his calves, Price to furnish the labor and the cattle, and the company furnishing the vaccine. McCready, if Price agreed to the plan, would come to Coyuntura, bringing a supply of vaccine and all necessary equipment with him. He would help with the work.

"We want a controlled test," McCready wrote. "In order to control we must vaccinate a number of calves and also have a number that are not vaccinated but otherwise living under the same range conditions. I am writing you because I know of your interest in the matter, and because at Midlands you seemed receptive to the idea."

"I'm going to take John up on it," Price stated, overriding his father's reluctance and Harvie's strenuous objections. "I'll write him tonight and tell him to come on. We're going to have to do this pretty soon if we do it at all."

Jim Harvie was still filled with objections. "We'll have to round up," he said. "That'll mean more work. An' it's comin' on toward the middle of August. We're goin' to have to put a hay crew to work an' we got all this ridin' to do an' . . ."

"We're going to do it," Price said, closing his mouth with a snap that meant finality.

"So we're goin' to," Ben Utt drawled, looking at Harvie with a twinkle in his eyes. "Jim, for a little feller, you can find more fault an' do more work than anybody I ever seen. I'll bet if Granny made a panful of bear sign you wouldn't see nothin' but the holes. You'd

101

never see the dough a-tall. When's this feller comin', Price?"

"I'll write him tonight and take the letter to town tomorrow," Price answered. "He ought to be here in about two weeks."

"Well," Utt drawled, "I'll guarantee that we'll be ready for him in two weeks. You know, Price, them X Bars an' Keys are gettin' so they're kind of spooky. There ain't many of 'em in the country neither. They're kind of driftin' back where they come from."

"We're doing a pretty good job of holding them off the water," Price commended. "If it would rain we'd have harder work."

"Yeah," Utt agreed. "They're goin' back where they can get a drink without havin' a rope drug offen their rumps. You know it ought to rain pretty soon. Notice how burnt the grass is gettin'?"

"An' short, too," Harvie added. "You're goin' to have to move some of our cattle pretty soon, Price."

"There's been rain in the hills," Price said. "There's plenty of grass up above the Mule Pens."

"But you can't hold cattle in the hills when it snows," Harvie announced. "You can't do that, Price."

"Jim," drawled Ben Utt, "yo're a damned pessimist!"

Price wrote his letter that night. In spite of what he knew, in spite of the work he had done, of the knowledge he possessed, he was still uncertain. McCready's letter had said that the vaccine was perfected. Perhaps it was. Perhaps the vaccine was a sure preventive of blackleg. But if that was true, why did the Flag company want to try it on a lot of calves?

102

Why didn't they release it in place of testing it further? The knowledge that Price possessed worked two ways: he could understand the making of a vaccine, its application and what a vaccine would do. He could understand, too, that there was many a slip between the first slow beginnings and the perfected serum. Suppose that John McCready was wrong? Then Price was gambling with his calves, with his whole future, and, worse than these, he was gambling with his father's happiness. Price Thorn was a young man. If something went wrong he could make it up, could bounce back. But Will Thorn was old and all the bounce was out of him. And so, in trepidation, Price wrote, accepting McCready's proposition, taking a chance, putting on a bold front and never for an instant letting anyone see that there was a doubt in his mind.

The following morning while Price was preparing to go to town to mail the letter, Will Thorn spoke to his son. "I wish you'd take Neil in with you, Price," he said. "I couldn't buy the boy a pair of boots at Pichon. Bacon didn't have any that would fit him."

"Sure," Price agreed. "Tell Neil to get saddled. I've got to order a pair of boots myself."

Accordingly, when Price rode away from the Teepee, Neil Redwine rode with him.

The man and the boy talked on the way in to Coyuntura. Neil, with the adaptability of youth, was fitting into the life at the ranch. He was doing another thing too: since Price had spoken to Will concerning the boy, Will Thorn had, seemingly, taken a new lease on life. He did not do a great deal of work at the ranch, he did not ride much, but his slumped shoulders were straighter and his eyes brighter than they had been in a long time. Neil Redwine was filling a need in Will Thorn's life; he was giving Will an incentive. The boy idolized the old man and Will Thorn had responded to the lad's devotion. Price was more than pleased with the success of his idea. He would have liked to spend more time with his father but the constant press of work precluded that, and so he was glad that Will was adopting Neil.

On the way to town Neil spoke of his life back in Iowa. He was an orphan and he had lived with an uncle on a farm. Price gathered from the boy's talk that the uncle was good enough but that the uncle's wife had made things tough for the boy. When uncle and aunt decided to migrate to Kansas, Neil cut loose and pulled out on his own. He had been bumming his way west, intent on becoming a cowboy, when he was taken off the train in Coyuntura.

"Gee, Price," Neil said with the familiarity of youth, "I won't never forget the way you took care of that brakeman. He'd slapped me a couple of times an' you knocked him down just like there wasn't anything to it."

Price grinned ruefully. "It wasn't as easy as that, kid," he returned. "That brakeman could hit pretty hard. Tell me . . . What do you think you'll make of yourself?"

Neil considered gravely. "I think I'll be a cowman like Mr. Thorn," he answered at length. "That's what he wants me to be. He's teaching me things every day."

"You'll have to go to school this winter," Price decided. "We'll get you some place to stay in Coyuntura."

"An' leave Mr. Thorn?." There was rebellion in the boy's voice.

"Maybe he'd stay with you," Price suggested. "Anyhow, you could come to the ranch every Saturday. What do you think of that?"

"Mr. Thorn could teach me all I'll need to know," Neil answered sturdily. "I don't think I'd like it in town."

Price said nothing more. This was something that Will Thorn would have to handle. The boy's loyalty and his adherence to Will Thorn pleased Price.

It was noon when the two reached Coyuntura. Price posted his letter and took Neil to a restaurant. When they had finished their lunch they started along the street to Coyne's saddle shop. Coyne employed a bootmaker and Price wanted to order a pair of boots for himself, as well as to ascertain if there were a pair in the shop that would fit Neil. As they walked along the street they passed a window display of pictures. Coyuntura had a photographer, a visionary man who did odd jobs and occasionally took pictures of a wedding or of cowboys in town for a bust and wanting to celebrate in every way possible. Just in front of the photographer's shop Price was accosted by an acquaintance and while Price and his friend talked, Neil looked in the window. As he searched the display his attention was drawn to one picture in particular. The photographer, anxious to ply his art, had taken a picture of the dead bank bandit. There was the man, bearded, dead eyes closed, face peaceful, hands folded

105

across his chest. Neil stared fascinated. When Price had finished and was ready to go on down the street, the boy was reluctant to leave.

"Did you see this, Price?" he asked.

One quick glance was enough for Price. "I've seen it," he said shortly. "Come on, Neil."

The boy followed after the man. "I . . ." he began. "Say, Price, didn't you . . ."

"I don't want to talk about it, kid," Price said curtly.

Heeding the tone of Price's voice, Neil said nothing more, but plainly there was something on his mind.

At Coyne's, Price was measured and left orders for a pair of boots. The saddle-maker had none that would fit Neil and so Price took the boy across the street to Brumaker's store and calling the storekeeper to him, gave Neil into the merchant's charge.

"Fit him out with a pair of boots, Howard," Price said. "If you haven't any boots that will fit him, give him a pair of shoes and I'll order him a pair of boots. I've got to go on to the bank."

Leaving Neil in Brumaker's charge, Price left the store. In the bank he talked to Pearsall, telling the banker about the chance he had to vaccinate his calves. Pearsall was frankly skeptical.

"You'll kill some calves, Mr. Thorn," he stated. "I don't like to tell you your business, but after all I'm interested and I don't think I'd do it."

Price, producing McCready's letter and some of the literature that McCready had enclosed, attempted to convince the banker of the worth of the plan. It took him a full hour to win Pearsall's reluctant consent to

106

the experiment. At the end of that hour Price bade the banker good-bye and went out to get Neil. It was long past noon and even if they should leave town immediately he and Neil could not hope to get back to the Teepee before dark.

Neil was not at Brumaker's. Brumaker had fitted the boy with a pair of boots and Price paid for them. "The kid wanted to write a letter and I let him use the desk," Brumaker said. "He's just gone to the post office, I think."

Price thanked Brumaker and went out of the store, intent on finding Neil and leaving town. Turning from Brumaker's door he was confronted face to face by Ed Pothero. Kuhler and Jule Pothero stood just behind the fat man. Price stopped short.

A little further back along the sidewalk Joe Nixon stood and with Nixon there was a square-shouldered, chunky man with a close-cropped gray mustache. Price did not know the heavy-set man and scarcely looked at him. He was occupied with the Potheros and Kuhler. Despite Donancio's warning and the suggestion that his carrying a weapon might be overlooked, Price was unarmed. He had not thought it necessary to wear a gun; still did not think it was necessary. The little three-sided indentation, that formed Brumaker's entrance-way was behind him, but Price did not back into it. Instead he faced Ed Pothero squarely.

"I been lookin' for you, Thorn," Pothero growled, his scowl almost obscuring his beady eyes. "Wanted to talk to you."

"I've been at the ranch," Price said smoothly. "You might have ridden over."

Pothero disregarded that. "I've had my fence cut," he said harshly. "My remuda was stolen. I found horses all over the top of the Rana hills. My cattle have been choused around till they're so wild a man can't come close to 'em. A fellow that'll do that ought to be strung up."

"You seem to have had some tough luck," Price said quietly.

"Luck, hell!" Pothero snapped. "It was done deliberate. You done it!"

The fat man was advancing and, before that advance, Price retreated a step. Now he was almost in Brumaker's entrance, glass on either side of him, the door behind him. The retreat was strategic. Price knew that he was facing a showdown and he did not propose to be jumped from in front and from each side. Pothero did not interpret the retreat in that light. He advanced threateningly.

"I'm goin' to beat all the hell out of you, Thorn," he snarled. "I'm goin' to put the fear of God into you so you'll leave my stuff alone."

"You want," Price commented, measuring distances, "to be sure you can do that before you start, Pothero."

"Damn you!" Ed Pothero bellowed, and charged in.

Price had anticipated that move and he was prepared. Smoothly as a machine going into action, he dropped his chin behind his shoulder, thrust out a long left arm and moved his right foot back. Ed Pothero ran into the clenched fist at the end of the left arm. It was

108

like running full tilt into an iron bar. But there was nothing barlike about the looping right hand that Price brought from behind him and drove; that was more like encountering a five-pound rock at the end of a swiftly whirling sling. Price had picked his target: the spot just above Ed Pothero's fat belly, just beneath his breast bone. Timing, shift of weight, impact, all were perfect. Ed Pothero, struck squarely on the plexus, lost all his breath in one gigantic grunt and sat down on the sidewalk, paralyzed, motionless for the moment.

His position stopped Hank Kuhler but did not hamper Jule. Jule was coming in, following his brother; and willingly, a cold rage possessing him, Price went to meet Jule. Jule's fist opened a cut below Price's right eye, high on his cheek, but in perhaps two seconds Price Thorn struck Jule Pothero six times, the blows sounding with a sharp "plop . . . plop . . . plop" as they found flesh. Jule recoiled from the attack and Price, all caution gone, followed his advantage.

Hank Kuhler clawed at Price as Thorn went past. Kuhler's raking fingers furrowed Price's cheek, almost tore an ear from its moorings, but Price was swarming over Jule Pothero, hard fists finding their mark, striking home. In the flurry of that brief attack Jule Pothero's nose was smashed into his face, his eye cut, his soft belly hammered unmercifully and finally a swinging left fist squarely on the mark, just on the angle of his jaw, finished him. His head twisted to the right, snapped back and his eyes glazed. Jule Pothero was out, just as surely as a lamp blown out by a single puff.

Kuhler, behind Price now, was clawing at his hip. Whether for a gun or a slingshot Price did not know and did not care. Hank Kuhler had a long neck with a prominent Adam's apple. Against that bobbing bulge Price exploded a fist and then struck Kuhler twice more as he fell. Kuhler lay prone, breathless, his head feeling as though it were cut off from his body by one vast pain.

Ed Pothero was scrambling up now. He reached his feet, half turned as though to run, and Price pounced on him. There was more than two hundred pounds of Ed Pothero. There was one hundred and eighty pounds of animated fury holding him. Pothero was jerked back, heaved up and sent flying to smash into the hitchrail. The hitchrail checked him momentarily and then he crashed through it to lie in the dust of Coyuntura's main street, stretched out and motionless. Price, legs spread wide, breathing hard, hatless and with blood flowing from the cut under his eye and from the furrows beside his ear, occupied the sidewalk in front of Brumaker's store, and in his doorway Howard Brumaker, eyes wide, spoke three words.

"My great Jupiter!" Brumaker exclaimed in awe.

Donancio Lucero, running toward Brumaker's, reached the corner of the store and slowed his pace to a walk. Coyne was coming from his saddle shop and Pearsall had emerged from the bank to stand on the step, a pencil poised in his hand as though he were engaged in computing interest. Donancio, strolling up to Price, half extended his hand and then, as though he

110

knew that a touch would bring another explosion, spoke soothingly.

"Price . . ."

Price Thorn turned, cocked and ready for action, potentially as dangerous as a loaded gun. For a moment he looked at Donancio, not recognizing the officer, and then he relaxed. "Why . . . hello, Donancio," Price said.

Donancio Lucero grinned, seeing the sanity return to his friend's eyes. "You've had plenty exercise, Price," Donancio commented: "Looks like you've done a day's work. Suppose you come up to Doc Cirlot's an' get patched up."

Donancio extended his hand and placed it on Price's arm. At the edge of the walk Hank Kuhler was sitting up, holding his neck with one hand and gulping like a chicken with the gapes. In the street Ed Pothero, apparently expecting a fresh attack, had rolled over and covered his head with his arms, Jule Pothero, face turned skyward, was still listening to the birds. Donancio held Price's arm gently.

"Three of 'em," marveled Howard Brumaker. "He whipped 'em standin' on a dime."

Pearsall had come across the street and was standing at the edge of the walk looking at Price, respect in his eyes. There were four men on the porch in front of Coyne's shop.

"Come on, Price," Donancio urged. "Come along, now."

Reluctantly Price moved under the urge of the hand. Donancio swung in beside him, grinned at Pearsall and

111

Brumaker, and made a little wry face. "Jus' like dynamite," Donancio said.

Pearsall opened his mouth to speak, thought better of it and turning abruptly went back across the street and into the bank. As Price and his conductor entered Cirlot's drug store, Jule Pothero sat up and gingerly put his hand to the side of his head.

Doctor Cirlot was briskly efficient. He took Price into the little office behind the drug store and went to work. He stopped the blood running from the cut on Price's cheek, using a styptic pencil and collodion, and he applied iodine to the scratches, and bandaged the ear. Donancio stood by while the surgery took place, the little half-grin never leaving his face. When Cirlot completed his work, Donancio asked a question.

"They jump you, Price?"

"I guess so," Price answered. The anger had run out of him, leaving him strangely weak. "I came out of Brumaker's and there they were. Ed Pothero gave up a lot of head about what he was going to do and I kind of lost my temper."

"Don't never get mad at me, Price," Donancio said seriously. "I ought to arrest you for disturbin' the peace." He grinned amiably.

Price returned the grin. "All right," he agreed.

"Daddy Burns would fine you ten bucks," Donancio said. Daddy Burns was Coyuntura's fat and wheezing Justice of the Peace. "I'd have to pay it. I saw you put Pothero through the hitchrail an' it was worth ten bucks. I ain't goin' to arrest you, Price, but I wish you'd get out of town." The grin had vanished from Donancio's face and it was entirely serious.

"I don't run," Price said curtly.

"No," Donancio agreed. "I wouldn't ask you to run, Price. But . . ."

"They're through," Price announced. Some of the anger was returning and with it a feeling of accomplishment. "Look, Donancio, when a man sets out to be tough he's got to stay that way. Pothero bragged about what he was going to do. He's been softened up and everybody knows it. He's not tough any more. There's no need for me to run."

There was an odd expression in Donancio's eyes as he scrutinized Price. "You think that, don't you?" Donancio asked. "I'm not asking you to run, Price, but is there anything to keep you in town?"

"No," Price answered truthfully.

Neil Redwine came in. The boy was panting, almost breathless. "Are you all right, Price?" he gasped. "I was in the photographer's lookin' at the pictures. Are you all right?"

"I'm all right, kid," Price answered. He looked from the boy to Donancio and then on to Doc Cirlot's whisker-rimmed face. Gently he heaved himself up out of the chair. His muscles were stiff and there was a pain in his middle where Ed Pothero had dealt him a blow. "I guess you're right, Donancio," Price said. "I'll go along home."

"Sure," Donancio agreed, his voice marked with his relief. "There's nothin' to keep you in town, Price."

"How much do I owe you, Doc?" Price asked.

"It's been a pleasure," Doc Cirlot said seriously.

Flanked by Neil and Donancio, Price left the drug store. Ed Pothero, Jule, Hank Kuhler, were not in sight. From Coyne's porch a man, the short chunky man who had been with Nixon, detached himself and came striding across the street. At Brumaker's he intercepted the little party. Price and his companions stopped. The chunky man held out his hand.

"I'm Tate Merriman," he announced. "Run the Key. I'll be movin' some cattle tomorrow an' the next day, Thorn; that is, if I can get close enough to 'em." Merriman grinned ruefully.

"Why . . ." Price said, "I'm glad to meet you, Mr. Merriman."

Merriman shook hands awkwardly. "Thought I'd tell you," he said, and then, with a snort, "The Potheros set out to be tough. Huh!"

Merriman turned and stumped back toward Coyne's. Price looked at the rancher's square shoulders, then at Donancio and at Neil. "Your horses are just up the street," Donancio said. "So long, Price. I'll be out to see you in a day or two." The undersheriff squeezed Price's hand and swung off across the street, headed for the Cliff saloon. Price stood and watched him.

"It's going to be mighty dark before we reach the ranch," Neil Redwine said.

Price looked at the kid, grinned and started up the walk again. His hat, retrieved from Brumaker's sidewalk, sat rakishly on the bandage that Doc Cirlot had applied to his ear.

"We'll pull out right away, Neil," Price said. "You're going to be a mighty stiff kid tomorrow. This is the longest ride you've made. Are you good for it?"

"Sure, Price," Neil Redwine answered sturdily. "Sure I am."

CHAPTER
EIGHT

Serums and Viruses

Price Thorn and Neil Redwine jogged out of town side by side. From where he stood in front of the Cliff saloon, Donancio watched them go. When the man and the boy were out of sight, Donancio, accompanying himself by a tuneless whistle, strolled casually into the saloon. Ed Pothero and his brother were sitting at a table away back in the room. Hank Kuhler stood at the bar. Hank was trying to drink whisky. He could not throw his head back and gulp it, as was custom; Hank's neck was too sore for that. Accordingly he had to sip the liquor and follow every mouthful with a chaser and a wry face. Donancio standing stiff-legged in the middle of the room, made an announcement.

"Enrique an' me," commented Donancio, "don't like fights in town, an' we just hate 'em out in the country. An' we don't like people to get killed unless we do it, an' we generally do." With that, Donancio stalked out, leaving a scowling pair of Potheros and a sore necked Hank Kuhler.

Price and Neil did not talk a great deal as they rode away from Coyuntura. They had more than thirty miles to go and it was past four o'clock, nearly five. Their

116

horses were no longer fresh and so they could not push on as rapidly as they had coming in. Still neither mentioned the long ride, Neil from force of pride, Price because he didn't think of it. Neil broached tentative questions about the fight and Price answered them shortly.

"What does Ed Pothero look like?" Neil asked. "I ain't never seen the Potheros or Kuhler."

"They got legs an' arms an' faces," Price answered. "They're just ordinary looking. Ed Pothero's fat."

Neil asked other questions and finally gave up when Price cut him off. They rode on, steadily putting the miles behind them. Trot and walk, trot and walk, the never-ending, patient gait of the cowpony bit into the distance. The sun went down and they rode through the twilight. Twilight ended in quick dusk and dusk in night, and still they rode.

"Gettin' pretty sick of that saddle, kid?" Price Thorn asked.

"I ain't hurtin' the saddle any," Neil Redwine answered with asperity.

Good kid! thought Price, No yelps out of him.

Muralla Butte shown black against the sky when the two rode in to the Teepee. "Go on an' get Granny to feed you," Price ordered Neil. "I'll look after your horse."

The boy, almost played out, sagged when he dismounted. For an instant he clung to the stirrup and then turned and shambled off toward the bunkhouse. Price, pulling free a latigo, chuckled to himself. The kid was going to do all right. He surely was! Ben Utt came

117

strolling up to the corral, stopped, peered inside and then opening the gate came in. He reached Price and stopped, peering steadily at his bandage.

"Somethin' happen to yore head?" Utt asked.

"Unsaddle the kid's horse and I'll tell you," Price said.

Utt went to work. Now Jim Harvie made his appearance at the corral. "The kid come in, lay down, an' passed out," Harvey announced. "I pulled his boots off him an' covered him up. What happened in town, Price?"

Price came out of the corral, carrying his saddle. Ben Utt too emerged, and the horses, freed, went through the gate and in the sand close by lay down and rolled. Before he answered Harvie's question Price put his saddle and gear on the long pole under the shed. "I'll tell you," he said. "The Potheros and Kuhler jumped me."

"Jumped you?" Harvie hauled Price around so that the light from the bunkhouse dimly illuminated him. "Yo're all bandaged up. How bad are you hurt, Price? What happened?"

"I'm not hurt much," Price answered. "And I think the Potheros are done fooling with us. I think they got all they wanted."

"Come on into the bunkhouse an' tell us," Harvie demanded, grasping Price's arm. "Come on, Price."

Price allowed himself to be led. In the bunkhouse, with Granny and Duke as well as Ben and Jim interested listeners, Price related the events of the day. He did not boast of his prowess. Indeed, when he

118

described the fight he did so in a very few words. "Ed Pothero started it and I knocked him down. Then Jule jumped in and I got a couple of licks and was lucky with him. Kuhler got hit in the neck and it kind of made him sick and so they quit," Price said briefly. "The kid and I left town right after that. I had Doc Cirlot patch me up and we pulled out."

"Three of 'em," Granny marveled.

"I'd of liked to been there," mourned Jim Harvie. Utt said nothing, but looked speculatively at Price.

"I think the Potheros are done," Price said. "Merriman came up afterwards and shook hands and said he was going to move some cattle. He won't side with the Potheros any more. The Potheros started out to be tough but I think they've had it taken out of them." Price could not quite keep the triumph from his voice. He stood up. "I'm going up to bed now," he announced. "I'm tired. Granny, you'd better let the kid sleep late tomorrow."

With that, Price walked out of the bunkhouse. For awhile after his departure, Granny, Duke and Jim Harvie kept the ball of conversation rolling. Ben Utt had nothing to say. Presently he arose; looking at Jim Harvie, he nodded toward the door and walked out. After a moment Harvie followed. He found Ben squatted against the building and as Jim joined him the gnarled face of the Texas man was illuminated briefly by the match he touched to his cigarette. Jim Harvie squatted down beside Utt and there was silence between them.

119

Utt broke the silence. "Price thinks because he licked them fellers, they're all done," Utt announced.

"Uhhuh," Harvie agreed, inhaling smoke from his cigarette.

"A fist fight don't settle nothin'," Utt commented mournfully. "Price is too young to know that."

Jim Harvie's affirmative grunt came again.

"The only way to settle a thing for keeps is to kill the other feller," Utt said, meditatively.

"You figgerin' on killin' the Potheros?" Jim Harvie demanded.

"I've heard of worse ideas," Utt drawled. "I don't think I'll do it though . . . Not unless I have to."

"Then you think that the Potheros have just *started* to make trouble," Harvie suggested.

Ben Utt puffed twice, inhaled, and answered. "They just started," he affirmed. "Jim, them fellers will stay quiet till the chance comes, then they'll make hell look like a winter holiday."

"How?"

"How do I know? Whatever way they can. They'll lay back now an' just rock along, but when they git a chance . . ." Utt let Harvie's imagination complete the sentence.

"What we goin' to do?" Harvie drawled at length.

"Look after things," Utt drawled. "It's goin' to be tough, too. Price won't like bein' looked after. He thinks it's all finished."

"Well," Jim Harvie began and then, "Ben you talk like you'd been there."

"I've saw some trouble," Utt admitted. "I was just ahead of trouble when Price hired me. Hank Kuhler knows me. Likely he'll try to start the trouble thataway."

"Thataway how?"

"Sendin' word back to Texas that I'm here," Utt drawled. "If he ain't already done it. I ought to of pulled out right after we got the heifers here, but damn it, I like Price!"

Jim Harvie said nothing more. Whatever there was in Ben Utt's past that would cause him grief, Harvie did not want to know it. It was none of his business. Utt smoked awhile longer, threw away his cigarette, and got up.

"Well, I ain't a-goin'," he announced with utter finality. "I'm goin' to stay here an' see it through. 'Night, Jim."

"Good night, Ben," Jim Harvie answered.

Up in the ranch house Price Thorn's light blinked out.

The following morning the work went on as usual. The Teepee rode the country, the water, the rincons and the canyons of the Ranas, looking after cattle, following out the never-ending, patient program of the man who raises beef. Within four days the riders saw new animals in their country, heavy bulls, carrying the X Bar and the Key brands. The X Bar and Key cattle were fewer too. Apparently the campaign of riding the water holes had been a success.

"They've quit," Price exulted to Jim Harvie. "They've thrown enough bulls in here to take care of what cattle they've got, and Merriman has pulled a bunch of Key cattle out of here. I knew they'd quit, Jim. No danger now of us not having a calf crop."

Jim Harvie, remembering what Ben Utt had said, made no answer to Price's declaration.

It was a week after the fight that Lunt Taliferro came to the ranch. Lunt, having made his usual haul to Pichon, rode over from the little settlement to bring Price a telegram. The message was from John McCready, saying that he would be in Coyuntura on August twenty-sixth. The Flag Company was going through with their end of the contract.

"Several new people in town," Lunt said conversationally. "There's a deputy sheriff from Texas stayin' at the hotel. I was in there last night an' heard him talkin' to Donancio. He's come over lookin' for somebody."

Ben Utt, mopping the last of the fruit juice from his plate with a piece of biscuit, lifted his head. Then, when Taliferro said no more, the tall man put the biscuit in his mouth, chewed and swallowed, and picking up plate and utensils, carried them to Granny's wreck pan. He strolled on out of the kitchen and Lunt went on with his gossip.

When, later, Price finished his meal and went out of doors, Ben Utt stopped him. "I'd like my time," Utt said quietly. "I'll go along, Price."

Price looked at the man, nodded, and said, "Come up to the house."

In the little room off the living room that served as an office Price paid the tall man. Ben Utt, sitting on the edge of the battered old table that served as a desk, swung one long leg. "I want to buy a couple of horses," he said.

"You can have any horse on the place," Price announced. "You can't buy them."

"No," Ben objected, "I want two horses an' I'll buy 'em. How much for that black Nigger horse I been ridin,' an' that bay Juniper horse?"

Price grinned. "Five dollars apiece," he said promptly.

Utt also grinned. The horses were worth fifty dollars each in any man's money. "All right," Utt announced. "Here you are. Make me out a bill of sale, will you?"

Price wrote out the bill of sale and Utt, taking it, thrust out his hand. "It's me that deputy's lookin for," he said casually. "So long, Price."

"I hate to lose you, Ben." Price took the extended hand. "You've been a mighty good hand. If ever you want a job . . . Why don't you stick here and we'll fight it out with them? I'll back you."

Utt shook his head. "Too expensive," he answered. "They don't want me very bad anyhow. An' you ain't losin' me, Price. I'm jus' temporarily mislaid. *Adios.*"

With that he turned abruptly and walked out of the office. Sometime during the night he departed from the Teepee. No one saw him go, no one knew where he went. Simply he rolled his bed, borrowed a frying pan and a lard bucket, a can of coffee and some salt pork, and disappeared. Granny had a few harsh remarks to make when he looked into his bread box and found all his cold bread gone, but aside from that not a great deal was said around the Teepee.

"Ben's gone," Price told the crew assembled at the corral that morning. "I don't know when he left or where he went, and neither do any of you."

"Sure not," Jim Harvie agreed, and Will Thorn nodded solemnly.

So it was that when a short time after dinner Donancio Lucero and a blond and sunburned individual, with the twang of Texas in his voice, rode in to the Teepee, they met with very little information. The Texan, introduced as Bill Slater, stated that he was a deputy sheriff, that he had been sent to Coyuntura because of a letter received by his superior, and that he was looking for a man named Ben Utt.

"He works here, don't he, Price?" Donancio interpolated. "You got Utt on your payroll?"

"No," Price said. "He asked for his time and bought two horses and pulled out of here. I don't know where he went."

Donancio and the Texan exchanged glances.

"What is he wanted for?" Price asked. "Have you got extradition papers for him?"

Slater shook his head. "Nope," he answered cheerfully. "The sheriff sent me over to see if Ben was here. If he was I was goin' to have him arrested an' then I'd get out the papers an' such. Tell you the truth, I don't want him very bad. He killed a man over by Marfa that sure needed killin'. I think Ben could come clear on a self-defense plea except that the family of the man he killed are kind of big bugs an' got a hell of a drag."

124

"Well," Price said again, "he's not here. You can look around of course, and we'd be glad to have you stay with us until you're satisfied, Mr. Slater."

Slater grinned. "Thanks," he said. "I got to stay a few days to satisfy them folks. I don't think I'm goin' to look very hard, though. No, I don't think I will."

"How about you, Donancio?" Price asked. "Can you stay awhile with us?"

"I'll stay two days," Donancio Lucero announced. "You remember you invited me to look at your cattle, Price?"

Price nodded and laughed. He was pleased with the attitude of both officers. Slater was a good man and so was Donancio. Both would do their duty as they saw it, but they weren't going a lot out of the way to find Ben Utt.

At supper that night, in the course of the conversation, Slater told Price a lot about Ben Utt. Utt had worked over most of West Texas. He had been in trouble, not of his own making, once or twice. The word had gone out that Utt was a bad man to crowd and for the most part he had been left alone. He had, when just a kid, been in a big gunfight and had killed a man. He had also served a term with the Rangers and held a good record. From that he had gone to a deputy's job and from the deputyship to running a little horse ranch.

"He run into this Norris abusin' a horse," Slater said. "Ben made Norris stop an' Norris got pretty salty. Ben had to knock him loose from his badness. Then three or four days later Ben was in town an' he an'

125

Norris had a run-in an' Ben killed him. I guess Norris was layin' for Ben. If he was, he found out it was a mistake. Ben pulled out because he knew that the Norrisses run that part of the country. The first word we'd had about it was a letter that come in sayin' that he was over here."

"Who wrote the letter?" Price asked.

"It wasn't signed," Slater said dryly. "I'd never of come, only one of the Norris boys is county commissioner an' he saw the letter an' made the sheriff send me."

"Well, Ben's not here," Price said.

"I know he ain't," Slater agreed, "but I got to stay awhile to make it look like I done my duty. If ever you should see Ben again I wisht you'd give him Bill Slater's regards."

"I don't think I'll see him, but I'll do that if I happen to," Price agreed.

Slater sipped his coffee thoughtfully. "You know, we're goin' to have an election over our way this fall," he said, putting his cup back on the table. "I wouldn't be surprised if after election the district attorney wouldn't dismiss the indictment against Ben. Wouldn't surprise me at all. Tell him that too, will you, Thorn?"

"I don't think I'll see him," Price said again, keeping his face sober. "I'll tell him if I do."

"An'," Slater emphasized the word, "*if* the indictment is dismissed and *if* you do see him, you could tell him that job's still open at the horse ranch. My dad owns it." An infectious grin spread over the young deputy's face, and Price returned the grin.

126

"He's a good hand, Ben is," Price said noncommittally.

When Donancio and Slater left the following day, Price went with them, driving a team and buckboard to Coyuntura to meet John McCready. McCready arrived the next morning, a small, brisk, efficient young man who carried all his necessities with him. At Cornell, Price Thorn and John McCready had been the two Westerners in the Agricultural College. While they had not roomed together, a similar background had thrown them into mutual companionship. Price had gone on from college to work with an Easterner who raised purebreds. From that position he had sailed for the Argentine on a three-year contract with a big cattle company. McCready had stayed with his first and only love, veterinary medicine, and now was active in the Flag Company, one of the pioneers in the field of vaccines and serums for cattle and horses.

The two men shook hands when McCready got off his train, looked at each other and grinned, and McCready said, "You'll have to stake me to a bed, Price. I've got everything else I need."

"Guess we can do that," Price announced, and led the way up the platform toward the baggage office.

When the train pulled out the depot agent helped the two load McCready's trunk, his grip, his sacked saddle and sundry boxes into the back of the buckboard, and they left the depot. There was nothing that McCready wanted in town and so the two drove right along, arriving at the Teepee in time for a late dinner. After dinner John McCready made himself pleasant to Will

127

Thorn and to the crew. He did not say a great deal but his slow smile, his deftness as he saddled a horse, the general impression that he made, quite won him a place with the riders.

"Mebbe this stuff is all right, Price," Jim Harvie admitted, drawing Price aside while McCready talked to Will Thorn. "Yore friend kind of acts like he knowed what it was all about, anyhow."

"He does," Price assured. "He's a good man, Jim."

That afternoon John McCready rode with Price and they looked at cattle. McCready was satisfied with what he saw and as they returned to the ranch he outlined his plan of work.

"We'll vaccinate your calves, Price," he said. "We'll get all of them that we can, and we'll mark those that are vaccinated. Then we'll wait and see what happens. I understand that there was a lot of blackleg in this country last year. Chances are that there will be a recurrence of the disease. Our company doesn't yet claim that the vaccine will give one hundred percent protection, but its protective rate is very high. If we can check your losses from blackleg against the losses of others who have not used the vaccine, we'll really have something to go on."

"We can do that, I think," Price returned. "But John, suppose these others want to vaccinate. Then what?"

McCready shook his head. "That's the tough part of it," he said. "We can't run an experiment that way. We've got to go through with the original plan, otherwise we'll have no unvaccinated animals to check against. Next year, if we prove this thing under field

128

conditions, we'll have it on the market and everybody can buy it. This year it's an experiment. I don't mind telling you that we're doing this same thing in Wyoming and in Oregon too. We're going to be sure, Price."

"Will you be back if the blackleg hits?" Price asked.

McCready shook his head. "You can check it," he said. "I'll have to be in Wyoming this fall. You are the only trained man that is cooperating with us, Price, and there are only two agents in the field."

Price nodded and McCready asked, "When do you want to start work?"

"Tomorrow," Price answered. "We'll begin roundup then."

And they did begin the next morning. Leaving Will Thorn and Neil Redwine to hold down the headquarters, Price, McCready, Duke, Harvie and Tony pulled out. They took a pack outfit in place of a wagon for they were going to work in the hills and the crew was small. They went to the west end of the country that day, made camp, and in the afternoon, leaving Duke with the remuda, began work.

McCready had made compact outfits for each rider. These consisted of a syringe, extra needles, vaccine in bottles, disinfectant, and a leather case to carry the equipment. Aside from that, all that was needed was a good horse, a saddle, a rope and pigging strings. McCready demonstrated on six calves, taking the first two himself and letting each of his companions vaccinate one under his direction. McCready quite won the Teepee with his first calf.

The first animal to get the vaccine was a four-hundred-pound, brockle-faced steer calf and McCready, mounted on Doughboy, loaned by Price for the occasion, came up on his calf in less than twenty yards. Doughboy, intent on giving his rider a throw at the calf, ran full out, straight across a little sand flat where the rats had built tunnels. The horse went into the sand, fetlock deep at times, but John McCready, riding light, paid no attention to the danger but built a little loop above his head and dabbed it down on the calf. Doughboy turned, faced the calf and squatted. The calf at the end of the rope, bucked and bawled. McCready, coming out of his saddle, pigging string in hand, went down the rope, flanked the calf, and kneeling on the heaving red side, tied the feet. The cow, anxious and worried pushed her nose almost into the kneeling man's face.

Getting up from the calf McCready walked back to his saddle and possessing himself of the leather case came back. The rest of the Teepee men had dismounted and formed a little circle around the calf.

John McCready, kneeling, fitted a needle to the syringe, drew the syringe full from the bottle, and addressed his audience. "We use five cubic centimeters, one syringe full," he said. "First you get any air out of the syringe," (a little gout of colorless liquid came from the needle as McCready touched the plunger), "then you inject the vaccine here."

With his left hand he took a fold of skin at the calf's shoulder. The needle flashed and then was covered by red skin, the plunger went home, the needle was withdrawn and McCready stood up. "How do you want to mark the ones we vaccinate, Price?" he asked.

"Bob their tails," Price answered, and with opened knife in hand he bent down to perform that operation.

"Good," McCready said. "Now I'll disinfect this needle and do another calf, and then you take one, Price."

He turned the calf loose and it loped off to its anxious mother. Returning the hypodermic and vaccine bottle to the case, McCready went back to his horse, mounted, and rode off, coiling his rope.

Jim Harvie, coming up to Price, made comment. "Keep him here for roundup, Price," Harvie said. "You could use him heelin' calves next spring."

That afternoon the Teepee worked a circle of flat country. They did not handle many calves for the work was new and strange. Tony broke a needle and was much concerned until McCready helped him recover the broken tip and fit another to his syringe. Jim Harvie, going after a calf across a dogtown, had his horse fall. Jim was thrown clear and was not hurt, but he lost his case and spent half an hour looking for it, finding it, eventually, in a prairie dog hole. That night at supper there was much conversation about the day's work.

Duke had cooked supper and the remuda was grazing, about half the horses hobbled, and a stake horse kept up by camp. The meal was eaten as dusk came down and when it was almost finished a tall rider came into camp, dismounted and stalked toward the fire.

"Got a place for another man on yore crew, Price?" Ben Utt asked. "Looks like you might be short-handed."

"You bet I have," Price Thorn answered.

CHAPTER
NINE

Blackleg!

The Teepee vaccinated three hundred and twenty calves. They did not try to get the remainder, about thirty head. These were missed somewhere in the drag that the crew made. McCready stayed with the men all through the work, directed it, seeing that it was done correctly. And while they vaccinated, the Teepee had visitors. Tate Merriman and Joe Nixon rode into their camp one noon, ate with them, and went out to see just what this was all about.

Merriman was not impressed. "I've seen a lot of things tried for blackleg," he said that evening, speaking to Price and John McCready. "I've tried a lot of things. My experience is that if the weather breaks bad in the fall, if you start gettin' cold days an' then it turns off warm again, an' then cold again, that you're goin' to lose some calves. Some years are worse than others. I've had pretty good luck takin' a piece of rope an' tyin' it through their briskets. That seems to help some, but a man is bound to lose a lot when there's blackleg in the country."

"Bleedin' 'em by cuttin' off the end of their tails, is good too," Joe Nixon stated with conviction. "It don't seem reasonable that squirtin' a little water under their hide is goin' to stop blackleg."

"It's not water," McCready explained. "See here, blackleg is caused by a certain germ. We know that."

"You mean one of them little bugs you can't see?" Nixon interrupted.

"Something like that," McCready said, impatient at the interruption. "What we do is to take a great number of these bacteria and kill them. Then we inject the dead germs into a calf. The calf builds up a substance in its blood that fights the poison of the germs. Then, if living germs attack the calf that substance is already in the animal's blood and the germs are killed. That's the way vaccine works."

Merriman shook his head. "Looks dangerous," he commented. "I don't like it. Seems to me that you'd spread blackleg."

"We stop it," McCready said firmly.

"Mebbe," Nixon drawled. "We'll see if the blackleg gets into the country. Say, Price, I left that grulla horse an' that ol' saddle at the ranch. That grulla's kind of a mean horse, ain't he?"

"Is he?" Price asked innocently. "I've never noticed. You know, Joe, I wouldn't pass out a mean horse to a friend or to somebody I didn't know."

Remembering Dynamite and the ride Price had made, Joe Nixon had the grace to blush. Merriman, who had heard the story, laughed at his rider's discomfiture. Price laughed too, and presently Nixon could not keep from joining in the merriment at his expense. "That grulla throwed me once between the ranch an' the wagon," he confessed. "He done it easy, just kind of shucked me off."

"What are you going to do for grass, Thorn?" Merriman asked. "If it don't rain pretty soon we'll all be out of grass."

"There's still plenty in the hills," Price answered.

"You'll have to come out of them before winter," Merriman said. "You'll have to get down into a winter country."

"We will," Price assured. "One thing sure, if it doesn't rain we'll all be in hard shape. We'll have to make the best of it. Are you putting up hay?"

Merriman said that he was, and added the information that the Potheros also were haying. Price knew that Will Thorn had hired a hay crew before he left on the round-up. How much hay the two Teepee vegas would cut was problematical, but he thought enough to go through the winter.

"Most of what I've got are young cattle," Price told Merriman. "We'll have enough hay to feed the weak cows and cripples."

The talk ran on. Merriman suggested that he had a calf buyer coming and that he might send him over to see Price. It was a friendly gesture and Price said that he would be glad to see the man. When the Key owner and his cowboy left the camp, Price had a very definite impression that he was a friend, and said so to Jim Harvie.

Harvie grunted. "He's yore friend now because you licked hell out of the Potheros," Harvie said. "You do

135

somethin' he don't like an' see how far he sides you. He ain't stuck on this vaccinatin' neither."

Harvie, having adopted John McCready as a friend, was thoroughly sold on the vaccination idea. Now he continued, speaking scornfully from his height of acquired knowledge. "Merriman'll go out of here an' do some talkin' an' if somethin' goes wrong with this plan of ours, he'll bring the whole outfit down on you. Yo're popular right now, Price. The whole Rana thinks yo're a swell feller; but just you wait till somethin' goes haywire."

McCready, at Price's elbow, spoke quietly. "He's right, Price. I'm afraid I talked over Merriman's head when I tried to explain this serum to him. There's no one who knows more than an ignorant man when he thinks he knows something and unless I'm mistaken, Merriman thinks he knows that vaccine is not good for blackleg."

"Wait till he begins to lose calves, and ours stay well," Price prophesied. "Then he'll know we're right."

"Maybe," McCready said skeptically, "but I wish that we hadn't done this, Price. You're a friend of mine and I don't want you to have any trouble on my account."

"Trouble?" Price scoffed. "There's no more trouble in this country. I've settled that." There was an arrogant tone in Price's voice and a cocky set in the way he held his shoulders and head, and McCready looking at Jim Harvie could not repress a faint smile which Harvie returned. Both men hoped against hope that young Price Thorn was right.

The crew finished with the work and went to the ranch. McCready stayed another day, visiting with Will Thorn and Price, and then Price took his friend in to Coyuntura and put him on the train. The two talked as they waited on the station platform, McCready rehearsing for the last time the conditions of the experiment.

"There is one thing I wish we had been able to do," the veterinarian said. "I wish that we had been able to vaccinate all your cattle. The blackleg doesn't discriminate, you know, and there is a chance that the older cattle will be hit too."

"Can I get more vaccine?" Price asked.

"Perhaps," McCready said.

"Well," Price listened to the approaching train blow the long station signal, "it's generally the young stuff that comes down with it, and if the vaccine works on the calves I might be sending in for some more for the cows and the heifers."

"I'll try to get it for you," John McCready promised. "Here's my train, Price. Take care of yourself and keep a close check on things. Write to me."

"I'll do that, John," Price agreed. "So long, and we'll be looking for you back."

When the train departed, carrying John McCready and his luggage, Price went back up town. He hadn't much to do before he drove back to the ranch, but he put the team in the livery and gave instructions that they be fed, and then leaving the barn, went into Brumaker's store and left an order.

Leaving Brumaker's he went to the courthouse and visited the sheriff's office. Donancio was out but Enrique was at his desk working on a letter, and Price sat down to wait until the sheriff had finished. Presently Enrique laid aside his pen, leaned back in his chair and surveyed his visitor.

"How are theengs, Price?" Enrique asked.

"Pretty good," Price answered. "We've been busy at the ranch."

"I heard," Enrique said. "Do you theenk that will work, Price?"

"I believe so," Price said sturdily.

Enrique shook his head. "I don't theenk anytheeng will stop blackleg," he announced. "I have seen everytheeng tried."

"This is new," Price explained, and plunged into an explanation of the principles of vaccination. Enrique listened, occasionally asking a question. Price tried to answer but while Lucero was shrewd and a good officer, he was no scientist. Price talked over his head and Enrique got a very garbled idea of what vaccination was all about.

There was a blue bandanna handkerchief on the sheriff's desk and the officer folded it and pulled it through his fingers as Price talked. Finally Price announced, "That's as good as I can explain it, Enrique," and the sheriff nodded absently and changed the subject.

"You see any handkerchiefs like thees, Price?" he asked.

138

Price examined the bandanna and returned it to the top of the desk. "I guess so," he answered. "They're common enough."

"Not so common," Enrique shook his head. "There ees none like theese een town. None een theese country."

"That right?" Price looked at the handkerchief with renewed interest. The neckerchief looked ordinary enough. There were white figures printed on the blue background and in the center of the outlined blue square was a white horse.

"Come to think of it, I don't believe I ever did see one with a horse on it," Price commented.

"That handkerchief," Enrique said, "was found where the bank robbers changed horses."

"The hell!" Again Price carefully examined the blue and white cloth. "You know, Enrique, the man that shot Billy Wayant was wearing one of these. He had his face covered with it."

Enrique held out his hand and Price returned the handkerchief. "There was no need to shoot Billy," the officer said. "Billy deed not have a gun."

"I know it," Price's voice was sober. "Do you think you'll ever find the men that did that?"

Enrique shrugged. "We keep tryeeng," he answered simply.

There was more talk in the office and then Price, knowing that his groceries were ready, took his leave. He picked up the buckboard and team at the livery barn and drove to Brumaker's. While his order was being loaded into the bed of the buck-board, Price went across the street to the bank, announcing to Pearsall that the vaccinating was finished. Pearsall replied that he was glad of that, that a number of men had been in to speak to him about it.

"Merriman was in here," the banker continued. "You know, Thorn, I think that business was dangerous."

"Why?" Price asked, surprised.

"Well," the banker explained, "it's dangerous starting a disease."

"But we weren't starting it," Price said, the expression on his face showing his astonishment.

"That's the way Merriman had it," Pearsall announced. "This fellow that came out to your place, talked to Merriman and he told Tate that you took the germs that cause the disease and shot them into the calves. It looks to me like that would give the calf blackleg."

"But that's not right at all!" exclaimed the indignant Price. "You vaccinate the calves, just like you vaccinate for smallpox."

"The way I understand smallpox vaccination, the doctor gives his patient a light case of smallpox," Pearsall answered. "If this is the same thing, it's dangerous."

"It's not the same thing," Price said. "Listen, Mr. Pearsall." For the second time that day he explained the theory of blackleg vaccination. He was eager and earnest and when he finished, Pearsall nodded.

"Well," the banker said, and there was still doubt in his voice, "I guess you know what it's all about, Price,

140

but that's not the way Merriman has it. He's going to be hard to convince differently, too."

Price, recalling McCready's declaration concerning ignorant men, made no answer. He talked a little longer with the banker and then left.

On the way across the street to Brumaker's from the bank, Coyne came out of his shop and called to Price. He had Price's boots ready and when Price went to get them the bootmaker gave him a pair to deliver to Tony Troncoso. "Tony wanted this three row stitchin' an' the white inlays," the bootmaker announced. "I never put inlays in a boot unless they're ordered. Tony wanted these extra tight, too. He must have a girl."

Price laughed, said that he did not think Tony was courting anyone, and paying for both pairs of boots, left the saddle shop.

All the way to the ranch, Price was absorbed with his thoughts, and when he reached the Teepee there was a little wrinkle of worry on his forehead. Price had not liked Pearsall's attitude toward the vaccination experiment and he had not liked what Enrique had to say about it; but he made no comment to the others as he retailed the news from town.

Late in August and all during the first week of September the Rana country was blessed with rain. Indeed the blessing was so great that it almost became a curse. On Monday of that last week in August, a little cloud showed up atop the Ranas and spread and spread. Rain came from the cloud, at first a steady drizzle that made the cowmen grin and go cheerfully about their work, water dripping from their hat brims and the long skirts of their pommel slickers dragging in the mud. Then the cloud opened up and it really began to rain. Arroyo Seco and Arroyo Grande were raging yellow torrents, impossible to cross. The Teepee was cut off from Pichon and from Coyuntura. There was water everywhere, in the water holes, in the dry lakes, even in the Teepee kitchen where the roof sprung leaks and Granny Davis puttered and fumed, setting buckets and wash tubs in place to keep from being flooded.

Indeed there were only three bright spots in the whole affair. The first and most important of these was that the rain came in time. It was not too late to make grass and if winter held off and there was no freezing weather for a month or so, there would be plenty of grama in the Rana country. The second bright spot was that the Teepee did not have much hay down. The little that had been cut was washed away. The vegas were lakes of water dimpled by the continuing rain, and the haycrew folded up their tents and put away mowers and rakes and sat idly by awaiting the end of the deluge. The third cheerful thing in the rain was Tony Troncoso's new boots. Cheerful, that is, to all but Tony.

Tony had come down from the Mule Pen camp to the ranch and was staying at headquarters. Despite the weather, the Teepee functioned as usual and that meant ride. For a day or two Tony wore his old boots, hoping to save his new ones, but the old boots were worn out and did not even pretend to keep Tony's feet dry. So on the third day of the rain Tony pulled on his new foot gear, the pride of his heart, grunting and tugging on the

142

lugs as he donned the boots, for, even as Coyne's bootmaker had said, the boots fit close.

Arrayed in the glory of new boots, a hat that would shed water (due to the grease and smoke of many camps), and a long yellow slicker, Tony rode out. That night he pulled off his boots with an effort, for they were wet. More than that, his feet were tender, having been scalded not a little by the wetness of the boots and the fact that Tony had tried to dry them on his feet. The following morning, hearing sounds of woe from the bunkhouse, the Teepee assembled. Tony was trying to get into his boots.

Tony sat on the edge of a bunk. Duke, Jim, Ben Utt and Price gathered about him. Will Thorn was in the house, Granny was busy in the kitchen and Neil was helping Granny. With a strong and gnarled forefinger through each lug of his right boot, Tony lay back and pulled.

"Lays off like ol' Poco at the end of a rope," Harvie commented. "Pullin' that way he could sure hold a calf."

Tony grunted, getting a little red in the face.

"Naw," Ben Utt spoke with lofty scorn, "Poco can't pull that good. Poco couldn't pull yore hat off. Tony pulls more like the work team. Seems to me like them boots is a leetle close, Tony."

"Little grease might help," Duke suggested.

"Shot up!" Tony snapped, and heaved again.

"I could always make it by wigglin' my toes," Utt drawled helpfully. "Gosh, but Tony's strong. Makes me think of that strong man I seen in the circus onct. He

143

just helt out his hand an' turned around an' set down on it. Kept himse'f sittin' there in the air, holdin' hisse'f up for half an hour."

Deliberately Tony freed himself of the boot, stood up and strode through the door, leaving both boots and tormenters. Returning with two table knives he inserted them in the boot lugs, got his foot in position and heaved again.

"Just lookit that knife bend," Duke marveled. "Tony sure is strong!"

"Damn eet!" Tony snapped, giving up once more.

"Now me," announced Jim Harvie, "I allus liked my boots to fit near but I didn't want 'em so damned close I couldn't git into 'em. What you goin' to do now, Tony?"

"Poot on thees boots," Tony answered grimly.

"I got a scheme," Utt stated. "Wait a minute, Tony." The tall Texan strode away only to return with the kitchen broom and the bunkhouse broom. The handles of these he inserted in Tony's boot lugs and then, with some dexterity, Utt proceeded to place the brooms on two chairs so that the boot hung from the handles, suspended by its lugs.

"Now," drawled Ben, "climb up on a chair, Tony, get yore foot in the boot an' kind of jump down. That'll put her on."

Tony, seeking any means that would get him into his boots, climbed on a chair. There, with Utt and Harvie balancing him, he reached out gingerly with one stockinged foot, got it partially into the boot and,

144

resting his hands on Utt's and Harvie's shoulders, shifted forward until his weight was above the boot.

"Jump!" snapped Utt.

Tony jumped. His foot went almost into the boot, the lugs broke and Tony sat down.

Ben Utt surveyed the catastrophe. Tony sat on the floor, almost crying with rage, unable to get the profanity that choked his throat out and into use. The boot, with both lugs broken, was almost on, would be nearly impossible to remove. Mr. Utt drawled ingratiatingly, "We showed you how, Tony. We got to go now. You come on out when you get yore other boot on . . . or when you get that'un off. We better go boys."

Ben Utt headed the procession toward the door and on the floor Tony wailed his lament. "Damn eet! My new boots! Oh by damn eet!"

The weather cleared in September's second week, turning off soft and warm. Grass grew rapidly. It was almost like spring. All through the Rana country riders could see cows grazing and when they lifted their heads it was to look inquiringly at the approaching cowhand as if to say, "Why bother me? I'm getting in shape for winter. Let me alone."

With the creeks and lakes full it was necessary to ride bog again, and Price, at Ben Utt's request, put Ben up in the Mule Pen camp. Ben was still not looking for company.

When the weather cleared off, so too did Tony Troncoso's temper, and having repaired the lugs of his new boots, he wore them regularly. All through September the spirits of the Teepee stayed high, and toward the last of the month Price had a stroke of luck. A calf buyer, sent out by Pearsall, visited the ranch and contracted Price's calves for November delivery, making an earnest payment of a thousand dollars. Price was elated when he went to town with the calf buyer, walked into the bank and deposited that check. Pearsall felt good too.

"You've made a good deal," the banker told Price after the calf buyer had left them. "Your calves will bring you better than eight thousand dollars. That will go quite a ways toward paying the bank, Price."

Price Thorn nodded. "And next year's calf crop will see us clear," he said. "I tell you though, Mr. Pearsall, if I can keep on owing the bank money for the next ten years, I'll be worth quite a little at the end of that time. You can't beat an old cow, Mr. Pearsall. If you stay with her and treat her right, she'll make you money."

The banker nodded soberly. "If nothing goes wrong," he agreed, and then, weariness in his voice, "But there are too many things that can go wrong. Drouths and disease and sheer human cussedness are the ruin of the cow business, Price. I've banked in a cow country for a long time. I've never seen it fail. When a man is on the road up, something happens to him. How many cowmen do you know of that died wealthy?"

Price grinned and shrugged. "Not many," he admitted. "Most of them go broke." He was sober for an instant, and then the sunny smile broke over his face again. "But look at the fun they had, Mr. Pearsall," he said, with the incurable optimism of the cowman.

146

"They all had a swell time making it and then going broke."

Pearsall could not restrain his smile. "You'll make a good cowman, Price," he said. "You've got what it takes to get along, I think. Don't start selling next year's calves before they're dropped, though. It isn't good business."

"I won't," Price assured. "So long, Mr. Pearsall." Turning, he left the banker, his hat sitting cockily on his head and his boot-heels thumping on the linoleum floor of the bank. Pearsall, watching him go, shook his head.

Price went back to the ranch from town, still feeling that he was on top of the world. That feeling persisted. He worked with the crew, watching the cattle put on their winter tallow, watching them grow their winter coats. September passed and October came and one morning there was frost on the ground and the re-employed hay crew shivered as they took the frosty seats of their mowers. Two days the cold weather held and then broke into balmy warmth again for a day. Then again forthcoming Winter snapped a loop at the Rana country. For a week the days were alternately warm and cold and at the end of the week Price Thorn and Jim Harvie, riding from the ranch, went through the range toward Seco Spring. They crossed the line of posts where once Ed Pothero had built a drift fence and dropping down into the lower country, saw three ravens fly up. Both turned their horses and rode to investigate. In a little draw they came upon the thing the ravens had left. A calf lay there, swollen, bloated, the hide already broken where a coyote had fed. It was a Merriman calf. The Key brand was plain upon its hip and, looking at it, both Price Thorn and Jim Harvie knew what had killed it.

"It's come, Price," Jim Harvie said solemnly.

Price nodded. "Blackleg," he said.

CHAPTER
TEN

We'll Fix Price Thorn!

One calf dead of blackleg does not make a blackleg epidemic. No matter what the precautions, blackleg may get a calf or two, may even kill mature animals. But the calves are particularly susceptible to the disease and when it is unchecked, blackleg will kill ten or fifteen calves to every older cow it drops. Price and Jim Harvie left the dead calf and went on to Seco Springs. They did not talk a great deal as they rode, but Harvie, after a lapse of time remarked, "That might be a start, Price."

And Price, agreeing with Harvie: "Maybe we'll see just how good this vaccination works, Jim."

They were back at the ranch that night eating supper when they found that their brief sentences had confirmation. Ben Utt, arriving from the Mule Pen camp, washed and seated himself at the place Granny had laid for him. Utt's hair was slick with the water he had put on it, and his face shone from the scrubbing, but neither slick hair nor shining face could keep the worry from his eyes.

"I found three calves today that died of blackleg, Price," Utt reported. "There was two X Bars an' one of ours that didn't have the tail bobbed."

Price nodded. "All in a bunch?" he asked.

"Pretty close together," Utt answered. "What are you going to do, Price?"

"We've done all we can," Price said slowly. "We aren't going to turn a hand."

"Not even on the calves that we didn't vaccinate?"

"No, Ben, not even on them. If some of them got blackleg and we tried anything and the sick calves didn't die we'd never know whether we saved them or not. We wouldn't know about the vaccine."

Ben Utt thought that over. "It looks like a pretty expensive experiment," he drawled. "Kind of tough on the. Teepee if that vaccine don't work."

Price's face was grave. "Did you ever see anything that was really good for blackleg?" he demanded, his eyes watching the men around the table. "Have any of you ever seen anything?"

Ben Utt shrugged. "No," he answered honestly. "I've tried a lot of things an' it always seemed to me that the calves died just the same."

"How about you, Jim?" Price looked at Harvie.

Harvie shook his head. "No," he answered slowly, "I got to say I ain't."

"Then all this docking tails and putting a rope through the brisket, and the other things that have been tried, are just a waste of time," Price said slowly. "Isn't that so?"

"But by Gosh you can't just sit an' see 'em die without tryin' somethin'!" Ben Utt expostulated. "You got to do *somethin'*, Price!"

150

"We've done something," Price answered. "We've taken our shot. Now we'll stay with it."

Utt drank coffee and put down his cup. "Well," he drawled, "they're yore cattle an' yo're the boss. An' . . . anyhow, Price, I figger like you do: if this vaccine don't work, then nothin' will work. As good a man as John McCready wouldn't be backin' no snide outfit."

And that was the way things stood at the Teepee.

During the following week, with the weather continuing alternately cold and warm, the blackleg spread. Because of his agreement with McCready, Price was anxious to check up on the losses of the other cattlemen in the Rana. He could best do that by waiting until the end of the epidemic and then getting a calf tally from his neighbors, together with an estimate of their losses. His immediate work was to check his own bunch and see what was happening, and this he did to the best of his ability. During the week, riding steadily, Price failed to find a single vaccinated calf, a single calf carrying a Teepee brand and a bobbed tail, that had died of the disease. He did find three of the heifers he had shipped into the country, that had died of blackleg.

On Saturday of that week he went over to the Key to visit Merriman. Riding in to the Key headquarters about ten o'clock he found the house deserted and all the Key men in the corral. There were a bunch of calves penned and Merriman and his men were working with the calves. Price went to the corral fence and stopped, looking through the bars.

Nixon was roping for Merriman and there was a flanking crew at work, just as though the Key were branding. But there was no fire and no hot irons being applied to the calves. Instead, when Nixon had snaked out a calf and the flankers had thrown it, Merriman, bloody knife in hand, bent down and made a slit in the calf's dewlap. Through that slit he pulled a piece of rope, a rope yarn from an old worn-out rope that had been untwisted. The rope yarn was smeared with axle grease and Merriman pulled it through the slit dewlap and tied it loosely. Then the calf was turned loose and another one dragged up.

Finishing with a calf, Merriman straightened, wiped the sweat from his forehead and seeing Price at the fence, came over toward him. The Key owner's face was definitely unfriendly.

"Morning, Mr. Merriman," Price greeted.

"Mornin'," Merriman grunted.

Price wanted to make conversation and did not know where to begin. Merriman helped him out. "Well," the Key owner snapped, "we got the blackleg all right. Pothero's been losin' calves an' so have the Luceros an' everybody else. I suppose *you* ain't lost any?"

"I've lost a few," Price answered. "I found three of the heifers I shipped in, that had died, and there have been a couple of calves that we didn't vaccinate."

"An' none of them calves you stuck a needle into have died?" Merriman asked.

"I haven't found any," Price answered honestly.

"You will!" the Key owner prophesied. "What are you doin' for it?"

"We've done all we're going to," Price answered.

152

Merriman's eyes were definitely hostile. "You've done enough!" he snapped. "You brought the blackleg into the country. You ought to be doin' somethin' to stop it."

"*I* brought it in?"

"Yeah, *you!* That fellow you had here said himself that the stuff he was shootin' into yore calves was the bugs that caused blackleg."

"But they were dead!" Price said in astonishment. "They . . ."

"How do you know the bugs was dead? All you had was his word for it. See here, Thorn. I've tried to get along with you. This is open range an' all, but I don't see where you got a right to spread blackleg over it, For awhile I kind of throwed in with the Potheros, but when you licked the three of them I thought you was all right an' I done my best to get along. Now I'll tell you that you'd better get them blackleg calves rounded up an' off the grass, an' you'd better start doctorin' 'em. Otherwise the cowmen around the Rana are goin' to do somethin' about it."

The attack was direct and fierce. Price reacted to it instantly. He was young, he could not see Merriman's viewpoint and he could not believe that Merriman meant what he said. There must, Price thought, be something else under Merriman's talk, something that he could not see. His voice was as angry as Merriman's when he answered.

"It's all of one piece," Price snapped. "I get it now, all right. You and the Potheros and some others tried to crowd my old man out while I was away. You damned near did it. Now you're trying again. I'm not getting my

153

calves off the grass, Merriman, and my calves are not spreading blackleg. They'll be the only bunch in this country that won't come down with blackleg. You'll see!"

He did not wait for Merriman to answer, but turned abruptly and, leading his horse out from the corral, mounted. As Price gained the saddle Merriman called to him. "You'll find out whether you can get by with this, Thorn! You think you know a hell of a lot, but there's others just as smart!"

Price made no answer but rode away and Merriman turned back to where a flanking crew had a calf on the ground.

The Key owner bent down over that calf and then straightening, threw his knife to the ground and snarled at Joe Nixon. "You go on an' work these calves over. I'm goin' to the Potheros."

With that he strode away and Nixon, looking at the flankers, drawled a statement. "The old man's mad," he said. "There'll be blood on the moon over this."

A flanker, nodding solemnly, spat tobacco juice into the corral's dust and agreed. "Hell to pay, Joe," he agreed. "Let's finish up these calves we got."

Tate Merriman made time going to the Potheros' X Bar. He rode in shortly after the Potheros had sat down for dinner, tied his horse to the fence and walked into the kitchen where the men were eating. Ed Pothero greeted him and invited him to sit down with them, making a place for Merriman beside him. The Key man took a chair, loaded his plate and, between mouthfuls, spoke his errand.

154

"Price Thorn come over this mornin'," Merriman announced, "I was doctorin' calves in the corral, puttin' a piece of rope through their briskets. I asked him what he was goin' to do about this blackleg an' he said he wasn't goin' to do a thing more than he'd already done. An' he brought it into the country, damn him!"

Ed and Jule Pothero exchanged glances and Ed spoke soothingly. "Has Thorn lost any cattle?"

"Said he'd lost three of them heifers he shipped in. It's that damn' business he done a month ago that's started this. That fellow he had here told me with his own mouth that they was shootin' these blackleg germs into them calves. That's what's started this. Hell, Ed! I'm losin' calves every day. If this keeps up I won't have a damned calf left. I'll be broke an' the bank will be closin' down on me. We got to do somethin'."

Ed Pothero nodded his agreement, and Merriman, with a sympathetic listener, poured out the story of his meeting with Price Thorn, embellishing the tale as he told it.

"I'm goin' into town this afternoon," he said, "an' see the Luceros. They got cattle out here an' they're officers. I'm goin' to see if there ain't some way we can make Thorn pen his cattle, or at least doctor 'em."

"Stop back by an' tell us what Enrique says," Pothero suggested. "If the Luceros can't see a way out, mebbe we could all get together an' hold a meetin' an' do somethin' about Thorn."

"I'll do it," Merriman exclaimed. He had finished his meal and got up from the table. "I want a fresh horse, Ed. I'm goin' right on in to town."

When Merriman had ridden away, Ed Pothero, with his brother Jule, and Hank Kuhler, went into the house. In the kitchen the cook was cleaning up after dinner. The three men took seats around the living room, and Ed thoughtfully lit a cigar.

"It kind of looks as though Merriman had throwed back in with us," he commented, eyeing Jule and Kuhler. "It kind of looks like Price Thorn was ridin' for a fall."

Hank Kuhler nodded, and Ed puffed his cigar. "You know," he said, "that business of havin' a meetin' ain't a bad idea at all. If the rest of the cowmen around here throwed in with us, we could make it pretty tough on Thorn. Damn him!"

"He ain't lost any calves," Kuhler said cautiously. "Mebbe there is somethin' to this vaccinatin', Ed."

"An' what if there is?" Ed Pothero snapped. "I don't give a good damn about that. The thing I want to do is to get even with Thorn, damn him!"

"Me too," Jule spoke for the first time. "Ever since he killed Tip Carey . . ."

"Killed *who*?" Big Ed Pothero came to his feet and with a step reached his brother's side. "What's this about Thorn killin' a man?"

"Thorn killed that bank robber," Kuhler said, his voice uneven. "You knew that, Ed."

"I knew it." Ed Pothero's little eyes were narrowed slits. "Sure I knew it. But how come you knew the fellow's name? Tell me that! What's he to you?"

"Oh hell, Ed," Jule began. "You know how a fellow gets around . . ."

156

Ed Pothero's big hand shot out, settled on his brother's shoulder and Jule was jerked to his feet. "So that's what happened?" Ed Pothero snapped. "You was in on that, huh? It was you an' Hank an' somebody else with this Tip that tried to hold up the Coyuntura Bank. I knew you was up to some hell or other when you wanted to take a vacation. The cow business wasn't fast enough for you. You was in that, wasn't you?"

He shook Jule as he asked the question, handling his brother as a man might shake a child.

"Damn it, Ed!" Jule began. "Hank an' me . . ."

"You an' Hank!" Ed snarled. "You went out of here an' tied up with some of Hank's old friends an' tried to stick up the bank at Coyuntura. I know what happened. Which one of you downed Billy Wayant? Tell me that. Which one of you . . . ?"

Hank Kuhler was staring at Jule Pothero. Ed, catching that look, had his question answered. "It was you, Jule," he snapped. "You damned fool. You . . ."

"I thought he was goin' for his gun," Jule said surlily. "How was I to know he wasn't heeled?"

Ed Pothero released his brother and wearily sat down. "Of all the fools," he said. "You just can't keep out of trouble, can you, Jule? You an' Hank ain't never satisfied, are you?"

"What you goin' to do about it, Ed?" Jule asked nervously.

"What can I do?" Ed Pothero said helplessly. "There ain't a damned thing to do. Anyhow they ain't got anything to tie you up with the robbery, *or have they?*"

"Not a thing," Jule answered quickly.

"It was Tip that planned it," Hank said. "Him an' Bruce Quale. Bruce got away an' he won't be back, an' Tip's dead. There ain't a thing that can tie us up with it."

"Thank the Lord for that," Ed snarled. "If you two keep yore mouths shut you'll be all right, I reckon."

Jule sighed his relief. Ed was on his side and Jule Pothero, younger than Ed and raised by his brother, was profoundly relieved. "It was a kind of a fool play," he admitted. "But, Ed, if we'd got away with it you an' Hank an' me would of had plenty of *dinero*. We'd of been sittin' on top of the world."

"If you'd got away with it you an' Hank would of pulled yore freight an' I'd never of seen you again," Ed Pothero corrected. "But you didn't get away with it."

"What do you figger to do about Thorn?" Hank asked, changing the subject. "We was talkin' about him an' this blackleg, you know."

Ed Pothero turned, favored Kuhler with a hard stare that made the man lower his eyes, and then looked back to his brother again. "I'll work out somethin' about Thorn," he said. "I'll do the thinkin' around here an' I'll give the orders. If you'd talked to me before you tried this bank job I'd of thought out a way of makin' the business stick. I'll take care of Thorn all right. What we got to do is make it look like some of them vaccinated calves have died of blackleg. Then Merriman an' the Luceros an' everybody else will cut down on him."

"How you goin' to do it, Ed?" Jule asked. "Those vaccinated calves ain't dyin'."

158

Ed Pothero scratched his head. "I'll think of a way," he assured. "I'll figure out one. You leave it to me."

"Thorn bobbed the tails of the calves he vaccinated," Jule said. "Merriman told me that. An' Merriman said that Thorn didn't get all his calves. There might be . . ."

"Shut up!" Ed Pothero was making marks in the dust on the table beside him, drawing lines with the end of a fat fore-finger. As he drew, a little gleam of satisfaction came into his piggish eyes.

"Look here," he commanded. "We're losin' calves, ain't we?"

"Plenty," Jule answered. "If you ask me, we ain't goin' to have any calves left. We're . . ."

"Shut up an' look here!" Again Ed Pothero drew in the dust on the table top. Jule and Hank Kuhler, standing beside him, looked down at the marks he made.

"Here's the X Bar," Ed said, drawing an X with a bar below it.

"Yeah."

"An' here's a Teepee." Ed again drew an X with a bar below it, closed the bottom and put flaps from the top of the X to the lower legs of the letter. "That's right, ain't it?"

"Sure, you can run an X Bar into a Teepee," Jule agreed mystified. "But what's that . . . ?"

"We hair-brand some of our own dead calves over to look like Thorn's," Ed Pothero explained pityingly. "We run 'em to Teepee's an' we bob their tails. Nobody is goin' to get down too close to look at the brand on a dead calf, not when the calf's died of blackleg. You think the Luceros an' Merriman an' the rest of the men around here are goin' to stand for what they'll find? You think they're goin' to believe Thorn when he says his calves ain't dyin'? Not by a damned sight! They're goin' to believe Tate Merriman when he tells 'em that Thorn spread the blackleg by vaccinatin' them calves. The proof's goin' to be right there in the dead calf. Then what'll happen to Mr. Price Thorn?"

Hank Kuhler nodded his head. Jule's eyes gleamed. "They'll close in on him," he predicted. "They'll . . ."

But Ed Pothero's mind was far ahead of the other two. "We can put him out of business," Ed Pothero announced. "We can clean him out. Then mebbe the X Bar will have some country to run cattle over. Damn Price Thorn, I'll teach him to suck eggs!"

He got up and stamped out of the room, leaving Jule and Kuhler. They could hear the fat man leave the house and when they were alone, Kuhler looked speculatively at Jule.

"You had to give it away, didn't you, Jule?" Kuhler said. "You had to spill yore guts about Tip gettin' killed."

"He'd of found it out sometime anyhow," Jule answered surlily. "You can't keep a thing like that hid from Ed. He didn't take it very bad, did he?"

"He took it just bad enough so that I'd of hated to see him take it any worse," Kuhler retorted. "I wish you hadn't got so free with yore mouth."

"It was just a slip," Jule excused his error.

"Yeah, an' yore losin' that bandanna was just a slip, too," Hank Kuhler growled. "Enrique an' that brother

160

of his have been pluggin' along on that until you'd think they'd wore the damned thing out."

Jule was defiant. "Well," he growled, "Bacon didn't tell him nothin'. Bacon's got the fear of hell in him. I told him I'd speak up to his wife about him foolin' around that de Castro girl, an' Bacon's keepin' his mouth shut."

"For now," Hank agreed. "Just the same it would be a heap better if Bacon didn't know you'd lost yore neckerchief."

"He sold a half dozen of 'em," Jule answered. "How did he know that it was mine that got found?"

"Because you went over an' told him to keep his mouth shut about yore buyin' that bandanna, that's how! Bacon ain't a plumb fool. When the time comes he'll cut down on you, see if he don't. You'll pay Bacon plenty for keepin' his mouth shut. He's mean an' he's got a bad reputation."

"I know about him an' that de Castro girl," Jule persisted stubbornly.

"An' he knows about you an' a murder," Hank Kuhler snapped. "Which one would do the most damage, tellin' about the murder or about him foolin' around that girl? Better think that over, Jule."

Jule's weak face was sullen. "I reckon I've got to do somethin' about Bacon," he growled.

Kuhler took out a plug, bit off one corner and began to chew. "An' you better do it pretty soon," he said. "Bacon ain't talked yet . . . but he might."

CHAPTER
ELEVEN

Just a Kid!

Tate Merriman came back by the X Bar late that evening. He was still angry and his trip to town had not brought the expected results. Merriman was a man who went off half-cocked, the kind of man who leads a lynch mob; a man given to great enthusiasms and equally great hates. He was convinced that the vaccinated Teepee calves were spreading black-leg, and he expected everyone else to be convinced of that fact by his statement. Because the Luceros and others whom he had seen were not so convinced, Merriman was very angry and discouraged.

"The Luceros are throwin' in with Thorn," he told Ed Pothero. "They say they got to see where them Teepee calves have spread the blackleg before they'll believe it. I tell you, Ed, it's no use. The Luceros an' the rest of the men I saw today won't do nothin'. It's up to us to do it all ourselves."

"They got to see it, huh?" Ed Pothero asked, and when Merriman nodded, Pothero spoke again. "Don't shoot off yore head, Tate," he warned. "I reckon we can show them fellows all right. We can't do nothin' by ourselves. We got to have everybody with us."

"Wait, hell!" Merriman snapped. "I'm goin' to start ridin' with a rifle on my saddle. Every damned one of them Teepee calves I see gets shot."

"An' you get throwed in the jail an' Thorn goes right on," Pothero argued. "We can show the Luceros an' the rest what's happenin'. All we got to do is get 'em out here."

"An' while we wait, I lose calves!" Merriman snapped.

It took some argument on Pothero's part but he finally convinced the irascible Merriman that waiting was the proper procedure. Ed Pothero had built a plan and it would take a day or two for it to mature. He needed a little time.

Pothero's plan was a good one. He had his brother Jule and Hank Kuhler to help him in carrying it out. Not that Pothero trusted either Hank or Jule, but they were bound to him by the knowledge that he possessed, and too, they had a common hatred of Price Thorn. The morning of the day after Tate Merriman's visit to the X Bar, Ed Pothero, his brother and Kuhler left the ranch. Each knew definitely what they were to do.

Pothero's scheme was simple enough. The Rana country wanted to be convinced that the vaccinated Teepee calves were spreading blackleg. Ed Pothero was about to convince it of that fact. The three rode west and north and watched the country. When they struck the banks of Arroyo Grande they followed along for a distance searching for a dead X Bar calf that Hank had seen there. They located the calf under the bank and

163

Pothero, dismounting, took his knife from his pocket and spoke to his companions.

"You know what to do," he said. "You got to get four or five calves in here that have died of blackleg. Bring 'em here an' drop 'em off."

"While you hair-brand that one," Jule commented. "You take the best end of the job every time, Ed. Here Hank an' me got to pack calves that are dead of blackleg on our saddles an' you . . ."

"I'll be handlin' this one, won't I?" Ed snapped. "Mebbe you want to let this go. Mebbe you've forgot the beatin' Price Thorn handed out to you! I ain't forgot it. If you want to let it drop, you go on back home. But don't be surprised if the Luceros come lookin' for the men that was mixed up in the Coyuntura bank robbery. They might find out you was the ones."

With scowls on their faces, Hank and Jule rode off, and bending down, a broken blade of his knife opened, Ed Pothero began to pick the brand of the dead calf, cunningly changing the X Bar into a Teepee. He was almost finished when Hank Kuhler came riding in, carying a dead Key calf across his saddle, the calf wrapped in a gunny sack.

Under Pothero's direction Kuhler put the calf down, close to the other dead animal, and rode away again; and with Kuhler gone, Ed Pothero completed his hair branding and as a finishing touch, docked the tail of the calf he worked on.

Jule came in as Ed finished. Jule was lugging an X Bar calf, wrapped, as was the one Kuhler had carried. Jule too disposed of his burden under Ed's direction.

164

"Wish we could drag 'em with a rope," he said as he dropped the carcass into the sand. "It would be a lot easier to handle 'em."

"An' leave too plain a trail," Ed reminded. "No, we got to carry 'em in."

"I found a Teepee calf that's dead," Jule announced. "One of them that ain't bob-tailed. I didn't bring it because I didn't think you'd want it."

Ed Pothero considered the statement. "Any more dead calves near it?" he asked.

"There's one about a quarter of a mile off," Jule answered. "Where I got this one."

"Bob the tail on the Teepee," Ed directed. "Then leave it lay. Here comes Hank with another one. We got to make this look good, Jule. We don't want to over-do it. This one that Hank's bringin' will be enough."

"Then I'll go back an' bob that Teepee calf's tail," Jule said.

"An' me an' Hank will clean up around here," Ed agreed. "Then I'll get Tate Merriman an' show him these calves an' let him do the rest. He'll just be on fire!" Ed Pothero chuckled and Jule, grining sardonically, reined his horse around and rode away.

Hank Kuhler rode in, dropping the dead calf he carried, as Ed indicated. Then the two men fell to work. There were tracks around the spot that their horses had made. Ed Pothero, with Kuhler accompanying him, moved out and picked up a few head of cattle. These they drove along the arroyo bank, keeping the cattle in line as though this were a bunch they were moving to the ranch. Where the calves lay, they dropped the cattle

165

and rode down into the stream bed, as though examining the dead calves.

"An' that will do it," Pothero announced as he and Kuhler took their horses up out of the stream bed. "It'll look like we had picked up a bunch to take in an' doctor an' just stumbled on these. You go on to the ranch, Hank, an' I'll light a shuck for Merriman's."

Kuhler nodded his agreement and struck out for the X Bar and Ed Pothero, with a final look at his handiwork, rode off toward the Key headquarters.

At the Teepee that morning, Price Thorn lined out the work as usual. The Teepee was bringing cattle out of the hills and when the men had ridden off on the tasks assigned, Price too took his departure, leaving Will Thorn, Neil Redwine and Granny Davis to hold down the place. There was nothing unusual in the day to make Price do otherwise than he had done. He had no qualms and was not particularly worried as he rode away from the Teepee.

Price had been gone an hour when Neil and Will Thorn went to the corral. Neil had helped Granny around the kitchen and Will had taken his time in the house. At the corral old Will Thorn grinned at the boy with genuine affection. "What have you got on your mind to do today, son?" he asked.

"I got all the chores done," Neil answered. "I fed the chickens an' I got the colts fed an' everything. Do you think I could go out for awhile, Mister Thorn?"

166

"I reckon you could," Will agreed expansively. "Don't go too far, Neil. You take that Nugget horse of mine. He needs ridin'. He's gettin' kind of snorty."

Nugget was Neil Redwine's highest aspiration. The bright sorrel that Price had brought from Texas was a lot of horse and while Nugget was gentle as a dog he had a way of rolling his eyes and acting spooky when he was saddled, that made a man think he was surely going to take a ride. Will stood smiling his amusement while Neil saddled Nugget and the old man stood at the gate while, solemnly as though uncorking a bad one, Neil rode Nugget in the corral. When, at length the gate was opened and Neil and Nugget came through, Will lifted his voice in a yell.

"Ride him out, cowboy!"

Nugget, free of the corral and having looked around to see that all was well with the youngster on his back, made a show of shying at yucca, and then with Neil's shrill yell echoing Will Thorn's, the sorrel horse loped away, his gait gentle as a rocking chair.

With shining eyes, Will Thorn watched boy and horse disappear and then went back to the house. Granny was working around the kitchen, making pies. Will Thorn, possessing himself of a spoon, dipped it into the dried fruit filling that Granny had prepared, tasting a tentative spoonful.

"Yo're worse than the kid," Granny scolded. "Dippin' into pie fillin'! What's got into you, Will?"

"I just feel pretty good," Will Thorn answered. "Best I've felt in years. That's good pie filling." He took another spoonful. "You know, Granny," Will continued, holding the spoon poised before his mouth, "I think I'll go out an' run in some of those colts. I believe I'll tie up two or three of them an' get them used to a rope."

Granny, about to expostulate, thought better of it. If Will Thorn wanted to work with the colts, who had a better right? And too, Granny was mighty pleased that Will was taking so much interest. Neil Redwine was bringing about a change in old Will Thorn, a mighty big change.

Neil, riding east from the ranch, let Nugget lope until of his own accord the horse broke the gait. Nugget was a pacer and unlike a lot of pacers he worked in a straight line. There was no sprawl to Nugget and he picked up his feet cleanly. He seldom, if ever, stumbled and was as safe a horse as a kid could ride.

The day being what it was and the horse under him full of power and ginger, Neil paid no attention to time or distance. He played at being cowboy. He found a bunch of cattle at a water hole and riding in to them, cut out a cow and calf, just for the hell of it. He was tempted to try a loop at the calf, even taking down his rope, but when the rope was down, Nugget acted so heads-up-and-ready and there was so much power under him, that Neil thought better of it. He had never roped from a horse and he thought he had better take an older, less alert animal than Nugget for his first try.

So Neil let the calf go and rode out from the water hole, his rope dragging. He coiled the rope and took a try at a clump of bear grass, missing his loop by some eight feet and with Nugget turning so quickly as almost to unseat him, and doing a little nervous dance. That

168

cured Neil. No more roping off Nugget until he knew how. He coiled his rope and fastened it to the swell of his saddle and went on, looking for worlds to conquer, worlds that he was *sure* he could conquer.

A mile from the water hole and a good ten miles from the Teepee, Neil Redwine saw a horseman. He was just stopping to dismount and as Neil watched, the man swung down from the saddle. Neil lacked the experience that might have identified the rider. He knew that all the Teepee crew was out and this man he saw might be Price or Ben Utt. Neil put Nugget to a lope and came right along. He was going to make an impression on Price or Ben when he came up at a run, slid Nugget to a stop and nonchalantly gave a greeting. It was going to be quite a show!

Nugget moved along, the powerful heave of the horse thrilling his rider. The distance lessened and Neil, all ready to set Nugget back, hang him up on the reins and call "Hello," was grinning in anticipation. As he came up he saw that the horse was not one of the Teepee's and that the rider was bending over a calf on the ground. The calf was dead. Neil pulled Nugget up. The sorrel broke his lope, and the man on the ground, wheeling, confronted Neil.

Neil Redwine knew the man. He had seen him once before but he did not know the man's name. The boy was wordless and, on the ground, Jule Pothero was also speechless. It was Neil who spoke first.

"You . . ." he began, "Why, I saw you at . . ."

The boy did not finish his declaration. Fear flashed across Jule Pothero's face, fear and hatred. His hand flashed down to the heavy Colt in his holster. The gun jumped up and fell level, and a shot roared there above the dead calf. Nugget sat back and whirled, and Neil Redwine, losing his grip, toppled from the saddle. For an instant Jule Pothero stood there, gun hanging loosely in his hand, then with a curse, he jammed the weapon back into its holster, pulled his frightened horse down with the rein he held, and disdaining stirrup, flung himself into the saddle. The horse bounded away under the thrust of spurred heels. Jule Pothero did not look back, but bending low, rode like a man pursued.

By the dead Teepee calf, there was no movement. Neil Redwine lay on the grama sod, motionless, blood flowing from a wound just above his temple. Nugget, two rods away, looked at boy and calf, ears cocked, head lifted, eyes alert. Still there was no movement and presently Nugget, the big bright sorrel, lowered his head and cropped a mouthful of grama, tearing it with strong yellow teeth. He munched the grass, the curb chain tinkling against the bit, lowered his head, took another bite, and then spying another tempting clump, moved toward it.

About three o'clock Price Thorn, riding in to the ranch, was met by his father at the corral. Will Thorn looked worried, and Price, dismounting, asked the cause of his father's perturbation. "What's the matter, Dad?"

"Neil ain't come back," Will Thorn answered. "He went out about an hour after you left, and headed over east. Did you see him?"

"No," Price said. "What horse was he riding?"

"Nugget."

Price laughed. "Not much danger for him on Nugget," he consoled. "Nugget's gentle."

"I know it," Will Thorn fretted, "but Neil ought to be back by now."

"He'll come in," Price assured. "Likely he fell in with Tony or Jim. They were over east today."

Will nodded, but could not keep the worriment out of his eyes. Duke Wayant came in presently. He had seen nothing of Neil, and when Jim Harvie reported that he had not seen the boy, Will Thorn saddled a horse and Price also roped out a mount. They were about ready to ride when Tony came bobbing up from the creek. Tony likewise said that he had not seen Neil.

"I don't see notheeng but some cows," Tony announced. "The keed maybe ees gone to Mule Pens."

"You ride up and see," Price commanded. "If that little devil has gone up an' is staying with Ben and hasn't told us about it, I'll be blessed if I don't tan his britches."

"Somethin's happened to the kid," Will announced. "He wouldn't stay out like this."

"Well, it isn't bad anyhow," Price assured. "Maybe Nugget got away from him and he's having to walk in."

"Then where's the horse?" Will demanded.

"Taking his time about getting home," Price answered. "We'll lope out and see if we can find Nugget. Maybe . . ."

"We'll see if we can find the kid!" Will snapped. "Come on, Price."

Price was not unduly worried about Neil. He watched Tony saddle a fresh horse, and ride off toward the Mule Pens. Will Thorn was fretting and Price, speaking to Duke and Jim, told them to stay at the ranch. "I'll go along with Dad," he said. "He's like a hen with one chick when it comes to Neil. The kid will be in pretty soon."

Jim nodded and Price, joining his father, rode off toward the east.

There was a lot of country east of the Teepee and looking for one boy in that country, one active, well mounted boy, was like looking for a flea on a thick-haired dog. The kid could keep moving around and he would be difficult to locate. Price did not see the use of the expedition although he did not say so. They were four or five miles from the ranch when Will Thorn, drawing abreast of Price, spoke out. "You go over toward Arroyo Grande," he said. "I'll try down at the Consadine water hole. I'm kind of worried about the boy, Price. He was gettin' to where he could rope in a corral and I think he might have spread his loop at somethin' off Nugget and maybe got jerked down. Nugget is too much horse for the kid; I shouldn't have let him take Nugget."

This put a new aspect on affairs and Price agreed. "If he wanted to try his rope he might have hit one of the water holes," Price said. "I'll go over along Arroyo Grande, Dad."

Price turned his horse and loped away, and Will Thorn sent Muddy along toward the east.

172

When he reached the water hole where in the morning Neil Redwine had cut out the cow and calf, Will Thorn found Nugget. Nugget was at the water. The horse had hung up the trailing bridle reins on some obstruction and had broken one rein short. The sight of the big sorrel put panic into Will Thorn.

He caught the horse without difficulty but it was now five o'clock and the sun, setting early in October, was well down toward the horizon. Will Thorn had not a great deal of time and he knew it. Somewhere, he was sure, Neil Redwine lay hurt, and the chill of the October night would do the boy no good.

Still, frightened for Neil's safety as he was, Will Thorn was too old a hand to lose his head. He cut sign around the water and found where Nugget had come in. The horse had wandered in, not following any direct line. Will Thorn had not time to work the trail out. Reasoning that Nugget had been hung up — this because of the broken rein — Will Thorn also reasoned that the horse had not been far from the water hole. Nugget had come in from the east. North of the water, extending toward the east there was a line of broken country. That broken land was hardly the place where a kid would ride for pleasure. Will Thorn struck east, keeping south of the rough country.

The sun went down and the afterglow remained to light the sky. Riding along, leading Nugget, keeping a sharp lookout, Will followed into a gentle depression. Far down toward the end of the dip he saw something too big for a boy, lying on the ground. Will headed toward it, saw that it was a dead calf and was about to

173

turn out and continue east when he saw another object, close beside the calf. He rode in to investigate, stopped, and looking down, stared straight into Neil Redwine's white face and half-opened eyes.

Will Thorn got off his horse. Deliberately, because he could take no chances, he wrapped Nugget's one rein around his saddle horn and tied Muddy to a yucca. Then he bent down over Neil. The boy was breathing and that was all. Save for the almost imperceptible rise and fall of his chest, there was no motion. Will saw the bloody hole made by a bullet in Neil's head, just above the temple. There was not a great deal of blood but the wound looked bad. Indeed, seeing it, Will Thorn could not believe that Neil still lived, and put his ear to the boy's chest to make sure. The slow, steady thump of Neil's heartbeat came to his ear and Will Thorn straightened. His old face was like granite, seamed, wrinkled and gaunt, a face carved from stone.

Leaving the boy he went to Nugget, freed the horse from his own saddle horn and placing the single rein on the horse's saddle, tied it there. Nugget stood by. Returning to Neil, leading Muddy, Will bent down. He gathered the youngster's body up in his strong old arms, and then spoke to the horse.

"Muddy!"

Muddy cocked both ears at the command and stood still. Muddy was wise and he knew that something unusual was expected of him. Very deliberately Will passed the right rein around Muddy's neck, put the left rein up and holding Neil in his left arm, twisted out a

174

stirrup. He caught his toe in the stirrup, reached for the saddle horn and spoke to the horse again.

"Whoa, Muddy!"

Muddy stood and, carefully, Will Thorn pulled himself and his burden up and settled into the saddle. Now, reaching with his right hand, he possessed himself of the reins against the saddle horn, cradled his right arm under the limp body of Neil and pressed gently with his knees. Muddy walked ahead and Nugget, for all the world like a well broken pack horse, fell in behind.

They were just so, Will Thorn on Muddy, holding Neil, and Nugget trailing along, when with the dark all about them, they reached the Teepee. Price had come in, having covered the country out toward Arroyo Grande, and was on the point of organizing a search for his father. It was Price who came to Muddy's side, and into his son's ready arms Will Thorn lowered his burden.

"Where'd you find him?" Price demanded. "Is he hurt bad?"

Will Thorn dismounted heavily. "I don't know how bad he's hurt," he said, and there was no inflection in his heavy voice. "I found him out east of the Consadine water lyin' beside a dead calf. He's been shot."

"Shot?" There was complete disbelief in Price's voice. "Neil shot? Who'd do . . ."

"Shot," Will Thorn repeated heavily. "I'll find the man that did this, Price! I'll find him."

"But Dad . . ." Price began.

175

"Bring the kid along to the house," Will Thorn ordered. "An' Jim, you put a saddle on the fastest thing we've got an' head for town. Get Doc Cirlot out here."

Jim Harvie made no answer. He was already running toward the corral. Turning, Will Thorn followed Price toward the house where on the stoop, Granny stood with a lighted lantern in his hand.

Price carried Neil Redwine into the little room off the kitchen, the room that Will Thorn had given the boy. There, with Granny hovering anxiously, he lowered the boy to the bed and straightened up. Will Thorn, face gray and still with that granite look upon it, had come in and joined Price beside the bed.

"I'll get some water," Granny offered. "We got a little whisky too. I'll bring it." He hurried away. Neither of the Thorns spoke. Will's big hand went down and touched Neil as though the old man could not believe the boy lay there. Price watched his father anxiously. Presently Will spoke and as he did so relief flooded Price Thorn.

"Just a kid," Will murmured slowly, and his voice was almost normal. "He never hurt nobody, Price."

"No," Price agreed.

"An' he was shot," Will continued, as though he had not heard his son speak. "Somebody shot him."

"Maybe an accident," Price offered.

Will shook his massive head. "No accident," he disagreed. "If he'd been shot by accident, the man that did it would have brought him in. He was shot on purpose an' left there."

"But why?"

176

Again the massive head was shaken. "I don't know," Will Thorn answered. Suddenly his eyes met Price's. "But I'll find out," Will said simply. "I ain't been good for very much, Price. I've let things slide. I've been too easy-going and I know it. But I'll be good for this an' I won't be too easy."

Granny came back carrying a wash basin and towels, and a flask. Will pushed the flask aside. "I'll wash his head and then we'll wait for Doc Cirlot," he decided. "It's too dangerous givin' him whisky. Has Jim gone?"

"He's gone," Granny answered.

"Then stand here with that pan," Will commanded. "Turn his head, Price, and I'll wash the hole."

CHAPTER
TWELVE

The Teepee Takes a Stand

Doctor Cirlot reached the Teepee about three o'clock in the morning. Jim Harvie was with him, riding in the doctor's buck-board, his saddle and gear thrown into the bed. Jim had ridden Jefe into town, obeying Will Thorn's order to take the fastest thing the Teepee had. The big yellow horse had covered the thirty-two miles to Coyuntura in a little more than two hours and was, so Jim said, in the livery barn in town. It would be some time before anyone rode Jefe again.

Cirlot looked grave when he was shown his patient. He took the boy's pulse, counted his respiration and took his temperature. Examining the wound he removed the improvised bandage that had been put in place, and worked carefully, his fingers deft. Then he looked up at Will Thorn.

"How bad is it, Doc?" Thorn asked.

Cirlot shook his head. "Pretty bad," he answered gravely. "The bullet struck just behind the temple. It didn't go in, but there's a fracture. I don't know, Will."

"Don't know what, Doc?"

"Whether the boy will make it or not," Cirlot answered. "There is some pressure on the brain. That is

178

why he is unconscious. That pressure must be removed."

"Can you do it?" Thorn asked.

"I can try," Cirlot answered, "but it's a chancey thing, Will. The boy may die."

"Suppose you don't try?" Thorn asked. "Then what, Doc?"

"Then I don't think he'll get well," the physician said simply. "What do you want me to do, Will?"

It took Will Thorn a long time to answer. When he did speak it was to ask a question. "Suppose he was yore kid, Doc; What would you do?"

"I'd try to remove the pressure," Cirlot said steadily.

"Then that's what you'll do," Thorn stated. "Have at it, Doc."

"Not until daylight," Cirlot made answer. "We can't work until we have light."

Thorn nodded. They left Granny with the boy and went out into the living room. "Did you see Enrique in town?" Will Thorn asked Harvie.

"Him an' Donancio was both gone," Harvie answered. "I left word with the jailer."

"He'll be out," Thorn said. "Enrique's a good man." He was silent for a moment and then added, "Just the same, the Teepee's goin' to kill its own snakes. We always have."

Price made a movement as though to speak and his father forestalled him. "We'll help the officers all we can," he announced, "but whatever we find I want to know it first. That's my kid in there. When will you work on him, Doc?"

"Not until daylight," Cirlot answered again.

Price, leaving his father and the doctor together, wandered out of doors. Ben Utt followed him. They squatted down beside the step and Utt, rolling a cigarette, drawled words at Price. "Yore dad is takin' hold, Price," he said.

Price nodded, "Yes," he agreed.

"Must of been a mighty good man in his time." Utt lit the cigarette. "I'd kind of hate to bump up against him now if he was riled."

"Dad will go a long way," Price said. "A mighty long way."

"Unless I'm mistaken he'll go until he finds who it was shot the kid," Utt said. "I'd kind of hate to be that fellow."

Price, remembering the metallic gleam in his father's eyes, shook his head. "I wouldn't want to be him, either," he said. "We'll have to trail along with Dad, Ben."

"Whoever said we wouldn't?" Ben Utt demanded. "I'll go all the way."

"And so will I," Price agreed.

Morning was a long time in coming. It seemed to Price, waiting, that the night was endless and when at length the east turned gray and then a faded pink appeared, Price rubbed his aching eyes and could hardly believe that the night was finished.

With morning Granny made more coffee and the men drank. As the light grew, Cirlot went into the bedroom once more and there made a long, careful examination of the boy on the bed. When he finished,

180

he looked up at Will Thorn. "Do you still want me to do this, Will?" he asked.

"If it gives the boy a chance," Will Thorn answered. "Yo're the doctor. Yo're supposed to know. I'm just a cowman, but I'd say to go ahead. The kid has got to be all right or die; ain't that so?"

Cirlot nodded.

"Then go ahead!" Thorn commanded.

Cirlot took a long breath. He looked around at the men and then spoke. "I'll work in the kitchen," he announced abruptly. "I want a lot of hot water. I want some clean sheets. You'll put them in the oven and get them hot. Granny, I want you to scrub the kitchen table until you about wear it out. I want you to help me, Price, you and your tall friend." The doctor looked at Ben Utt.

Ben Utt reached back to his hip for his chewing tobacco, brought it out and lifted the plug to his mouth.

"And you won't chew," the doctor stated. "Now, Price . . ."

Already the Teepee crew had dispersed upon their various errands. Harvie had gone for wood. Granny was stripping the red and white oilcloth from the table. Will Thorn, striding away, returned with his arms loaded with old yellow sheets. Price, momentarily, wondered where his father had found them. There had been no sheets on the Teepee within Price's recollection; no sheets since his mother had died, years before. The fire roared in the stove and Tony came in with pails of fresh water and Doctor Cirlot spoke to Price and Ben Utt,

181

instructing them, telling them what they must do, how to go about the work that was to be performed.

It took time to make ready the Teepee kitchen for the operation, but when at length the preparations were complete, Dr. Cirlot ordered the men out of the room.

"Stay outside," he commanded. "You'd be in the way here. Find something to do and keep at it. We'll tell you when there's anything to report."

Tony and Jim and Duke filed out. Will Thorn, taking a chair, seated himself beside the door. "You too, Will," Cirlot ordered.

Will Thorn shook his head. "I stayed with you when Price was born," he said, "an' I was with you when my wife died. I reckon I'll stay now, Doc."

Cirlot's eyes were keen. Suddenly he nodded. "So be it," he agreed, "and now . . ." He turned to Price.

"Yes?" said Price.

"Now God help us!" Dr. Cirlot said. "Bring the basin with the instruments that we've boiled."

Price Thorn walked to the stove and came back with the wash pan, the sterile instruments steaming as he carried them. Dr. Cirlot, his hands scrubbed and still wet from that scrubbing, looked keenly at Price, then at Ben Utt, and then picking up a scalpel, bent over the inert boy on the table.

As long as he lived Price Thorn never forgot the next hour or more, and as long as he lived, he could never describe it. How can a man tell of the deft motions of a doctor's fingers, of the sheen of instruments in the morning light, of blood that wells up to be wiped swiftly away, of the pallor of a boy's face and the shine

182

of dead gray eyes seen through half-open lids? Prosaic words in a medical text might detail the things that Doctor Cirlot did there in the kitchen of the Teepee during those early morning hours, but those words could never picture the scene, could not portray the doctor, tense, alert, tuned like a fine violin; could not show tall Ben Utt, his empty jaws moving rhythmically as though he chewed; nor Price Thorn at the doctor's elbow, nor Will Thorn, pale beneath his tan but erect as a ramrod in his chair.

And then Doctor Cirlot was wrapping bandage about Neil Redwine's head and the doctor's face had lost its tense expression and Will Thorn was getting up and asking, "How about it, Doc? How about the kid?"

"I think," Doctor Cirlot said slowly, his bandaging finished, "that he's got a chance, Will. A good chance. We can't know yet for awhile, but I think he's got a chance."

Will Thorn gathered the boy up from the table and carried the inert figure into his own room in the front of the house. Neil was laid on Will Thorn's big bed and the doctor and Will sat down beside him. Out in the kitchen Price Thorn spoke to Ben.

"Let's get out of here," Price said.

"Let's," Ben agreed fervently, and then, when they were out on the stoop, "By Gosh, Price, I'd ruther . . . I'd ruther . . . Hell, I'd ruther lynch a horse thief than to do that again."

"And so would I," Price echoed.

The two went on from the stoop down toward the corral. There Duke and Tony and Jim Harvie and

Granny met them, filled with questions. Price could not answer the questions, nor could Ben Utt. All they could tell their questioners was that Doc had said that the kid had a chance and that Neil was still unconscious and they did not know how he would come out. They were at the corral, talking low-voiced, when across the little creek below the house, from the fringe of leafless cotton-woods that bordered the creek, a group of horsemen appeared and came steadily toward them.

"Enrique," Tony exclaimed. "Hee's . . ."

"An' Donancio," Price interrupted, "and Merriman and the Potheros and some more. It looks like Enrique's brought a posse with him."

Beside Price, Ben Utt spoke very slowly. "It looks like trouble to me," Ben Utt said ominously.

The approaching riders came nearer and Price walked out from the corral to meet them. They were a compact little group and there was nothing of friendliness on any of their faces. Besides the two Luceros there were the Pothero brothers, Tate Merriman, and Dave Appleby of the O Slash.

Price stopping before them, spoke to Enrique. "You must have started early," he said. "I didn't look for you until after dinner. Doc Cirlot operated on the kid. He just finished. We don't know yet whether the kid will make it or not."

"What keed?" Enrique demanded, a puzzled frown crossing his face.

"Neil Redwine," Price answered, and then: "Didn't you know about it? Didn't you come from town?"

184

"We have come from Merriman's," Enrique answered. "What is the matter with the boy?"

"He was shot in the head yesterday," Price answered briefly. "If you didn't come out about the kid, what did you come for?"

"To see you about the blackleg," Merriman answered, before Enrique could answer. "By Glory, Thorn, yore calves are spreadin' it just like I said they would. I found the proof yesterday."

Price fixed the speaker with cold eyes. "That's a damned lie!" he declared, his voice level. "I know you, Merriman, and I know what you and the Potheros are up to. You tried to hog this range once and I called your bluff. Now you're trying another stunt. It won't work either. What are you going to do about this kid that was shot, Enrique? Are you interested in attempted murder in your county, or are you like all the rest of these: just set on trying to hog grass?"

Enrique scowled. Price had said the wrong thing. Enrique Lucero was straight as a ruler's edge and Price Thorn, in his hasty sentence, had questioned that straightness.

"I'll see about the boy," Enrique answered, clipping the words. "But I'll see you about theese blackleg too."

Price realized that he had said the wrong thing, but in his anger and pride he would not back down an inch. He did not try to conciliate Enrique. "Get it off your chest," he ordered. "What about the blackleg? You've all lost calves. You've done a lot of damned fool things, choused your cattle and bled 'em and put ropes through their briskets, and they died just the same. I

185

vaccinated three hundred and twenty head and so far I haven't lost a one that was vaccinated."

"That's what *you* think!" Merriman snapped. "Right now there's one of your vaccinated calves layin' in Arroyo Grande, an' there's three calves that it give the blackleg to, layin' alongside of it."

Price's eyes widened. "You're crazy," he snapped. "I . . ."

"We seen it, Price," Donancio interrupted quietly. "Enrique an' me wouldn't believe it until we went to look."

"But . . ." Price began.

"It's there, Thorn," Appleby interrupted. "Merriman found me in town yesterday and I came along just to see. I reckon Tate's right. Yore calves are spreadin' the blackleg."

Price shook his head. "There's something damned funny about this," he declared. "We've been riding. We've been working our cattle down out of the hills. I'm going to ship calves pretty soon and I've kept a close check. I've lost some calves that we didn't vaccinate, and I've lost a heifer or two, but all those vaccinated calves are all right. I haven't lost a one of them. We bobbed the tails when we vaccinated and . . ."

"And this calf in Arroyo Grande has got a bobbed tail," Donancio Lucro declared. "All of us here saw it."

Price knew Donancio and Enrique. He knew that Donancio was not lying. The statement hit him like a blow. He had nothing to say.

Enrique drove the blow home. "We talked eet over before we came here," he said levelly. "You have got to

186

keep your calves penned, Price. We can't afford to lose calves because you make theese experiment."

"But . . ." Price began again.

"An' you won't ship 'em!" Ed Pothero spoke for the first time. "You're not goin' to drive across our country an' spread blackleg, an' yo're not goin' to put them calves into the pens we'll have to use when we ship."

Price looked searchingly at Ed Pothero. The man was grinning a little, his face creased with the smile. All the anger welled up in Price Thorn. From Pothero he looked to each of the others in turn, examining their faces. On every face he saw determination written.

"I think this must be your bright idea, Pothero," Price said at length, his voice very quiet. "I suspect you thought that one up yourself."

"It don't make any difference who thought of it," Merriman snapped. "We got to protect ourselves."

"And so I don't ship," Price drawled on, not heeding Merriman. "And the bank calls my note that's due when I sell the calves, and I turn back my down payment and someone of you fills my calf contract. Mighty nice. Yes, you've got it all figured out. The only thing you overlooked was me."

"You might say that I'd anted a chip too," Ben Utt's drawl was placid as he spoke from where he stood just behind Price.

"Me, I play theese game, *tambien.*" That was Tony.

Price glanced around hastily. They were all there, all behind him, the whole Teepee. Fat Granny Davis with his flour-sack apron, little Jim Harvie, tall Ben Utt, Duke Wayant — just a youngster but his face as stern as

Utt's — and more than any of these to Price: Will Thorn. The whole Teepee was there. It came as a shock to Price but an even greater shock was in store.

Will Thorn's voice had a ring in it when he spoke, a depth and a strength that Price had forgotten. "Price has told you," Will Thorn said, and there was no anger in his voice but only that underlying steel like the faint cocking of a gun or the tap of a spur as a rider crosses stones. "I reckon that finishes yore business, gentlemen. You'll find that yore cattle are usin' range where I control the water. If you're afraid for 'em, yo're welcome to move 'em. When shippin' time comes, we'll ship. Did you have any more business here?"

"Will . . ." Enrique began.

"You rode for me when you were a kid, Enrique," Will Thorn said, his voice kindly. "You an' yore brother are officers an' there's work for officers here at the Teepee. Providin' you want to do it?" The last sentence was a question.

"Will . . ." Enrique began once more.

"Yo're welcome to stay Enrique, you an' Donancio, if you want to do that work," Will Thorn drawled. "An' the rest of you can git out. Now!"

"By God . . ." Ed Pothero began, "we . . ."

Enrique held up his hand. The sheriff seemed to collect his companions with his eyes. He turned his horse and rode off a little distance, Merriman, Appleby and Donancio following him. The Potheros did not move.

"Pothero!" Enrique snapped.

188

Ed Pothero heeded that command. He turned his horse, as did Jule, and they too joined the sheriff. Price, with his father beside him and the rest of the Teepee standing by, watched the little group of horsemen as they conferred. Then Enrique and Donancio came riding back and Merriman led the others away toward the creek.

"About theese boy that was shot," Enrique said, dismounting. "When deed it happen, Will?"

"Yesterday afternoon," Will Thorn answered. "I found him."

He talked rapidly then, detailing to the officers what had happened, how Neil Redwine had gone out and failed to return, how, worried, he and Price had made a ride, how he had found Neil. All through the recital Will Thorn was as impersonal as though he spoke to a total stranger.

"You'll want to see the place where I found Neil," he completed. "I'll go down with you. Doc Cirlot is stayin' with the boy. Do you want to talk to Doc?"

Enrique signified that he did, and Will Thorn took the officer to the house. Price followed after his father and the sheriff and Donancio fell in beside Price.

"This blackleg business . . ." Donancio began unhappily. "You know, Price . . ."

"Pothero's sold you a bill of goods, Donancio," Price said. "He's done a nice job, but don't you think for a minute that we'll pen our calves in a vega and let 'em lose weight, and don't think we won't ship!"

Donancio shook his head. "Merriman says they're spreadin' the blackleg," he stated. "I wouldn't believe it

189

but I saw that calf of yours, bob-tail an' all, an' I saw the other calves right with him. We got to work this out someway, Price. We got to!"

"We'll work it out, with no man telling me my business," Price answered, his voice stony. "Do you want to go in, Donancio?"

They were at the house now, ready to mount the stoop. Donancio shook his head. "No," he answered. "Price, will you go look at those calves? They're in Arroyo Grande. You . . ."

"I intend to look at them," Price said. "I want to find out what's queer about this. I want . . ."

"You can't fight the whole country, Price," Donancio pleaded. "You can't buck us all. We've never had blackleg so bad before. We're all losin' calves. We can't let you ruin us. You an' me have been friends, Price. You know . . ."

"I know that you came out here telling me what I could and couldn't do," Price replied heatedly. "Maybe you call that friendship; I don't. Here's Enrique. I'll saddle a horse and go with you. So will Dad. And don't try to tell me my business, Donancio. This whole country isn't big enough to do that!"

Will Thorn and Enrique Lucero came out of the house and Enrique joined his brother while Will came to Price. "I'll take them down and show them where I found the boy," Will announced, and Price nodded agreement.

Side by side the two Thorns went to the corral and there saddled mounts. Enrique and Donancio led their horses down to the pen and stood waiting, undergoing the hostile looks of Tony, Ben Utt, Duke and Jim. Granny had gone back to the house and was staying with Doctor Cirlot who had promised to remain with Neil until Will returned.

When the Thorns were ready they mounted and joined the officers. It was noticeable that there was no mention made of fresh horses for the Luceros, nor, although it was almost noon, did either Price or Will suggest that the Luceros stay to dinner. Indeed it was a very business-like party that rode out of the Teepee toward the east.

In about an hour the four men reached the little swale wherein lay the dead Teepee calf. When they reached the calf Will pointed out the spot where Neil had fallen, and answered the questions that Enrique asked. Price, while he listened to what his father said, examined the calf and so too did Donancio and Enrique. Price could hardly believe what he saw. There was a Teepee calf with a bobbed tail, and dead of blackleg. It seemed impossible and yet there was the evidence.

"You see, Price?" Donancio said, pointing to the calf. "You wouldn't believe what I told you."

Price nodded, and his face was set in stubborn, hard lines. "I see all right," he agreed. "That doesn't change things. I'm not going to be penned in and broke because of one calf. And those vaccinated calves can't spread blackleg. It isn't possible."

Nevertheless Price's faith, his assurance, was shaken. Suppose he was wrong? Suppose, just suppose, that there had been a slip-up in the vaccination? Suppose those had been live, instead of dead, blackleg bacteria that had been shot into the calves' shoulders? Donancio, seeing the struggle on Price's face, wisely said nothing more.

Will Thorn finished his explanation of what had happened, as he believed, and Enrique scouted around. Donancio too walked about, looking at the land around the site. There was a little bunch of brush off to the south of the dead calf, and Donancio, seeing something white in the brush, picked it from a thorny growth. It was a bit of hide and hair. Donancio dropped it and the brush caught it again.

Will Thorn was anxious to get back to the ranch. He asked Enrique if he could be of further help and when the sheriff curtly shook his head, Will mounted and started for home. Price also mounted when his father did, but, in place of going back toward the ranch, rode east. His confidence shaken by the thing he had seen, Price was determined to investigate the calves that Donancio had told him lay in Arroyo Grande.

The two brothers, left alone at the scene of the crime, talked together concerning it. Neither Donancio nor Enrique could puzzle out a reason for Neil Redwine's having been shot. It seemed possible to the officers that the shooting had been accidental. Unlike Will Thorn, they were prone to that theory, believing that whoever had discharged the gun had been frightened when the boy fell and had run away. This seemed plausible to both officers, for in no other way could they account for the shooting. However it was almost as bad to shoot accidentally and run away as to

192

shoot deliberately and then depart. They made a careful circuit of the dead calf and determined that three sets of horse tracks, as well as those they had made, were present. The unraveling of those tracks was the problem to be tackled next. Donancio and Enrique lost no time.

Around the calf the ground had been trampled by Will Thorn, by themselves and by Price. Accordingly they gave up that jumble and determined to follow the horse tracks as best they could. They followed one set of tracks for a distance but when they began to wander, as a horse will when he grazes, they returned to the body of the calf. They had followed Nugget's tracks.

Back again at the calf they discussed the next trail to follow. "Will came in from the ranch an' went right back," Donancio said. "Those are his tracks coming in from the west. There's no need to follow them."

Enrique nodded agreement. "We take theese others then," he said. "Did Price say anytheeng to you when he saw his calf weeth the tail bobbed?"

Donancio shook his head. "He looked mighty funny," he observed. "Like he couldn't believe what he saw. I guess it was quite a jolt to Price. He'll get another when he sees them calves in the arroyo."

"He needs jolteeng!" Enrique snapped. "Hees kind of cocky!"

"Uhhuh." Donancio fished out the makings. "You know, Enrique, I don't quite get it all. Price was so sure he was right an' that his calves couldn't spread blackleg, an' Merriman's so sure they did. I don't get it."

"We can't take chances," Enrique returned. "Thees ees a bad year, Donancio. Everybody ees looseeng calves. We have got to keep the Teepee from spreading theese blackleg."

"If they're spreadin' it," Donancio agreed. "I ain't ... Say!" Turning abruptly, Donancio walked to the brush clump and returned carrying the little tuft of white hair. "Look here, Enrique," he ordered.

Enrique took the hair tuft and examined it. His eyes strayed to the dead calf, and then sought his brother's face.

Donancio nodded. "It come off the calf," Donancio said. "It sure did, *bermano mio.*"

"Then . . ." Enrique began, and stopped.

"Then mebbe the kid came ridin' in an' saw somebody bobbin' the calf's tail," Donancio concluded, "an' that somebody, not wantin' to be caught, shot the kid."

"Go on," Enrique ordered.

"So," Donancio possessed himself of the tuft of hair and twisted it in his fingers, "the hombre rode away, makin' tracks, an' left the kid there. Who's been pushin' this idea of the Teepee calves spreadin' blackleg, Enrique?"

"Merriman," Enrique returned promptly.

"An' who's behind Merriman?"

"The Potheros. You theenk, Donancio, that theese calf was not one of those that Price vaccinated?"

"It couldn't be. Not if this tail bob was cut off after it was dead," Donancio assured. "Price was awful careful markin' the calves when he vaccinated them."

194

"Then . . . ?" Enrique raised heavy black eyebrows.

"Then this was a calf that Price didn't vaccinate. It wasn't marked. It died of blackleg just like all the others died. I bet you . . ."

"What you bet me?"

"I bet you that one of the Potheros or Tate Merriman found this calf an' bobbed the tail an' was caught by the kid, an' shot him."

Enrique walked toward his horse.

"What you goin' to do?" Donancio asked. "Tell Price about this? Are you?"

"No!" the older Lucero snapped. "We let Price sweat awhile. Eet weel be good for heem. Hee's too beeg for hees pants. We see eef we can follow theese trail. An' Donancio . . ."

"Yeah?"

"Eef you are right about thees, next fall you weel run for sheriff, an' I weel be your deputy."

Donancio grinned. "OK," he agreed. "It's my turn to be sheriff anyhow."

CHAPTER
THIRTEEN

Time Enough to Kill a
Man Tomorrow

When Price left Will Thorn and the Luceros, he rode on East. Striking the bank of Arroyo Grande he followed down toward the south, his mind a turmoil filled with indecision. He had talked up to Enrique, to Merriman, to the Potheros and to Donancio, talked badly because he thought that he was right. The sight of that Teepee calf, dead of blackleg and with its tail bobbed, had kicked out the props from under his beliefs. Price thought, just as he had said, that the ranchers of the Rana, egged on by Ed and Jule Pothero and led by Merriman, were again engaged in the business of crowding the Teepee. That had made him pretty hot. He was willing to go a long way to keep the territory that was rightfully the Teepee's, willing to back up his claims and beliefs with gunsmoke if necessary. Now, after seeing that calf he was not sure. There was just the possibility that Merriman was right.

Price knew a good deal about the new business of vaccinating calves for blackleg. With a college training behind him, a good mind, and the information that John McCready had passed out, Price knew just how

196

the vaccine was made and just how it reacted. His work in the laboratory had familiarized him with the process of vaccine manufacture. He knew that blackleg bacteria were taken, killed, filtered and put up in standard doses to be injected into a calf. He knew that following the injection the calf immediately began to build up a resistance to the virus that had been shot into its shoulder. He knew that, because the bacteria were dead, the calf's blood became loaded with antitoxin, a material that counteracted the action of the virus and that this antitoxin continued to form until any live blackleg germs that might infect the calf were killed by the antitoxin. That meant that the calf was immune to blackleg. All these things Price knew and had tried to tell Tate Merriman and Enrique Lucero and Claude Pearsall.

But there was a chance that he was wrong. Suppose those germs injected into a calf were not dead? Suppose they had not been killed but were living? Then inoculating a calf would just be giving that calf blackleg. That is what it would amount to. And Merriman would be right and Price would be wrong and the whole thing would be a dismal failure; not just failure, disaster!

Worried as he was, Price did not stop to reason that, had the vaccine contained living blackleg bacteria the calves would have come down with the disease shortly after vaccination. He did not think of that. As he rode down Arroyo Grande he was thinking only that perhaps Merriman had been right and he himself wrong.

197

When he reached the spot where the dead calves lay, he did not dismount. He saw the X Bar calf and the Key calf and then, close against the bank the calf that carried the Teepee on its hip. That calf's tail was bobbed as Price could see, and Ed Pothero had done an artistic job with the hair branding. Price gave one sick look at the calf, turned his horse, and riding back across the little stream, headed for the ranch.

He had gone some distance before good sense began to overcome the sick sensation he had experienced when he saw the calf. He should have, he told himself, stopped and made an examination, dismounted and looked the calf over thoroughly. He was tempted to go back. And then he had another idea. Between where he was and the ranch, there was another calf, the one beside which Neil Redwine had been shot. He could just as well stop and examine that calf as ride back to Arroyo Grande. And so he went on, changing his course slightly toward the north.

Price missed Donancio and Enrique Lucero. Those two astute gentlemen, keeping still and using their eyes, were following a horse trail toward the east. They lost the trail in a maze of cattle tracks nor could they find it again and so, extremely irritated, they decided that they must do a little waiting and a lot of thinking. Price missed them but he did not miss the calf. He rode up to where the animal lay, stopped his horse and, dismounting, tied the animal to the identical soapweed that Will Thorn had used. Having done that,. Price advanced upon the calf and stood looking down at it, his legs wide spread, trying to decide just what to do.

198

All the external symptoms of death by blackleg were on the calf. Price could see them. The calf was swollen, bloating somewhat in the time it had lain there. Price steeled himself to make an autopsy. It would be a nasty, stinking job, probably a useless job because it would tell him nothing that he did not already know. Still there was a chance that he might discover something new and so he bent down, caught the calf's tail and pulled, intending to get the body in a better position.

He hauled the calf around and then stopped, the tail still gripped in his gloved hand. There, just where the calf had been, right against the imprint left in the grass by the calf's body, was a stockman's knife, one blade opened. Very slowly Price let go the calf's tail and bending further, picked up the knife.

The knife told him nothing as to ownership. There was nothing about it to identify the man who had possessed it. There were thousands of good, sharp, three-bladed knives all across the ranges. A good knife is as much a cowman's tool as a rope or a saddle or spurs or pinheeled boots. There were knives like this on sale in Brumaker's store, Coyne carried a supply of them, Bacon at Pichon had just such knives as this one that Price held. But why was it here?

Price looked at the knife as though it could answer him, studying it, turning it over in his hand. Then he bent down and picked up the tail of the dead calf and looked at the end. The tail was bobbed but there was no scar there on its end, no mark of healing. Instead the end was raw dried flesh and Price, dropping the tail, had an answer. The knife had been dropped when the calf's tail had been bobbed and the bobbing had been done *after the calf was dead*.

The first feeling that Price experienced was one of intense relief. He had not been wrong! The calf that was dead was not a vaccinated calf! Everything was all right.

Following the relief came the feeling of anger. Someone had pulled this trick. Someone had bobbed the tail of this dead calf to make it appear that a vaccinated calf had died of blackleg. Who would pull a stunt like that? It did not take Price long to get an answer. The Potheros! The Potheros were bucking him, had bucked him all along! One of the Potheros had found this calf and cut off the end of the tail!

And now Price Thorn's eyes narrowed. Standing there, the knife in his hand, he came to the same conclusion that, earlier in the day, Donancio Lucero had reached. Neil Redwine, riding out on Nugget, had come down on a man bending over this Teepee calf and that man, surprised, had straightened up and pulled a gun and shot the kid! It all added up. It was all there. The only question that remained was which of the Potheros had done the shooting? Which of them had dropped Neil?

Price Thorn did not care a great deal. It did not make much difference to him which of the Potheros had been at the calf when Neil came up. They were brothers, Ed and Jule Pothero. They were tarred with the same stick. The same sort of dirt was on them both. It was time for a showdown now. As far as Price was concerned it was past time for the showdown. He

200

would hunt the Potheros just as a man might hunt a dog that was killing cattle, and when he found them, alone or together, he would accuse them of this thing they had done and abide by the consequences of that accusation.

Closing the knife Price thrust it into the pocket of his trousers, turned and, untying his horse from the yucca, mounted. For a moment he sat there in his saddle, undecided. Should he ride to the X Bar now? Should he? Price was perfectly willing, but once more the cold reason that dominated him when his first anger was gone took charge. If he went to the X Bar and demanded a showdown, if it came to shooting, and Price was certain that it would, then what? Suppose that he came out on the short end? Then all this business about vaccinated calves spreading blackleg would keep right on rolling. Then the Potheros and Merriman and Enrique and Donancio could make the accusation stick. There was first the Teepee to consider. Price knew that he must go back to the ranch, talk to Ben Utt and Jim, to Will Thorn, and tell them what he had found, what he had learned; and when that was done he could go to the X Bar. After all, the Potheros were not going to run away. There was time enough! Time enough to kill a man tomorrow. Price started his horse west, toward home. Above the Ranas, clouds had formed and the wind that blew from the hills was chilly.

And in the meantime Donancio and Enrique Lucero, having lost the trail of the horseman, having done some methodical swearing and even more methodical thinking, were adding one more bit of evidence to that they already held. Donancio and his brother, when the trail was lost, discussed the next step. They were in possession of one bit of evidence. They knew that the tail of the Teepee calf had been bobbed after that calf was dead. They believed they knew that Neil Redwine had seen a man bobbing that tail and that the man had shot Neil. Both officers strongly suspected the Pothero brothers, but they also considered Tate Merriman as a likely suspect. It was Enrique who got the idea of going back to Arroyo Grande and looking at that bunch of dead calves once more.

"Mebbe," Enrique stated, "we see sometheeng that we don't see before. We can ride back that way, Donancio, an' eet weel be just as short."

Donancio agreed and so, their horses weary, the two officers headed back east.

Unlike Price, when they reached the dead calves, the two men dismounted. Examining the calves closely Enrique saw something that had been missed on the first cursory inspection. *"Mira!"* he commanded Donancio. And when Donaicio came to look, "Theese ees a hair brand!" Enrique announced.

Good a job as Ed Pothero had done, it would not withstand careful and close inspection. The X Bar was there, worked over into a Teepee. Donancio swore softly and taking out his knife skinned out the brand and, rolling it carefully, tied it to his saddle.

"An' now?" he suggested.

"We go to the Key," Enrique said. "Eet ees late an' I want to show Merriman w'at fools he ees. Us too. I theenk you weel run for sheriff, *hermano. Ya lo creo!*"

202

"An' tomorrow?" Donancio suggested.

"Tomorrow we weel see the Potheros," Enrique announced. "I don't know how theese weel look in court, Donancio, but I theenk we arrest theese Potheros for shooting that keed."

Donancio nodded. He knew Enrique, and knowing Enrique he was certain that his bulldog older brother, having set his teeth in this thing, would worry and tug at it until it came out.

"Why not the Teepee?" Donancio asked. "Price would like to know . . ."

"Price theenks we are crooked," Enrique snapped. "We weel let Price alone awhile. Mebbe he weel learn better."

That was that. With a grin, Donancio climbed into his saddle and side by side the two brothers rode toward Tate Merriman's Key headquarters.

"Merriman," Donancio drawled as they rode along, "is sure goin' to be disappointed about this. It's pretty near goin' to break his heart to find out he was wrong about them calves."

Enrique grunted his disgust at Donancio's facetiousness. Donancio, glancing sidelong at his brother, grinned. Enrique had his back up; Price had hurt Enrique's pride, and too, Enrique had been sold on the idea that the vaccinated calves spread blackleg. It was as much a jolt for Enrique as it would be for Tate Merriman.

When Price reached the Teepee he found that Doctor Cirlot had departed, a messenger having come out from town to bring the doctor back to Coyuntura. Lunt Taliferro had brought the message to Cirlot and thoughtful as always, Lunt had brought the mail for the Teepee. There was a little pile of it on the living room table when Price walked in and dropped his hat on a chair.

Duke Wayant, Tony and Jim Harvie had been asleep while Price was gone. Ben Utt having stayed with Will Thorn, came in to talk to Price. Will was sitting beside Neil, watching the boy.

"He ain't moved since Doc left," Ben Utt informed Price, speaking of Neil Redwine. "He's just lay there. Doc said that it would take a while for him to come out of it, if he come at all. Doc can't tell how much damage was done to the kid's brain, but he's kind of hopeful. He says that if the kid is quiet an' keeps holdin' on like he is, he's got a chance. Doc will come back tomorrow."

Price nodded. "How's Dad?" he asked.

"Weary," Ben answered. "He's just sittin' there' beside the kid, watchin' the kid breathe. Say, wasn't it great the way the old gentleman backed you up out there? He was all ready to go to war, he was."

"The kid has done a lot for Dad," Price said. "If Neil dies . . ."

"Hell, he ain't goin' to die," Utt snapped. "You look all done up, Price. Why don't you get some sleep?"

Suddenly Price realized just how tired he was. He had been up all the night before. It was evening now. He had been running on nerve and anger, and his supply of both was well-nigh exhausted. "I'll go in a

204

minute," he said. "Ben, that calf out there, where Dad found the kid, had died of blackleg all right, but somebody had cut off his tail, after he was dead, to make it look like he was one that we'd vaccinated."

"The hell!" Utt exclaimed incredulously.

Price nodded. "That's right," he said. "I think one of the Potheros did it. I think Neil must have come down on him while he was bending over the calf and he shot the kid to keep him from talking. I found his knife." Price pulled the knife from his pocket and went on talking, telling Utt how he had come to find the implement, how he had gone to Arroyo Grande, the whole story of his day. Utt listened, turning the knife over and over between his fingers.

"An' so?" Utt drawled when Price finished.

"So I'm going to have a talk with the Potheros tomorrow!" Price stated levelly.

"Hmmm," Ben Utt hummed deeply in his throat. "I'll just go along," he said then. "Here's the knife, Price. You go get a little sleep."

Price went to his room. Utt heard the bed creak as the younger man stretched upon it and then, going out doors, Ben Utt set down on the back stoop and rolled a cigarette. He was there, consuming his fifth smoke when Granny Davis came out.

"It's spittin' sleet outside," Granny announced. "Better come in, Utt." He stood for a moment watching the overcast sky, then, "I got some supper ready," he said. "You reckon I'd better call Price an' Will?"

"Sure, call 'em," Utt said.

Granny went back into the house and Ben Utt, getting to his feet and tossing aside his cigarette butt, walked down to the bunkhouse to summon Tony, Duke and Jim Harvie.

The meal that was eaten in the Teepee kitchen was a very quiet one. No one had much to say while they listened to Price recount the story he had told Ben Utt. Price did not mention his determination that the Potheros were the ones concerned. He did not need to. In each of the men about the table that suspicion was raised, lifted until it became a certainty.

"We'll go callin' on the X Bar tomorrow," Jim Harvie declared as he put his plate in the wreck pan. "That right, Price?"

"Somebody will go over there," Price answered. "No need of all of us going."

Harvie grunted, answer enough to show the determination in his mind. As if anyone could leave Jim Harvie out of a thing like this; Jim Harvie who had been with the Teepee so many years!

The meal finished, the Teepee separated, Utt, Harvie, Tony and Duke going to the bunkhouse to smoke and talk; Will Thorn and Price remaining with Granny in the kitchen. They were in Granny's way and he said so.

"Get out if you ain't goin' to help!" Granny ordered.

A good cook is boss of a kitchen and Will Thorn and his son left. They went into the living room where now a lamp was lighted, and each disposed himself in a chair after Will Thorn had peered into the bedroom and saw that Neil had not moved. Price, sitting beside the

206

table, idly picked up the little pile of mail and spoke to his father.

"You're going to have to rest some, Dad," he said. "You've been up all yesterday and last night and today. You can't stand it."

"I can't sleep either," Will Thorn said. "Seems like I can't get the boy off my mind. Just a kid, Price. He makes me think of you before yore mother died. Always into somethin' an' always callin' me 'Mister Thorn,' an' thinkin' everything I did was just right."

"He'll be following you around again in a couple of weeks," Price assured sturdily. "You go lie down on the couch awhile. I'll call you. I'm going to get some rest myself tonight."

"An' see the Potheros tomorrow?" Will Thorn asked sharply.

"Maybe!"

The older man got up, came over and stood beside his son and put his hand on Price's shoulder. "Think it through before you jump," he warned. "You might be wrong."

"If I am they'll have a chance to tell me so," Price answered. "You go lie down, Dad."

Leaving Price, Will Thorn went to the couch, sat down on it, and presently stretched out and relaxed. "I won't go to sleep," he said. "I'll just stretch out awhile."

"All right," Price agreed.

Within minutes Will's regular breathing told of sleep and Price smiled gently. The old man was worn out with his vigil. He got up, walked to the bedroom door

207

and looked in. Neil Redwine was a long, quiet shape covered by the bedding.

Back at the table once more Price picked up the mail. There was a saddle catalog for Jim Harvie. Jim collected saddle catalogs from all points in the country and once every eight or nine years bought a saddle from Coyne and then complained that it did not suit him. There was a bundle of newspapers. There was a letter from the calf buyer, which Price opened and read. The man who had bought the calves would expect delivery in Kansas City stockyards on November twentieth. Have to start that work pretty soon, cutting off the calves and trailing them to town. Price's brain was dead tired. He could hardly keep his eyes open. He laid aside the letter from the buyer and looked at the last letter in the pile. It was addressed to one Carl Langstreet in Monroe, Iowa. The letter had been forwarded twice and finally stamped with the red letters that the post office uses: "Return to sender. Addressee unknown." Up in the left-hand corner was written: "Neil Redwine, Teepee Ranch, Coyuntura, New Mexico."

Neil had wanted to impress his friend, hence the return address. Price turned the returned letter over slowly. It was almost as though that quiet, white-faced boy in there on the bed had spoken. Indecision filled him for a moment and then thrusting a finger under the flap, Price ripped the letter open, took out the written sheets and unfolded them.

There was nothing of any importance on the first page. Neil had written to his friend Carl to tell him that at last all his ambitions were realized. He was on a real cow ranch in a real cattle country. He had a horse and a saddle and pair of boots. Neil amplified the importance of his position in the letter. As Price read it he could not keep back a smile. From what the letter said, Neil was a real top hand. Price turned the page and read on.

"The way I got here was funny," Neil had written. "I bummed my way on freight trains. The day before I got here I was in a jungles up at La Junta, Colorado. A jungles is a place where hobos hang out when they are not riding freight trains. I was in this jungles and I heard some men plan a bank robbery. They talked about how easy it would be. I got to look at them. There were four of them and when they seen me and the Kid I was with, they chased us out. So I got in a box car on a freight train and we left La Junta. We got away down the railroad to Coyuntura and the brakeman found me and pulled me out of the box car. He hit me twice and then Price Thorn — he's the son of the man I work for — came over and licked the brakeman and took me back to camp and I've been here ever since. But the funny thing is that the bank they planned to hold up was in Coyuntura and when they held it up Price killed one of them and the photographer took his picture after he was dead. I saw the picture in a window when Price and me came to town to get me some new boots. You have to have boots when you punch cows because shoes have low heels and will go through a stirrup. Mr. Thorn says that every cowboy needs boots . . ."

The letter went on. Price did not read further. So Neil Redwine had seen the men who had tried to rob the Coyuntura bank, had heard them plan the job and that day in Coyuntura he had tried to tell Price about it. Price placed the letter on the table, looked at his father and then went into the kitchen.

Granny had finished in the kitchen and had gone on out, leaving a lamp burning. Price got a drink from the water bucket and then carrying the lamp, walked into the little room that Neil had used. He put down the lamp and sat down on Neil's cot and looked around.

Boy-like, Neil had decorated his room. There was an old pair of spurs hanging from a nail in the wall, a piece of hair rope festooned below the spurs. There were pictures cut from magazines pinned up above the bed and beside the window. A bandanna lay on the bureau and reaching out Price took the neckerchief and idly unfolded it. How much had happened at the Teepee since that night when he had brought Neil to camp. How much that was bad and how much that was good! Neil Redwine had been the making of Will Thorn. Neil had brought Will back again, and now, with the boy lying there in the front bedroom scarcely breathing, either going down toward death or up and back to life, Will Thorn had taken hold once more, was himself again. Neil had done that. Price unfolded the bandanna and spread it out upon his knees. There, in the center of the blue field was the white silhouette of a horse!

After a little time, carrying the bandanna, Price went back to the front room. Will Thorn sat up as Price entered, stretched and rubbed his eyes.

210

"Must have dozed off," he mumbled. "How is he, Price?"

"Just the same," Price answered. "I think he's resting, Dad. I think maybe this is sleep. Where did the kid get this bandanna?"

Will glanced at the blue square that Price held up. "Over at Bacon's in Pichon," he said. "Neil saw it when I was there with him an' I could see that he liked it, so I bought it for him. Why, Price?"

"Nothing in particular," Price answered. "I'm going out and get Jim to come in and sit with the kid. You and I have both got to get some sleep."

Leaving his father Price went out through the kitchen. When he stepped out on the stoop he saw that snow was falling, light feathery flakes. Through the snow Price walked down to the bunkhouse to get Jim Harvie.

Behind him, ghostly through the falling snow, the lights shone in the ranch house. There was a kid lying in there, a kid that was, perhaps, dying. And if this kid died — Price's boots scuffed the snow — then Will Thorn would die too; drop back into the lassitude, the lethargy of his former existence and, an old, old man, pass out of the picture.

CHAPTER
FOURTEEN

Brothers

When Ed Pothero and his brother Jule got back to the X Bar after their expedition to the Teepee with the Luceros, they had a definite feeling of accomplishment. Tate Merriman had done more than they really expected him to do; he had interested Appleby and he had brought the Luceros out with him to look at the dead calves. It seemed to Ed and Jule that everything was working out just the way they wanted it to, and they were in good spirits when they reached home.

The two men unsaddled, telling Hank Kuhler about the success of their expedition as they did so. Kuhler stood by in the corral, listening, his face expressionless.

"Just the way I'd planned it!" Ed exulted, pulling his saddle from his horse, "Everything went like greased oil. Young Thorn bristled right up to the Luceros an' talked big, an' it didn't sit a bit good with Enrique. Then the whole Teepee outfit backed Thorn, even the old man. It looks to me like we was goin' to have the law with us for once. I never seen a madder Messican than Enrique was."

"Worked good, huh?" Kuhler commented. "Nobody looked close at them calves?"

212

"Hell, no. We didn't get off the horses. Just looked at 'em an' went on. Did you bob the tail of that other calf, Jule?"

"Yeah," Jule said laconically, "I bobbed it."

"So much the better," Ed Pothero commented. "The Thorns got some other troubles too, Hank. Somebody taken a shot at that kid that's been stayin' there. Hit him in the head an' Doc Cirlot done some kind of operation. Guess the kid ain't goin' to live. They was all stirred up about that an' the Luceros stayed to look into it."

By this time Ed Pothero had disposed of his riding gear and now he started toward the house. Jule, still unsaddling, taking his time, waited until his brother was gone. "I shot that kid," he said hoarsely, when Ed was out of earshot. "I was bobbin' the tail of that calf an' the kid came ridin' up. Know who he was, Hank?"

"No." Kuhler was looking at Jule with wide, questioning eyes.

"He was one of them kids that we run off when you an' Tip an' me was plannin' that Coyuntura job with Bruce. He knew me. I had to let him have it."

Hank Kuhler said nothing and Jule, after a long silence, spoke again. "Damn it, Hank! I know it looks bad, shootin' a kid; but what else was there for me to do? He'd of run an' blabbed to Thorn an' then we'd of been in it clear up to our necks. What else could I do?"

"I don't know." Kuhler shook his head. "But Ed said that you didn't kill the kid. Suppose he gets well? Then he'll talk . . ."

"He ain't goin' to get well!" Jule snapped. "He's hit in his head. He's goin' to die. By God, Hank . . ."

Kuhler stilled the explosion with a lifted hand. "All right," he interrupted. "All right. He's goin' to die then. But what are you goin' to do about Bacon?"

"Bacon?"

"Yeah. He was over here today while you an' Ed was gone. Come walkin' up to the house big as life an' set down to talk. Give me a cigar an' kind of beat around an' then come out with it."

"Out with what?"

"He wants a thousand dollars," Kuhler said. "That's what he comes out with! He wants a thousand dollars or he's goin' to tell Enrique Lucero about sellin' you that bandanna an' about how you come an' told him to keep his mouth shut about it."

Jule Pothero leaned against the corral fence. "My good gosh!" he ejaculated.

"Yeah," Kuhler grated, "my good gosh, an' then some. Where you goin' to get a thousand dollars?"

"Ed . . ." Jule began.

"Ed will just naturally beat the hell out of you an' let you lie in jail," Kuhler snarled unfeelingly. "Damn you, Jule. You blabbed about Tip to Ed. You went up to Bacon's an' let him in on the whole thing by tellin' him to keep his mouth shut about that bandanna. Now you shot this kid at Thorn's. Yo're a fool. You don't need to think Ed will help you out!"

"But Ed's got some money in the house," Jule expostulated. "He's got three or four hundred dollars. I've seen it. He keeps it . . ."

214

"What good is that goin' to do you?" Kuhler interrupted bluntly. "Bacon wants a thousand, an' anyhow Ed ain't goin' to give you what he's got. I'll tell you somethin', Jule. I ain't so damned sure of Ed."

"What do you mean?"

"Ever think that you and me are the only ones that know what Ed's doin'?" Hank Kuhler bent down, picked up a straw and began to twist it in his fingers. "Ever stop to think of that, Jule?"

"Sure, but he had to have some help," Jule answered.

"He don't need help no longer," Hank said significantly. "If you an' me was out of the way, Ed wouldn't have a thing to worry about. We're the only ones know about stampedin' those Teepee heifers an' about this blackleg business."

Jule shrugged that off. He was not worried about what he and Hank Kuhler knew. The thing that preyed on Jule's mind was the fact that he needed some money, needed it to keep Bacon's mouth shut. If he could give Bacon a little, stall him along for awhile, the opportunity might arise . . . Jule's eyes narrowed. He had shot twice when he was in a panic. He could shoot again and so still forever Bacon's mouth.

"I'm goin' to ask Ed for some money," he said bluntly.

"An' tell him what you want it for, I reckon?" Kuhler jeered.

"No! An' damn you, Hank, don't you talk to him neither!"

"I ain't likely to," Kuhler shrugged. "It looks to me like it was about time for me to pull my freight around here."

"You won't run out on me," Jule snapped. "You won't do that, Hank!"

Kuhler did not answer that but walked to the gate, and Jule, glaring after the man, slowly finished his unsaddling.

Jule Pothero did not immediately speak to his brother concerning his wants. When he finished at the corrals he went to the house and ate a little. The Potheros had a native cook, a man, and the meal was redolent of chili and garlic. When he finished eating, Jule went out again. The day was well along, not many hours remained until sundown. There were clouds over the Ranas and the air was cold. It looked as though there might be snow. Jule paid no attention to the weather. He loitered in the barn for awhile and then, nerving himself, went back to the house. Ed was in the front room.

The Potheros were not good housekeepers. The front room was dirty, a littered, filthy place. Ed was sitting at his battered desk, his feet cocked up on the top, his spurs dug into the wood. The older Pothero was smoking a cigar and as Jule came in, Ed removed the cigar and spat. An ugly yellow stain appeared.

"It ain't goin' to be long now," he greeted his brother. "Thorn is goin' to try to ship around the middle part of November an' when he does that we'll set up a deadline an' he won't come across it. I got Merriman an' the Luceros sold on the idea, an' Appleby is goin' to stir up the lower country. Mr. Price Thorn's goose is just about cooked."

216

Jule sat down on the desk and turned his head so that he faced his brother. "What am I gettin' out of this?" he demanded.

"We're pardners, ain't we?" Ed asked expansively. "You got a half interest in the ranch."

"An' I never get nothin' out of it," Jule responded. "I need some money, Ed."

"What for?" Ed Pothero was nothing if not parsimonious. Getting money out of Ed Pothero was like getting a straight tip on a race horse.

"Never mind what for," Jule snapped. "I need it. I want two hundred dollars."

"Yeah, an' I want the world with a rope tied around it," Ed answered. "I ain't got two hundred dollars to give you."

"Yes you have."

The two brothers glared at each other for a moment. It was Jule who first lowered his eyes. "I ain't drawed a cent from this place," he said defiantly. "I got some comin'."

"You'll get what you got comin' when I sell the calves," Ed snapped. "Now shut up about money. I got enough trouble without you bellyachin'."

"I got to have two hundred dollars," Jule said obstinately. "I got to have it."

"Try an' get it!" Ed flicked the ashes from his cigar. "I'll give you what you got comin' when I sell the calves an' not before, an' that's that!"

Jule slipped off the desk. "All right," he grated, "an' I'll . . ."

"You'll do yore work an' keep yore mouth shut!" Ed flung the words at his brother. "Now get on out of here an' let me alone!"

Jule walked out of the room. In the kitchen, Kuhler, dallying with the dipper from the water bucket, grinned at him wisely. Jule scowled at Kuhler and went on out.

Jule did not see Ed again until the evening meal. All three men sat down at the table in the kitchen and ate together. Halfway through the meal Jule dropped his knife and fork in his plate and got up from the table, knocking over his chair with his abruptness.

"I'm sick an' tired of this!" he snarled. "Chili an' beans for breakfast, dinner an' supper! Garlic in everything but the coffee. To hell with this layout!" Having so declared himself, Jule stamped out of the house.

Ed Pothero and Hank Kuhler exchanged looks. "Pretty snorty," Ed observed. "He braced me for some cash awhile ago."

"Give it to him?" Kuhler drawled.

Ed Pothero grinned flatly. "You know I didn't," he answered. "What would he do with cash?"

"He might spend it," Kuhler observed, dryly. "It wouldn't hurt you to loosen up once in a while, Ed."

"You get paid regular," Ed retorted. "Loan him some money if you think he needs it so bad. Hey, Juan! Bring me another cup of coffee!"

Jule did not come back into the house. Kuhler and Ed Pothero finished their meal and Ed lit a cigar while Hank rolled and lighted a cigarette. They smoked in the kitchen while Juan, the cook, did the dishes and cleaned up. Juan went on out to the bunkhouse where he slept alone, and Ed Pothero talked expansively to Kuhler.

About eight o'clock Hank went out, coming back in to say that it was sleeting. He put more wood on the fire in the stove and poured two cups of coffee, and he and Ed drank. Ed declared his intention of going to bed, and having finished his coffee and his third cigar, got up and went through the front room to the bedroom he occupied alone. Kuhler, morosely nursing a smoke, sat up awhile. He heard Ed Pothero fussing about, undressing, heard him blow out his lamp and heard Ed's bed squeak as he got heavily in. Still Jule did not come back. Finally Hank Kuhler gave up waiting and went in to his own bed in the room he occupied with Jule.

Hank had gone to bed and was almost asleep when he heard Jule come in. Jule did not light the lamp but undressed in the dark. Once, in moving about, Jule stumbled over something and cursed savagely under his breath. Kuhler stirred.

"Where you been?" he asked sleepily.

"Out talkin' to Juan," Jule answered.

"What's it doin' outside?"

"It snowed a little an' then stopped," Jule answered. His bed springs creaked as he got under the covers. Hank Kuhler turned over. From the front of the house came Ed Pothero's stentorian snoring.

Jule Pothero did not sleep. He lay in his bed, turning restlessly, tossing and twisting under the heavy covers. There were a lot of things for Jule to think about, a lot of worries. If Ed had given him the money he asked for, Jule thought, he could have gone up to Bacon's and stalled the storekeeper along. He could have gotten by for a while longer anyhow. But Ed, damn him, wouldn't part with a cent. Ed wouldn't even give a man tobacco money. And Bacon knew too much and so did Hank Kuhler. And if he told Ed about what Bacon knew and about shooting Neil Redwine, then Ed would have even more on him than he already had. There was just one thing to do and that was to figure out some way of keeping Bacon quiet. He couldn't just ride to Pichon and kill Bacon. There were too many people in the little town and someone would see him. Bacon had to be killed, Jule was resolved of that, but it must be done so that no one knew. And that would take time. If he had a little money he could buy that time. And Ed had money. There was money right here in the house, right in the front room. Ed thought that it was hidden but Jule had seen his brother push a roll of bills behind one of the newspapers tacked to the wall. He knew just where that money was.

The night wore on endlessly as Jule turned and tossed and Ed Pothero snored a heavy, basso growl and Hank Kuhler added a high pitched nasal diapason. The alarm clock in the kitchen ticked the seconds away and Jule Pothero thought and planned and, presently, relaxed somewhat. About four o'clock, with the darkness lessening, Jule sat up in his bed. He looked over to where Kuhler slept. In the gloom he could faintly discern the outlines of the man. Jule pushed

220

back the covers and, noiseless in his stockinged feet, got up.

He did not dress completely. He slipped into trousers and shirt and picked up his gun belt from the back of a chair. After a moment's hesitation he put on the belt, the gun sagging heavily against his leg. It was lighter now, light enough to see the chair and the beds. There was a skiff of snow on the ground and the snow caught the beginning of the morning light and, diffusing it, made the whole world a lead gray. Now, moving slowly and avoiding all sound, Jule Pothero opened the bedroom door and stepped out into the living room.

He crossed the living room toward the desk. Just beyond the desk was the newspaper tacked on the wall. Behind the newspaper was Ed's money cache. Jule stepped on a loose board that squeaked unnervingly. He stopped, panic stricken, waiting. Nothing happened. There was no sound from Ed's room. Jule went on. He rounded the desk and paused, hand extended, listening. Still no sound. Jule touched the newspaper, pulling it up gently. With his left hand he reached behind the paper and found the little packet of bills he had seen Ed Pothero place there. He had withdrawn the packet and was turning, when Ed spoke.

"What in hell are you doin' there?"

Jule wheeled like a flash. Ed Pothero, his belly protruding like a round drum covered by the flannel of his underwear, his feet in socks, a gun in his hand, stood in the door of his bedroom. Ed's eyes were narrowed. "You . . ." he began.

Jule did not let his brother finish his sentence. Frantically, panic dictating his movements, he jerked the gun from its holster at his hip, whipped it up and shot twice, the explosions thundering in the room. In the doorway Ed Pothero sagged, reached out a hand toward the door jamb for support, dropping the gun he held. "Why . . ." he began, and then, his hold on the door slackening, his knees buckled and he slumped down. Jule, his gun still lifted, stood motionless behind the desk.

He was there when an instant later Hank Kuhler came bursting into the room, gun in hand, and stopped short. "What the hell . . . ?" Kuhler exploded.

"He seen me," Jule Pothero said blankly. "He come in an' seen me."

"My good Godfrey!" Kuhler ejaculated.

For an instant Jule Pothero hesitated. Then he lifted the gun in his hand, pointing it to Kuhler. Hank Kuhler interpreted the movement. His face was already white and his eyes wide with the thing he saw and he called sharply.

"No Jule! Not me. Not me. I'll help you, Jule!"

Jule held the gun on Hank Kuhler, his eyes indecisive. Then, slowly he lowered the weapon and spoke hoarsely. "You got to help me, Hank. You got to help me get away from here!"

There was relief in Kuhler's voice when he spoke. "I'll help you," he answered. "I'll go with you, Jule. We'll pull out together."

Jule Pothero looked down at his brother lying there in the door. "Why damn him," Jule said slowly, "he

222

wouldn't give me any money. His own brother an' he wouldn't help me out!"

"You've got to get dressed," Kuhler said. "We've got to dress an' get out of here, Jule."

"I got some money anyhow," Jule Pothero rasped. Still looking at his brother, Jule moved around the desk, the gun dangling in his hand. Kuhler backed away from the door and Jule came toward it, looking at Ed, turning his head as he progressed so that he could keep his eyes on the body.

"Come on, Jule," Hank Kuhler urged. "Come on."

Back in the chilly bedroom Jule Pothero dropped his gun down into his tangled bedding and slumped down. Hank Kuhler, watching him, sat on his own bed, dressing hastily. Presently Jule stooped and reached for a boot. Kuhler was already stamping into his own boots.

"I've wanted to do that for a long time," Jule said suddenly. "I never knew it but I've wanted to kill Ed for a long time. Ed never treated me right."

There was a plaint in the words and Kuhler spoke reassuringly. "Ed never did treat you right," he agreed. "We'll make some coffee an' then we'll pull out of here, Jule. We've got lots of time. We can get clear away. We can go up into Colorado an' meet Bruce, an' the three of us will get together on somethin'."

Jule Pothero nodded. He looked up at Kuhler and his eyes had lost their glazed expression. "Yeah," he said, "we'll go find Bruce. To hell with this workin' business. There's other ways of makin' money. Anyhow I won't have to stick around takin' orders from Ed an' listenin' to him tell how smart he is. I've kind of put it over on Ed. Look!"

From the bedding beside him, Jule Pothero lifted the little bundle of bills he had taken. It was a slim enough bundle, perhaps four hundred dollars in all. Jule eyed them and then looked at Hank Kuhler again. "We'll stop some place an' blow ourselves to a party," he announced. "We'll have some fun, Hank."

"Hurry an' get dressed," Kuhler urged. "Come on, Jule."

At the Teepee ranch, with the first hint of dawn in the sky, Price Thorn stirred himself and sat up. He had brought Jim Harvie from the bunkhouse to sit with Neil and he had covered his father's long body, on the couch in the living room, with a blanket. Then he himself had gone to bed. Despite his nap in the afternoon, Price was bone weary. His mind was singularly free from worry and he had slept, but now that morning was coming he was awake and alert.

Getting out of bed he slipped into trousers and shirt and went out of his room. Will Thorn still rested on the couch and when Price looked into the bedroom he saw that Jim Harvie, too, was sleeping, lying back in a big chair with a blanket over him. Price, his stockinged feet making no noise, went into the bedroom and looked down at Neil Redwine. The boy was motionless and had not changed save only that his eyes were not completely closed. Neil's face was waxy white, but his breathing was regular and, it seemed to Price, there was a little color in Neil's lips.

224

Price stole out of the bedroom without disturbing Jim Harvie, reached the living room and stood thinking. Then, decisively, he went back to his own room again. There he ran a comb through his sandy hair, tied the blue bandanna about his neck for a neckerchief, slipped into a coat, and picking up the belted Smith & Wesson, strapped it on. He put on his hat then, stooped and picked up his boots and, carrying them, went softly out of the house, closing the kitchen door noiselessly behind him.

On the stoop Price sat down and pulled on his boots. There was a light skiff of snow on the ground, a thin blanket that, once touched by the sun, would disappear. The whole world was lead colored, with a heavy cloud blanket hanging over it. Price stamped his boots gently to settle his feet into them, and without a backward glance went to the corrals.

Nugget had been left in for a wrangling horse. Beside Nugget there was a three-year-old that Duke was breaking in the corral. There were no other horses there. Price went to the saddle room, brought out his riding gear and, bridle in hand, approached Nugget. Nugget circled the corral, stopped, allowed himself to be caught, and stood with one bridle rein around his neck, while Price warmed the bit under his arm and then pushed it into the horse's mouth. He brushed off Nugget's back, placed his saddle blanket, heaved up his saddle and pulled the front latigo through the cinch ring.

With Nugget saddled Price led the horse out of the pen, placed his reins and, twisting out a stirrup, mounted. For a long moment he sat there on tall Nugget's sorrel back, looking at the sleeping Teepee; then, turning the horse, he rode away from the corrals, heading toward the southwest.

Nugget fretted because Price held him down. He tried to pace and was pulled up, and tried to trot and was firmly corrected. Then Nugget settled down into a running walk that covered country and Price let him keep the gait. Horse and man were two miles from the Teepee when they heard another horse coming from behind them. Both looked around and then Price pulled Nugget to a halt. Ben Utt, on the three-year-old bronc, was coming at a lope across the white flats.

Utt came up, stopped the bronc and scowled at Price. Price said nothing. Utt's frown became a reluctant grin. He chuckled dryly. "Thought you'd pull out an' leave me," he stated, "I was awake. I seen you go."

"Well . . ." Price said.

"You figgered," Ben Utt interrupted in a drawling voice, "that you'd save the rest of us the trouble. I know how you figgered."

Price said nothing. Utt's grin broadened. "Kind of feel like you'd been caught with yore hand in the candy case, don't you?" he commented. "You sure got big ideas, Price, goin' over to brace the Potheros all by yourse'f."

"It looked like it was my job," Price said.

"Oh sure," Utt waved one big knuckled hand, "an' you started out to do it before breakfast. How did you think you'd come out with the Potheros, Price? There's

226

three of them an' one of you. Or didn't you think about that?"

"Tell you the truth, I didn't," Price answered. He was grinning a sheepish grin at Utt now. "I guess I was kind of a fool, Ben."

"The kind of fool I'll hang around with," Ben Utt announced. "Well, no harm done. We'll rock along, Price."

Price started Nugget. The three-year-old colt fell in beside the sorrel horse. Ben Utt chuckled. "Jim," he observed, "is goin' to be awful sore about this. So is Tony an' mebbe even Duke ain't goin' to be too well suited."

"They've got no business in a deal like this," Price said shortly.

"No," Utt agreed, "they ain't. You figgered you'd take it off all our hands, didn't you, Price?"

"I didn't think much about it," Price answered. "Last night I made up my mind I'd ride over to see the Potheros, so this mornin' I set out."

"An' now you got company," Utt said cheerfully. "Yo're a hard kind of fellow, Price. You got some rock in you some place."

"Well?" Price said defiantly.

"Well," Ben Utt drawled, "I like rock. You don't object to me sidin' you?"

"No."

"Good enough." Utt's voice showed his satisfaction.

The two rode along in silence for a time. "I ought," Price said suddenly, "to hunt up Donancio and Enrique and tell them what I know. That's what I ought to do."

227

"You goin' to do it?" Utt's tone was sharp.

"No."

A small, satisfied smile stole across Ben Utt's rugged face. "I didn't think you would," he approved. "Comes to a showdown you kind of like to shoot yore own skunks, don't you?"

Price nodded. "But this isn't up to you, Ben," he said after a moment of silence. "You're . . ."

". . . workin' for the Teepee," Ben Utt interrupted. "Damn this horse. Ridin' a green bronc is just like sittin' on a piece of rubber, just exactly. I wish that Duke had had time to teach this horse somethin'. I'd get along better."

Price grunted and the two men rode on in silence.

And when dawn broke at the Merriman headquarters Donancio and Enrique Lucero, sleeping in one bed, heard the cook's alarm clock and got up. They dressed and went to the kitchen washbench to make their toilets. There, in the kitchen, with the fire beginning to crackle in the stove, the Luceros met Tate Merriman. Merriman's eyes were sleep-filled and his face was rusty with the beard stubble that was on it. Tate Merriman's voice was harsh as he spoke to Donancio and Enrique.

"I'll go over to Potheros with you," Merriman snapped. "If what you say is right the Potheros have been makin' a fool out of me. I don't relish bein' made a fool of. We'll go right after breakfast."

228

CHAPTER
FIFTEEN

Fight on the Flats

Breakfast at the Key headquarters was a sketchy affair. The cook gave Merriman, Enrique and Donancio warmed-over biscuits, enough coffee to float a battleship, and big chunks of ham. The men ate in silence while from outside came the sounds of the ranch, the pound of hoofs as the horses were run in, the plaintive bellow of a milk cow separated from her calf so that the Key might have a little milk; the rasp of men's voices as the three cowpunchers that worked for the Key talked, surly before breakfast. Merriman bolted his food while the Luceros ate more leisurely.

"Come on," Tate Merriman grated, just as Donancio was considering a third cup of coffee. "We got a ride to make."

Regretfully Donancio put aside the idea of coffee and he and Enrique followed Merriman to the door.

"Pick what you want to ride," Merriman invited when the three reached the corrals. "That bay's a good horse an' that black is a good one. We'll be back here before noon, I reckon." This last to Joe Nixon who stood by.

Nixon nodded. Enrique was already in the corral where the wrangler was pulling out the bay horse.

Donancio slipped through the gate, Merriman following him. Enrique was bridling the bay.

"I'll take Honey," Merriman said, and the wrangler nodded and circled his rope, shooting it out toward the milling remuda.

When the saddling was finished, Merriman spoke briefly to Nixon, mounted, and joined the waiting Luceros. The three rode off together, heading south; and, watching them go, Nixon spoke to one of the other riders who stood beside him.

"The boss is kind of takin' it hard," Nixon commented. "Last night when Enrique told him that Pothero had been makin' it look like the Teepee calves were spreadin' blackleg an' that they really wasn't doin' it, Tate wouldn't hardly believe him."

The other hand nodded. "What we doin' today?" he asked.

"You," and Nixon grinned broadly, "are goin' to ride the Cienega. An' I hope you get back by sundown."

The other man swore mildly and spat into the dust of the corral. "So do I," he answered. "Well, the snow will be gone by noon anyhow, an' that's somethin'."

"Don't count yore blessin's before they're hatched," Nixon warned. "I'm goin' to eat some breakfast an' then get out."

Donancio, Enrique and Tate Merriman, heading south, kept their horses going right along. Merriman set the pace and apparently Merriman was in a hurry to reach his neighbors' ranch. The X Bar headquarters was sixteen miles from the Key, ordinarily a two hours' ride. Merriman kept up a gait that would cut down that

230

time, and Donancio and Enrique kept up with Merriman. So, on that frosty morning, three groups of riders were abroad, three groups of men were traveling.

It had taken Hank Kuhler and Jule Pothero some little time to get away from the X Bar. Desperate as was their necessity for leaving, still there were things that they must do. Jule Pothero's panic seemed to grow as the realization of what he had done became clearer. It was Hank Kuhler, level-headed and with an idea already forming in his mind, who kept things straight. Hank wrangled horses. Hank insisted upon the packing of a few personal possessions to take behind their saddles, and Hank dealt with the cook.

The shots had not wakened Juan, and Kuhler, slipping into the bunkhouse, threw a blanket over the sleeping cook, tapped him on the head with the barrel of his six-shooter and lashed the blanket around the man, callously indifferent as to whether Juan would smother or not. It was Kuhler who picked out the horses they would ride, choosing the best that the X Bar afforded, and urging Jule to saddle.

When they had saddled, when they had tied their possessions in saddle rolls behind their cantles, when they were mounted. Hank Kuhler led the way out of the corral and headed west. Jule rode beside him, slumped in his saddle, scarcely heeding their direction. Hank Kuhler eyed Jule speculatively and as he did so the idea that was in his mind germinated and began to grow. Here, right here, was an opportunity for Hank Kuhler. He must nourish it carefully until it bloomed.

It was a simple enough idea that Kuhler had. He wanted the X Bar. That was all. There was a good chance of his getting it. He would stick with Jule until opportunity offered itself, then, through that opportunity, he would get Jule to sign over a power of attorney. Armed with that, Hank Kuhler would run the X Bar and, eventually, he would own it. Reasoning his idea through, Hank Kuhler scowled and mentally swore to himself. Right here was the opportunity and he had almost muffed it. He pulled up his horse.

"Jule," he rasped, "we're damned fools, that's what we are!"

Jule stopped his horse but did not come back to Kuhler. Instead he waited until Kuhler came up to him.

"I reckon you think I oughtn't to of shot Ed," Jule said, dangerously. "Mebbe you . . ."

"No," Kuhler spoke swiftly, "I think we're damned fools for runnin' off with just a little money when we might have a lot."

A gleam of cupidity came into Jule Pothero's frightened eyes. "How do you mean?" he rasped.

"I mean that we ought to fix it up so that Ed would look like he'd killed himself. Fix it so it would look like he'd been cleanin' a gun or somethin'. Then you'd own the X Bar an' you'd have the cattle."

For a moment Jule pondered that, then he shook his head. "It's too dangerous," he answered. "I ain't goin' to stick my head in a noose for a few dollars. Not me. I'm too smart for that. I'm goin' to get out of this country. A way out of it." Once more Jule Pothero started his horse.

232

"No, but look, Jule," Hank jumped his horse ahead and swung around so that he blocked Jule's progress. "We can fix it. We can go back there . . ." Kuhler stopped. Jule's eyes were smouldering and his hand rested on his gun butt.

"You tryin' to get me hung?" he asked deliberately. "You want me to go back there an' then tell folks that I killed Ed. That's what you want! Damn you, Hank . . ."

Hastily Kuhler reined his horse aside. "That ain't right, Jule," he protested. "You know that ain't so. You know I'll stick with you. I'm yore friend. Why Jule . . ."

"Then shut up an' come on," Jule ordered. "Damn you, Hank, if ever I think that you ain't level with me . . ." Jule Pothero left the threat unfinished. His eyes had strayed past Hank Kuhler's face on toward the west. Now they squinted narrowly. Two horsemen had come up over a little rise a quarter of a mile west and were steadily approaching, coming straight on, the running walk of their horses biting into the distance.

"Price Thorn, damn him!" Jule Pothero rasped. "He's headed straight to us. Here's where I get even with that bastard!"

Hank Kuhler turned and looked. His face turned white beneath its tan. "Ben Utt's with him," he snapped. "Let's get out of here, Jule! Let's make a run for it!"

"No!" Jule Pothero growled, and pulled the gun from his scabbard. "We won't run. Let 'em come in. I've wanted to kill that sonofabitch for a long time an' here's where I do it."

He turned his horse a little as he spoke so that the animal's left side was toward the advancing riders. The gun he had drawn was beside his leg, hidden, and he spoke again from the corner of his mouth.

"You better get ready, Hank. You take Utt, an' by God if you don't get the job done, I'll kill you myself!"

Tate Merriman and the Luceros reached the X Bar while the sun was still half hidden behind the earth's curve. There was a streak of clear sky between the clouds and the horizon, and through that opening the sun shone bravely for the few minutes it had. The three men rode into the yard, stopped and, turning to Enrique, Merriman spoke.

"They ain't up yet. Nobody's built a fire."

"That's right," Enrique agreed. "We . . ."

Merriman interrupted. He turned from Enrique and, lifting his heavy voice, hailed the Potheros. "Hello the house! Ed . . . Jule . . ."

There was no answer. Again Merriman called and then, impatient, slipped down from his horse and, letting the animal stand, strode to the kitchen door. The tattoo he beat upon the panels echoed hollowly. Enrique and Donancio, also dismounting, came up and joined Merriman.

"Sleep like they was dead," Merriman complained. "Hey in there!" Again he beat upon the door.

Still no answer came. "I'll get 'em up," Merriman snapped, and turning the knob pushed the door open and walked into the kitchen. He crossed that room, went through the narrow hall beside which was the

234

bedroom Jule and Kuhler had shared, and so entered the living room. Donancio and Enrique followed Merriman. In the living room Merriman paused and looking back over his shoulder said, "I'll get Ed up. Hey, Ed! Get . . ." His shout died away. He was looking with shocked surprise at the open door of Ed Pothero's bedroom just beyond the desk, and from behind the desk the stockinged foot of a man protruded.

"That's . . ." Merriman began, and started forward. Donancio's hand on his shoulder stopped the rancher's progress. Enrique, stepping aside, circled the desk, halted, and then looked at his brother and Merriman.

"Ed Pothero," Enrique said quietly. "He ees dead!"

"Thorn!" Merriman burst out.

"Now wait," Donancio warned. "We'll look around a little before we start sayin' Thorn did this."

"He ees coming out of hees room," Enrique announced slowly. "Hee's gun, see?" Enrique pointed to where Ed Pothero's Colt lay on the floor, half hidden by his body.

"We better look an' see what happened to Jule an' Kuhler," Merriman snapped. "They both slept in the house."

With Merriman leading, the three went back down the hall. They opened the door of the other bedroom and stepped in. The room was in the wildest disorder. A glance showed it to be unoccupied. Enrique shrugged and turned to Donancio. "We go to the bunkhouse," he announced; then speaking to Merriman, "How many men deed Pothero have?"

"He had five an' himself," Merriman answered, "but after that business of him losin' his horses he fired three of 'em an' he hadn't got anybody to take their places. He was goin' to wait till he started to ship calves before he hired anybody."

"No cook?" Donancio asked.

"He had a Mex . . . he had a man cookin' for him," Merriman answered.

"I'll go find the cook," Donancio announced.

Enrique nodded agreement and Donancio went out. When his brother was gone Enrique began a careful examination of the disordered room. "No one ees hurt een here," he said at length. "Wheech bed deed Jule use?"

"That one, I guess." Merriman pointed to a tangle of disordered bedding on a bunk.

Enrique stepped over to the bed, bent down and straightened up with a brass cartridge case in his hand. Jule had jacked out the empty shells he had used on his brother, and reloaded while he sat on the bed.

"Thirty-two-twenty," Enrique said. "Their clothes ees gone."

"I don't sabe this," Merriman announced. "Ed is there dead, an' Jule an' Hank gone. I don't sabe this at all."

"I think I sabe plenty," Enrique announced.

Donancio appeared at the door, shoving Juan along in front of him. Juan, his eyes wide and frightened, was babbling Spanish. Enrique listened carefully and then turned to interpret for Merriman's benefit.

"Juan says he was esleep. He says somebodee throw a blanket over heem an' heet hees head an' he don't know notheeng onteel hee's wake up an' find hees tied een the blanket."

"This is a hell of a note," Merriman said.

Enrique spoke to his brother, low-voiced and in Spanish. He held out the empty cartridge case. Donancio took it, looked at it for a long time and then answered his brother, also in Spanish.

"Now we go back an' look at theese other one," Enrique said briskly.

Donancio went out. Merriman heard the outer door close. The rancher gave Enrique a helpless look and followed him into the front room once more, Juan trailing along. Juan threw up both hands and made an exclamation when he saw Ed Pothero. Enrique asked a question and Juan shook his head.

"He don't know," Enrique told Merriman, as though that explained everything.

Donancio came back in. "Two of 'em pulled out," he drawled. "There's no tracks headin' in here except ours. The snow is beginnin' to go, Enrique."

Enrique went to the front door, forced it open and looked out. "I theenk," he said slowly, not looking around, "that Jule or Kuhler keeled Ed Pothero. I theenk they have ron . . ." Enrique stopped short and held up his hand. Faint, from afar off, came the roll of gun fire. Shots, faint dots of sound in a desert of silence, and then just silence once more.

"We go now," Enrique said, breaking the silence and then, excitement showing in his voice for the first time, "Pronto! Pronto, Donancio!"

Price Thorn and Ben Utt, coming steadily toward the two men who waited for them, had no illusions. They were riding into the sun, but while they rode, before they had traversed the little distance, the sun went up behind the cloud bank. Ben Utt, close beside Price, spoke a warning. "That's Hank Kuhler with Jule Pothero," he announced. "They're waitin' for us."

"I see they are," Price answered dryly.

"Don't take any chances," Utt warned, and reined away a little. He did not want to be too close to Price. If trouble started, and it was bound to start, Ben Utt knew that with his green horse he would need plenty of elbow room. He took up the slack in his reins and held his horse up, letting Price get half a length ahead of him.

Price paid no attention to Ben Utt. Utt was competent and could take care of himself. Price was intent upon the two waiting men. His coat was open and the end of the blue bandanna tied at his throat fluttered in the breeze. Price too took up the slack in Nugget's reins and the horse, feeling the tension, tossed his head against the tie down. When perhaps thirty feet separated the two groups, Price pulled Nugget to a stop. The halt was unexpected. Jule had thought that Price and his companion would come right on up to them.

"Don't forget," Jule rasped to Hank Kuhler, his voice low. "I told you to take Utt!"

"Travelin' kind of early," Price called across the little distance that separated the four men. "Out lookin' for more Teepee calves to bob-tail?" There was anger in his voice, anger and accusation.

Jule Pothero turned his horse a little more, so that his side was toward Price. "Yo're out kind of early yorese'f," he called back. "Come on over here, Thorn, if you want to talk. I ain't goin' to yell at you."

Under the pressure of Price's knees, Nugget moved forward. Ben Utt's young horse, held too tight, fought for his head and Utt gave the horse slack as he followed Price. The distance was half of the original now, perhaps fifteen feet, and Price stopped again, Nugget hung up on the reins, held just so, ears pointed, shoulder muscles quivering.

"I'm close enough now," Price said. "I asked you a question, Pothero."

"An' I didn't answer it!" Jule was stealthily lifting his hidden hand. He would shoot across his body when the hand cleared.

Price could see the movement. His own right hand rested on the fork of his saddle, scant inches from the Smith & Wesson. "I found your knife," Price said casually, and then, "Get your hand out from behind your leg an' shoot, you damned kid-murderer!"

Jule Pothero jerked his hand up. As the muzzle of his gun cleared the top of his saddle, he pulled the trigger. Price with Nugget hung on the reins, picked the horse up with his spur and reined left. Nugget cut back to the left as though turning a calf. The shot that Jule Pothero threw across his body, slugged into empty air behind Price's cantle and Price Thorn's own gun was in his hand and his right side toward Jule Pothero.

At the explosion of Jule's gun, Ben Utt's young horse went straight up and came down bucking. Ben Utt lost his hat, his stirrups and his seat, in the first two jumps. On the third jump he quit the bronc up in the air, went off over the horse's shoulder as the bronc came down, and struck on his head and shoulder. Hank Kuhler, who up to this time had not made a movement, jerked out the gun he wore and leveled off at Utt, scrambling up from his fall.

Price, on Nugget, saw all this in one hasty glance. He saw Jule fighting his horse around so that he could get another shot. Price shifted aim and threw a shot at Kuhler that cut through the man's coat and thudded solidly into the cantle of his saddle. Kuhler, thrown off-balance, frightened by the sudden attack when he thought himself safe, missed his shot, brought his gun down for another and found lanky Ben Utt almost upon him. Kuhler's second shot missed by fractions of an inch. He had no time for another. Utt, swarming up Hank Kuhler, caught at his arm, and Kuhler's horse, frantic now, went into the air. Both men came down, hard on the ground. Price saw no more of that.

Jule had his horse around now and must have been shooting. When Price looked at Jule the man was just dropping his gun level. Nugget continued to turn and Price, reining him back short to the right, brought his right side to Jule again and with his arm extended, fired twice. Jule Pothero's gun hand jumped and then he folded forward over his horse's neck. The horse, close-reined, spun in a circle, straightened out, ran a dozen feet and reared. Jule Pothero, as the horse went up, slipped back over the cantle, over the animal's rump, to fall in a little huddle on the ground. The horse went on and Price, with one shot left in the Smith & Wesson, turned Nugget back. Ben Utt was just straightening up from Hank Kuhler and there was a foolish grin on Utt's face.

"I lost my gun when I got bucked off," Utt gasped. "Thanks, Price."

Nugget was sweating at the shoulders. Price slid a hand along Nugget's sorrel neck, straightened, put the Smith & Wesson back in his scabbard and slowly dismounted.

"I killed Jule Pothero, Ben," he said, his voice very low.

"A damned sight better than I done," Ben Utt said strongly. "All I done was choke Kuhler down. You watch him while I get my gun." Utt hurried away, stooped and picked up his gun, then came hurrying back.

Hank Kuhler was beginning to move, twisting on the ground.

"Lord, but that was sudden!" Ben Utt exclaimed.

There was silence for an instant and then Utt spoke again. "Jule had his gun out, layin' for you, Price," he said. "That Nugget horse is a handlin' fool. I seen you take that shot at Hank when I was on the ground. Thanks."

Price said nothing. He was looking over to where Jule Pothero lay. Beyond the man's body the horse that Jule had ridden had stopped and was looking back.

"And that about finishes it," Price said slowly. "I wonder why Ed Pothero wasn't along?"

Utt shrugged. "I dunno," he said. "Say . . . say, Price. You know . . . Lie still, damn you!" Hank Kuhler, eyes blank, was struggling to a sitting position.

"We might as well go on to the X Bar," Price said quietly. "We might just as well finish this, Ben. Where's Ed Pothero, Kuhler? Where is he?"

Hank Kuhler shook his head as though to clear it. Stooping, Ben Utt caught the man by the shoulder, and hauled. Kuhler, his eyes still dazed, struggled to his feet. "Where's Ed Pothero?" Utt demanded.

A little sanity had returned to Kuhler's eyes, a little light of reason. "Jule . . . ?" he began.

"Jule got himself killed," Utt snapped. "Where's Ed Pothero? Which one of you skunks shot the kid?" As he spoke, Utt shook the man he held, Kuhler's body limp and almost raglike. "Come on! Speak up. Where's . . ."

"Wait!" Price commanded. "There's somebody coming. See, Ben?"

Price was staring toward the west. There, against the horizon was a black spot that moved, rising and falling.

"Mebbe that's Ed," Ben Utt said grimly. "We'll wait an' see. Who was it shot the kid, Hank? Tell me, or by Glory I'll . . ." He did not finish the threat but shook Kuhler once more, and Hank Kuhler, with Ben Utt's harsh grip on his shoulder, Ben Utt's harsh voice in his ear, looked at the hard marble mask that was Price Thorn's face, and made answer.

"Jule shot him. It was Jule. He killed Ed this mornin'. He . . . Let me go, Ben! Let me go an' I'll tell you!"

242

"You bet you'll tell us," Ben Utt vowed grimly. "You just bet you will!"

"We'll wait till these others get here," Price said quietly. There's three of 'em and the man in front rides like Donancio Lucero."

CHAPTER
SIXTEEN

Shipping Time

Hank Kuhler sat down, glaring resentfully at Ben Utt. "You damned near twisted my neck off," he complained. "There wasn't no need of that, Ben."

"No?" Utt drawled. "An' you tryin' to shoot me? Mebbe I *was* a little rough, Hank."

Kuhler twisted his head experimentally and Price continued to watch the approaching riders. They came on, closing the distance, riding hard. "Enrique, Donancio and Merriman," Price announced. "All together." His statement was needless. The little group of horsemen was close now, Enrique already pulling in his mount. The horses stopped, Enrique got down, went directly to Jule Pothero, looked down at the man and then strode toward Price. Donancio, a quizzical gleam in his eyes, was standing, holding his horse and staring at Price and Kuhler and Utt. Merriman dismounted stiffly.

"Who shot heem?" Enrique asked.

"I did," Price answered. "I started out this morning to kill him, and Ed Pothero, too, if I could find him. Where is Ed? Kuhler says that Jule shot him." There was nothing soft about Price Thorn as he stood there,

244

nothing but hardness. Voice, eyes, face, posture, all spoke of a readiness, a determination, a purposefulness. Enrique Lucero, looking at Price Thorn, thought that he had never seen a harder man and Enrique had been an officer for a good many years and had seen some tough ones.

"So you shot heem," Enrique said softly. "Why, Price?"

"Because," Price answered, "he shot the kid. Because he had a gun hid behind his leg when I rode up, and he took a shot at me. Any objections to my shooting him, Enrique?"

Thoughtfully Enrique Lucero shook his head. "Not if what you say ees so," he observed. "Only Price, you are goin' to have to tell a lot of people about it. How do you know thees theengs?"

Price Thorn jerked his head toward Hank Kuhler. "Ask him," he said. "He's doing quite a lot of talkin'."

Enrique turned to Kuhler. "Go ahead," he ordered. "Tell us about it."

"An' speak out, Hank," Utt drawled.

Hank Kuhler looked at the group about him as though seeking some avenue of escape. There were five pairs of eyes fixed on his face and every pair of eyes was hard. Hank Kuhler swallowed his Adam's apple a couple of times, took a breath and said, "Well, I'll tell you."

From that start he continued telling the story, telling about Jule Pothero's shooting his brother Ed; about how Jule had threatened him and made him come along. Enrique, listening, shook his head. "You come

245

because you want to," Enrique stated with conviction. "Why you want to, I don't know but that ees why you came. Why deed Jule shoot Ed?"

"Ed wouldn't give him any money," Hank explained. "Jule knew where Ed had some hid and while he was gettin' it Ed caught him. Jule shot Ed then."

Enrique nodded and Price said, "Tell about Jule's shooting Neil Redwine."

"Well," Kuhler gulped down his Adam's apple again, "Jule done it. He told me so. Jule was bob-tailin' that calf an' the kid come up an' Jule shot him."

"When Jule bob-tailed the calf," Price repeated. "It was Jule and Ed and you . . ."

"*No es importante,*" Enrique interrupted. "We know about that, Price. We found out some theengs yesterday. I theenk we take theese Kuhler een to town an' put heem een the jail. I theenk you had better come along, Price. We have got a lot of theengs to do. We have got to get a coroner's jury an' we have got to hold an eenquest. Oh damn eet, Price, you make a lot of work for your friends. Nex' time you keel a man do eet een town, weel you?"

"I'll go to town with you," Price agreed, "but somebody's got to go to the ranch and tell Dad where I am. And I want to know about Neil. I've . . ."

"Look!" Donancio exclaimed.

There, over the little rise which so short a time ago Price and Ben Utt had topped, came horsemen. There were four of them and it needed no great knowledge to place the riders. The tall man in the fore was Will Thorn. The little man beside Thorn was Jim Harvie, and the two bringing up the rear were Tony Troncoso and Duke Wayant. They came on apace, stopped, ranging their horses in a little semi-circle, and Will Thorn dismounted.

"You all right, Price?" he demanded as he came forward. "Ben, you all right? What's goin' on here?"

"We're all right, Dad," Price assured. "I . . ."

He got no further. Will Thorn had reached Price's side and now he spoke again. "You oughtn't to of slipped off alone like that," he chided. "We were all comin' with you."

"I know, Dad," Price answered, "but I . . ."

"The kid woke up!" Will Thorn could not keep the elation from his voice. "Woke up an' looked at me. He knew me, too. He said, 'Hello, Mr. Thorn!' He's goin' to be all right, Price."

Father and son, two tall men, faced each other, looking into each other's eyes. Price's hand shot out and rested for a brief moment on Will's sleeve. That was all, but in the gesture Price spoke to his father, joined his father in the older man's happiness. Will wheeled to Enrique.

"Now," he demanded, "what happened?"

Enrique shrugged eloquently. "Price shot Jule Pothero," he answered. "He . . ."

"That right?" Will Thorn looked at Price again.

Price nodded. "Jule shot the kid," he said slowly.

Again Will faced Enrique but it was to Price he spoke. "What do you want to do, Price? Go back to the ranch with us?" In that moment Will Thorn was as hard, as competent as his son. The years had sloughed from his shoulders. Price thrilled to the older man's voice, his bearing. He knew that he had but to say the word and the Teepee and Will Thorn would back him against the world, fight for him, stick with him. He did not say that word.

"I'll go in with Enrique," Price said decisively and Enrique Lucero sighed deeply as though a weight were lifted from him. Enrique did not want trouble with Will Thorn, not now, not anytime.

Will Thorn accepted that statement, and Enrique, speaking quickly, added assurance. "Jule had a gun out," he said. "Price had to shoot heem. *No es verdad?*" Enrique looked at Hank Kuhler.

Kuhler nodded surlily. "Jule meant to kill him," he growled.

"You had better go back to the ranch, Dad," Price said. "You stay with Neil. I'll go in with Enrique and it will be all right."

Will Thorn shook his head. "I'll go with you," he said definitely. "Jim, you go back to the ranch, you and Duke. Tony will go along with Price and me."

"An' I theenk we had better go," Enrique said. "We have got theengs to do, Donancio."

Donancio came up at the command. To him Enrique gave orders. Donancio was to ride to Pichon and there assemble a coroner's jury. He would bring that jury, together with Anastacio Lucero, uncle of Enrique and Donancio, and Pichon's justice of the peace, to the X Bar. Donancio nodded understanding as his brother gave his orders, and mounting he rode off to carry

248

them out. Horses were caught then and Jule Pothero's body loaded on his mount.

When the preparations were complete Enrique spoke again. "We weel stop at the X Bar," he said. "No use to go to town an' then come out again. *Vamos, Caballeros!*"

And so they rode, Enrique Lucero and Will Thorn, Tate Merriman and Tony Troncoso, Price Thorn and Ben Utt, with Hank Kuhler in the center of the cavalcade and Jule. Pothero lashed across his saddle, bumping along on his horse which was fastened at the end of the lead rope that Tony held. Harvie and Duke Wayant, rebellious at being excluded from this, the final act of the drama but still obedient to Will Thorn's wishes, mounted their horses and rode off toward the west again, bound back for the Teepee. The horses' hoofs scuffed the grass and the sun was bright overhead, and against the cut banks, sheltered from the sun, the little rifts of snow lay white, prophesying Winter.

At the X Bar the group of horsemen left their mounts in the yard and carried Jule Pothero in and placed him on the floor of the room where his brother lay. Tony, a cigarette drooping from the corner of his cheerful mouth, brought blankets from the bedroom and spread them over the two dead men; and in the kitchen with Juan, still wide-eyed, wrangling a fire in the cook stove and promising coffee "pronto . . . pronto," Enrique Lucero sat down behind the table and looked around with bright, inquiring eyes.

"An' now," Enrique announced, "we find out before theese coroner's jury comes."

Find out he did. Price Thorn told his story simply. Told of his ride to Arroyo Grande where he had found the knife beside the dead Teepee calf, and the conjectures he had drawn from that discovery. Price told too of the blue bandanna in Neil Redwine's room, of where Will Thorn had bought that bandanna and of the letter that had come back from Iowa. Enrique listened, his face as impassive as the face of any of his Indian forebears, nodded, asked questions and grunted understanding when they were answered.

And then came Hank Kuhler's turn. Hank Kuhler talked. He lied when he thought he could, in a vain endeavor to protect himself, and because of what Enrique knew, of what Price Thorn knew and had told, was trapped in his lying. There in the little kitchen, with the aroma of coffee rising up from the cups that Juan had poured and distributed, the whole tawdry mess of the Rana was pawed over, aired and cleaned. When he was done with Hank Kuhler, Enrique spoke.

"So," he said, looking at Price, "me an' Donancio found out yesterday about theese hair-branded calf. Donancio has got the brand on hees saddle. An' Donancio find theese piece of tail where Jule has bobbed eet an' then shot the keed. Donancio ees pretty smart. I theenk he weel run for sheriff next time. He tells me what has happened and preety soon I beeleeve heem. Now I know he ees right. An' I know that Jule keeled Beely Wayant een the bank robbery, an' shoot

250

the keed an' keeled hees brother. Eet looks like you have done a preety good day's work, Price."

Enrique pondered a moment and then glared at Kuhler 'again. "You," he snapped, "you goeeng to plead guilty to bank robbery or accessory after the fac' or murder? You got your choice. Maybe you get tried for both."

Kuhler wilted in his chair and once more Enrique was silent. Then lifting his head he spoke once more. "Theese Bacon," Enrique promised, "w'en I get ahold of heem I make heem sweat, you bet." The sheriff grinned suddenly, got up and walked over to stand beside Will Thorn. His hand went out to rest on Will Thorn's shoulder and when Will looked up, Enrique said, "Jus' like old times, Will."

Price, watching the two — officer and ranchman — nodded. Enrique had caught it too. It was like old times. There had been grief and strife in the Rana, trouble and turmoil, and out of it all, Will Thorn had come back, the old Will Thorn, a man, and on his feet once more. Very slowly Price nodded his head again. It had been worth it. Well worth it.

A shout and the sound of traveling horses came from outside. In the little kitchen of the X Bar the men stood up.

"An' now," Enrique said, "we do eet all over again for Tio Anastacio an' the coroner's jury."

Beef is the business of the cattle country. Despite fire and flood, drouth or storm, murder or theft or accident, the beef moves to market. So it was that with

November half gone, Price Thorn brought the Teepee calves to Coyuntura and penned them in the stockyards. The Teepee, with help from Tate Merriman and from the Luceros, had rounded up, cut off the calves, and now they were in town. Nothing had hindered the roundup, nothing had stopped the drive. Where warfare might have flared, there had been only helpfulness, for all the Rana — Merriman, the Luceros, Appleby, all the cowmen in the lower country — knew that out of three hundred and twenty head of vaccinated calves, Price Thorn was shipping three hundred and twenty head. The thing that Ed Pothero had planned and striven to execute had not been consummated. The Rana country had some information, was getting educated, and in the bank Claude Pearsall had made a statement.

"The men that borrow money from me next year have got to vaccinate for blackleg," Pearsall declared. That was money talking. That was power. The Rana scratched its head and allowed that maybe, just perhaps, there was something in this vaccinating business. Anyhow it was a dirty trick that the Potheros had tried to play on Price Thorn. They deserved the killin' they got and Price Thorn was a mighty smart young fellow. Just about the best young cowman in the state, if you asked the Rana.

As for the blackleg, that scourge was done for the present. Cold weather, settling in, had checked the disease. Blackleg lay there in the Rana, in the soil, along the arroyos, in the corrals, dormant, deadly, hidden. It would be there a long time but never more did the

252

Rana need to fear it. Price Thorn had led the way; Pearsall had added his weight, the Rana was convinced. Blackleg might strike again but never as before, for now the cowman had a weapon against it: a syringe filled with a colorless liquid that, properly used, would stop the blackleg before it ever started.

There were cars on the siding for the Teepee calves and a dirty, sweating crew loaded those cars. The local, chuffing and puffing and tooting, came along and picked up the loads. In the cars the calves, tight-loaded, bumped together when the couplings went home, their eyes big and anxious, their pink nostrils wide. Beef is the business of the cattle country and the cowman ships his beef.

Price Thorn put his grip on the caboose step and shook hands with his father. "Tell the kid," Price said, "that I'll bring him a new saddle from Kansas City. Tell him I'll expect him to be ready to use it when I get back."

The grip of Will Thorn's hand was strong. Price mounted the step. The conductor, waving a bunch of yellow flimsies in his hand, signaled the engineer. Away up ahead the engineman answered that signal with his whistle. All along the length of the train the slack rumbled as the engine pulled it out, and Ben Utt, thrusting his head through a window of the caboose, called to Tony.

"Take care of them new boots, Tony. Take care of 'em till I get back, an' I'll help you put 'em on."